WHO'S KILLING
THE BROOKLYN DODGERS?

DONALD DEWEY

MILFORD
HOUSE

an imprint of Sunbury Press, Inc.
Mechanicsburg, PA USA

MILFORD
HOUSE

an imprint of Sunbury Press, Inc.
Mechanicsburg, PA USA

For information about special discounts for bulk purchases, please contact Sunbury Press Orders Dept. at (855) 338-8359 or orders@sunburypress.com.

To request one of our authors for speaking engagements or book signings, please contact Sunbury Press Publicity Dept. at publicity@sunburypress.com.

ISBN: 978-1-62006-759-8 (Trade paperback)

Library of Congress Control Number: 2018940784

FIRST MILFRED HOUSE PRESS EDITION: April 2018

Product of the United States of America
0 1 1 2 3 5 8 13 21 34 55

Set in Bookman Old Style
Designed by Crystal Devine
Cover by Lawrence Knorr
Edited by Lawrence Knorr

Continue the Enlightenment!

For Allen Ryan

CHAPTER 1

How remote can you be from things and believe you have some claim to them? I've had some practice in the question. The first time was when I was still at the Academy and fell for Rennie Miller. Rennie worked in one of those empty-space stores suburban malls call art galleries. They're usually hemmed in by a hair salon on one side and Key Food on the other, and their trade in yellow slashes and beige clouds depends on some soccer mom wanting more for her morning outing than wheeling a cart of cereal boxes and celery stalks out to the trunk of her car. Rennie's sales technique was to stand at her gallery window waiting for the soccer moms to notice her, decide she wasn't threatening, and wander inside in search of something exotic to put above the living room couch.

Skip the supermarket cart, and that's how I met her, too. I parked every morning near the gallery on my way to the Academy, took my lumps in the gym and classroom for four hours, then returned to my tenth-hand Cutlass trying to persuade myself that Nassau County was about to graduate the most skilled crime-fighter since Batman. It didn't take much to talk me out of that delusion. Sometimes I only had to sit behind the wheel for five minutes trying to turn over the engine, remembering the smarmy fireman friend of a neighbor's who had assured me the car had "world tours left in it." And it did—as long as it was in the hold of a tramp steamer. But anyway, one day Rennie had helped me postpone that Finley Moment by waving to me from her window. I suppose we had been working up to that commitment for a week or so—recognizing each other as I had locked up, a little nod, then a really BIG nod. Once I had even thrown her a shudder as my meteorological commentary before grabbing my duffle bag and hustling off to the Academy. But her wave had put an end to all those modest exchanges. Because she hadn't been able to keep her hand in her slacks pocket, I had been forced to enter the gallery.

The short of it was she thought I was a curiosity in my cadet uniform, I thought she was Genevieve Bujold between roles (I was really into *Coma* at the time). We went out together, we went in together, we stayed in together. She was there for my graduation from the Academy, I was there for a gallery opening of what looked like dozens and dozens of medieval battle helmets in Velcro. We started talking about sharing an apartment. Then we stopped talking about it, and so naturally that when we decided we had come to the end of the road, there was no shock involved. I told myself it must have had something to do with potential turning into reality: The Academy cadet becoming just another cop, the art gallery curator becoming just another manager of an identical shop in an identical mall three miles further east on the Island. If we couldn't be unique to the rest of the world, how the hell could we have expected to go on being unique to one another? I've always been good for lavishing big ideas on small events.

But back to the remoteness. About five months after Rennie and I had stopped seeing one another, there was a radio call in Valley Stream about a shooter blazing his way out of a bank. I heard the call sitting in a patrol car in Mineola with George Moreno, the two of us waiting for a high school to disgorge classes for the day. I heard the next call there, too—this one asking for some backup from Lynbrook because the shooter apparently had an arsenal of ammunition and had already taken down two cops. Most of the other details came later in the day, but what I remember from our stakeout was Moreno saying we should stop worrying about whether some 17-year-old dork was selling weed to his classmates and get over to Valley Stream to lend a hand. And I remember me just grunting, as in: "Yeah, and while we're at it, why don't we see what we can do about that crisis in the Middle

East?" What I learned later, at the end of my tour, was that the shooter had finally been taken down, but not before he had killed two passersby—a telephone repairman and Rennie Miller.

I went to the memorial service on Central Park West, but I didn't know what as. I might have introduced myself to the family as an ex-boyfriend, but that idea was scotched as soon as I overheard somebody pointing out a lanky, ashen-faced guy in front of the synagogue as "her fiancé." Simple friend wasn't much better because, the fact was, we hadn't talked once in the four months since we had split up and, besides, there were enough crying people (none of whom I had ever met) to qualify far more seriously for the title. I couldn't even pretend to be there as a representative of the county that had let down the Miller family: Whatever George Moreno had wanted to do, it *hadn't* been our call. I'm not saying feeling responsible for someone's death isn't worse, but that day mourning seemed like a natural privilege I was being denied. Was remoteness what Sister Mary Tierney had meant when she had been talking about Limbo?

All of which gets me to the Professor. Joe Carroll is my father-in-law. At least I think he still is. I've had different people tell me different things when it comes to a dead wife (mine) and daughter (his). I suppose the laws about it are written down in some cellar in Rome or Jerusalem, but I've never been obsessed enough with the subject to look into it. At this point, neither one of us has anybody else to leave our money to—not to mention no money to leave—so the titles don't mean much. The important thing is that, even with Jenny dead six years, we continue to *treat* each other like in-laws: I respect him for his field (European history) and not at all for his cantankerousness; he respects me for my doggedness (first as a cop, then as a private investigator) and wonders constantly why that burden has been placed on him. One of the advantages of not living with him (which I did for a couple of years) is that I no longer have to see him chewing over that question and coming to angry answers.

Since his retirement as head of the History Department at Adelphi, the Professor has had far too much free time on his hands. This has meant less of it for me. Even though he is still out on the Island in Garden City and I'm in Brooklyn, he uses his cellphone as though he can still shout down the stairs to me in his house basement. A bus just blew a tire outside his house and almost came through his window! Be sure to get my nose out of the *News* and buy the *Times* to read an Op-ed piece by "that Harvard conman" on economic development in Bulgaria! And whatever I do, don't waste my time going to see *Mission Impossible XIV!* These calls have usually irritated me twice over. First, because Joe Carroll feels at liberty to interrupt me for this drivel in the middle of my most delicate investigations. Nothing is as important as what *he* has just seen or thinks. He might not have students hanging on his every word anymore, but he still has Paul Finley. And if Paul Finley happens to be meeting with a client on a life-and-death matter? Well, that's just too bad.

And that's the other irritating thing about these calls: They have *never* interrupted Paul Finley on a life-and-death matter. But why tell him that? It wouldn't have made a difference anyway. Whether I had been advising a client how to avoid a hitman's poisoned-tip umbrella on his next spying mission in Moldova or trying to pretend my little Compaq has launched Finley Investigations into the high-tech era, the major point would still have been that Tom Cruise wasn't as good in *XIV* as he had been in the first six or seven, so I was better off saving my money.

When he hasn't been pressing me on his speed dial, Joe has been squeezing himself into crowds. Most of all, there has been the weekly Wednesday night salon at his place where he puts out the wine, cheese, and ashtrays, and waits for former colleagues and students, sometimes just neighbors, to fill up the living room with talk about everything from the Gallic Wars to the latest Mets free agent outfielder. Some weeks, only two or three people show up; other times, there'll be a dozen. The important thing—what makes it impossible to get the old man to the city or anywhere else on Wednesdays—is that everybody in eastern Long Island knows where wine, cheese, and talk can be had on a certain evening. If those who show up also bring along some beer and pretzels, that's okay, too. I always bring some gouda or taleggio because the host's idea of cheese is any cardboard sliced and packaged by Kraft.

When he's not acting as the home team, Joe is making sure others are entertaining him. He belongs to more groups and goes to more meetings than one of those networking compulsives. Start with all the academic associations at Adelphi and in the Tristate area where he is welcomed as a venerable presence. Then throw in the library and other civic organizations. If his local deli had a meeting to complain about wholesale prices, he would be there ranting about the salami supplier. You don't get to be called the Professor without having an opinion about absolutely everything.

And so what? Why should I sound so skeptical about all this? Wasn't Joe Carroll just doing what every mental and physical healer in the universe counseled—keeping busy, maintaining interest in everyday things, not wallowing in his retirement as a death sentence? Of course, he was. It was uplifting, worthy of a postage stamp for inspiring senior citizens. But for my taste, there was also a little too much mortality about it all—a reminder that my father-in-law was the closest thing to a family I had left since the accident that had killed Jenny and my daughter Susan and that without him I wouldn't even have some of his seventeenth-century kings to kick around. I didn't need an excuse for moroseness from among the living; in case you haven't been counting, I've already found enough excuses for that in the dead. And that's not including the walking dead that have become the daily fare of Finley Investigations—the cheating husbands and wives, the slumlords, the insurance company frauds, the surgeons who need nose candy to reach for a scalpel, the workout gurus who never saw a muscle they couldn't tear. I didn't need Joe Carroll and his therapeutic schedule telling me I had taken more than one wrong turn and probably shouldn't have had spells when I wondered what, aside from a few grains of sand, was the real difference between Bay Ridge and the Gobi Desert.

It was partly thanks to all these happy thoughts that I got involved with the Brooklyn Dodger killings.

CHAPTER 2

The Professor's favorite evening every year, what he might have even sacrificed a Wednesday salon for if necessary, was the Brooklyn Dodger Banquet. As you can imagine, there weren't too many life insurance salesmen hovering over the affair flogging long-term policies. At 76, Joe was only slightly older than the average age of the 100 or so who flocked to a downtown Brooklyn hotel room every spring to meet with the ever-thinning survivors of the teams that had played at Ebbets Field until 1957. There was drink and talk about Jackie Robinson, drink and food and talk about Duke Snider, drink and talk about Johnny Podres, and drink and drink and talk and a little more drink and talk about that cocksucker Walter O'Malley who had abducted the team west to resettle it in Los Angeles. The way the old man told it, the evening was as ritualistic as nine innings had once been in Flatbush. From the first order at cocktail hour, everyone did and said the same things, including announcements about what fatal disease had made it impossible for so-and-so to be there again to do and say the same things with them. It had gotten so familiar, he said, that the guests of honor no longer needed questions after dinner, they just stood at the dais podium and rambled on without interruption about the strategies behind some August 1953 game against the Cardinals, sure they were answering some vital question on the minds of the people listening.

If all this sounds like batting practice for a nursing home social, you couldn't tell Joe that. He was never bubblier than right before the Dodger dinner. For him, the evening was more than a chance to jaunt down memory lane, it also let him advertise his Brooklyn roots. It was one thing to drop in on me unannounced every few months and drag me out for walks to see where George Washington had once shot at the Redcoats or where Willy Sutton had once beaten a bank alarm or where Henry Miller had once written something that had made him famous; that was merely being a guide for the unenlightened. But when he got together with the old Ebbets Field crowd, he was peeling off his own part in all that white flight from Brooklyn to the suburbs in the '50s. Nobody wanted to hear how he had lived most of his adult life on Long Island or had risen through the university ranks or had published a dozen books or had raised a daughter. Least of all did *he* want to hear about it. He went back to the Dodger dinner like some Spaniards he had once told me about—the exiled revolutionaries who had sometimes slipped back across the Pyrenees from France to visit old village friends.

Except this time Generalissimo Franco had been waiting for them.

I first heard the news from a twilight state of mind. After six years, I've gotten used to living by myself again, but I still have a problem going to bed without the radio on. That means Mel Torme does a lot of crooning and Dizzy Gillespie a lot of blowing while I'm off in Nod. It also means I wake up every morning to an intruder on my night table sounding a lot like my high school chemistry teacher, Mr. Barone: "Thank you for rejoining us, Mr. Finley . . . As I was saying . . ." What the intruder was saying this time was that Ralph Carey, a one-time outfielder for the Brooklyn Dodgers, had been shot to death the night before in the press box at Citi Field after a game between the Mets and Cubs.

I popped up the way I usually did in Mr. Barone's chemistry class. Forget the jumble of teams, the wrong park, and a killing I felt I was the last one in the city to hear about. My immediate association was Ralph Carey and the Professor. For days, the old man had been going on about how Carey was going to be the special guest at the Dodger dinner and about how the other fanatics were grumbling that they should have found a better attraction than some guy who had been on the team for less than a month. Joe had thought that funny. "How many times they want to hear the same stories from Erskine and Newcombe?" he had laughed into his cellphone just the day before. "Somebody like Carey can give a fresh perspective. The guy who wishes he *had been*. Know what I'm saying?"

"In other words, you've already rationalized why some non-player is worth your $100."

"Screw you, Finley."

At the time, it had been a line just to get him off the phone so I could get back to finishing off my white paper on a sleazy dentist named Francis Forte and his Marquis de Sade notions of dental implants. But sitting up in bed while the announcer went on to talk about hurricanes in Florida, I had a belated attack of squeamishness. I shouldn't have mocked the old man's enthusiasms so glibly. I shouldn't have put a hex on them. I was sick and tired of people being disappointed because other people were getting killed on them. Loony, but that was my first reaction. And the second one wasn't much better—that as soon as the Professor heard the news, he'd be on the phone demanding I call the cops for information he couldn't get from CNN. Before I had even put my foot on the floor for launching a sparkling new day, my toes were squishing the overnight deposit that my pet cats Guilt and Irritation had left for me.

Naturally, I underestimated the aggravation. Instead of a phone call, there was a ring on the downstairs bell about ten minutes after I got out of the shower. "Who the hell do you think it is?" was the password for buzzing him in, unlocking the front door, and going back to my coffee on the kitchen table. As I waited for him to ride up to the third floor, I listed all the reasons I wanted him to know I was annoyed by his visit. The list seemed to start and end with the thought that Ralph Carey had nothing to do with me and, outside a dinner for the fatally nostalgic, not much to do with him, either.

That debating point evaporated as soon as I got a look at him. He charged into the kitchen so out of breath he seemed bent on rescuing me from a gas leak. Whatever wood was left on my second kitchen table chair groaned under the heavy weight he dropped on it. "Goddamn elevator's broken again," he said.

That reassured me. As long as Rudy the super was still sticking his mop in the elevator door upstairs so he wouldn't have to wait three seconds for the car, novelties like heart attacks weren't going to happen in front of my eyes. "It's not broken. But you're doing a good impression you are. Tell me this isn't about Citi Field."

"What the hell you think it's about? I got three calls this morning. The dinner's probably going to be canceled."

I said nothing, letting him play back his own voice for a second. It was a harsh, raspy voice in the best of times—not one that would have let you sleep in his class *a la* Mr. Barone; with his breathing settling down only reluctantly, it dropped a couple of more decibels to a growl. Joe Carroll hadn't borrowed anything from that Kennedy kind of Irish handsomeness; somewhere in his past, there must have been a Dublin fishmonger who had made a deal with the devil to win a lottery in exchange for rubbing some flounder genes into his next-born. From the side, Jenny had shown the same long cheek and jaw drop, but, thank God, without her father's pop-eyes. You didn't fall asleep in the Professor's class, as I had once told her because you might have lost your rod and reel. (That had gotten me a dishtowel snapped in front of my face.)

His breathing normal again, he realized what he had said. "That's a shitty way of putting it, isn't it? What I mean is, this has everybody excited. Gives them something to fret about at dawn besides taking a half-hour to piss. Got more of that coffee?"

"Take your Norvasc, instead."

"Already took it. You going to give me the goddamn coffee or do I have to get it myself?"

I got him his goddamn coffee while he added some particulars I hadn't been curious enough about to go running around the radio dial. Carey had been a baseball broadcaster for a minor league team in Nebraska, where one of his partners had been the latest play-by-play man for the Mets. He had taken advantage of his invitation to the banquet to come in a week early and see New

York. The first thing he had done was look up his old partner at Citi Field; he had been waiting to go out to dinner with him when he had been killed by a single shot to the head. It didn't seem to be a question of a stray bullet or a wrong target; the shot had been fired from within the press-level box where Carey had been sitting. "That's as much as the reports have," he said, his request already peeking out of his eyes as I handed him his mug. "Don't suppose you know anymore?"

"I don't have the hotline going before eight o'clock like you do."

"Get a little older and you'll find out that's the only time you want to talk to people."

He put the mug over his mouth before I could see how serious he was. "What do you expect me to do?"

We both knew the answer to that. For the better part of a year, I'd been dating Dana McGill, a lieutenant with the 107 in Fresh Meadows, on the doorstep of Citi Field. For almost as long, I'd stayed away from asking Dana to press those magic buttons that were supposed to produce shortcuts to all kinds of obscure information on behalf of my clients. In fact, I'd been so careful about crossing lines that even she thought me funny taking transarctic routes to something her Rolodex would have answered in five minutes. But for several good and bad reasons, both of us had observed that ground rule—one that the Professor was now trying to be cagey about asking to be waived. "So, I call somebody and find out they have a dozen leads," I said, knowing I was merely postponing the inevitable. "A) it was a nut job. B) it was some jealous husband who followed Carey here from Nebraska because he didn't want blood all over his wheat stalks. C) it was a nut job. I get this great intelligence and I pass it on to you and you . . . Help me out here, Joe. I don't see what I've accomplished."

"It was my idea."

"What was?"

He looked ashamed to remember. The banquet people had sent out a letter saying none of the special guests invited could make it, so it was up to club members to decide if they wanted to go ahead without a star attraction or call off the dinner for a year. Joe had countered with a proposal they invite a couple of scrubs who had never gotten to talk about what it had been like to be on the bench in Ebbets Field in the good old days. The crack occurred to me ("the same way it had felt sitting in the grandstand, only cheaper"), but I stifled it.

"You listening, Finley? The guy was only in town because I had this brainstorm. If he stayed home, he'd still be alive."

I was back at the synagogue saying goodbye to Rennie Miller. And I didn't like the feeling now in my Bay Ridge kitchen any more than I had liked it standing around on Central Park West 20 years ago. "Things so slow out on the Island? You got to invent responsibilities for yourself?"

A couple of years before, I would have shrunk before his glare. The two of us had spent so much time stoking one another's pain over Jenny and Susan that responsibility had turned into a street corner shell game: keep your eyes on the *real* guilt as opposed to the two sham guilts. It had taken us a long time to walk away from that hustle, and I didn't like seeing it sitting at my kitchen table again.

"I mean it. How do you know the guy didn't bring his problems with him? And if he didn't, it still has nothing to do with you. You want to be in charge of life and death so much? Okay, try this, then. You *don't* come up with your idea to invite Carey. So last night here's this psycho walking around Citi Field looking for a target and he spots this 10-year kid. He kills the kid because Joe Carroll didn't have the brains to invite Ralph Carey to his dinner. That kid's death is your fault too, right?"

"I'm not talking about fault . . ."

"So, who's talking about Carey still being alive if he'd stayed home?"

He took it too well: just staring out the window to the street while he sipped more coffee. "I'm still missing something here, Joe."

"Probably," he said tonelessly. "Will you make a couple of calls? I promised you would."

So, had I—if only to myself.

CHAPTER 3

I called Dana as soon as the old man left. She was out, and I didn't feel like mentioning Ralph Carey on her machine, so I just said hello and hung up. I was that kind of guy: The kind who called for no better reason than to wish people well on their day. If the phone companies had cooperated with reasonable rates, I would have done the same thing with everybody in the city. But since they weren't ready to cooperate, I had to get back to non-Ralph Carey work. At the top of the list was Shari Glynn.

I'd never realized I was fascinated by beads until Shari Glynn hired me. Shari, her husband Marty, and her sister Christine ran a store off Fourth Avenue called Beads, Beads, and More Beads. They sold beads—hundreds, thousands, of them, of all colors, sizes, and shapes, each with its own wooden compartment on one of the five long tables that barely left room in their store for a cash register. Did I mention the store was called Beads, Beads, and More Beads?

The first time I walked into the place, I had a flashback to dreary mornings when my mother had dragged me through Woolworth's, past separate cases for yellow jelly beans, orange jelly beans, white pineapple jelly beans, and purple jelly beans. They had always seemed ripe for some infinite combining if I'd had a big enough ladle. But since I had never become Ronald Reagan and had never found the right shovel, I had been forced to leave all those jelly beans back in Woolworth's until they had torn down the place and all my secret ambitions. What Beads, Beads, and

More Beads teased was that I had another shot, that I didn't have to be President of the United States to swing my jelly bean powers around. What's more, there were lots more kinds of beads than jelly beans. The table for the plastic beads alone had sectioned off trays for berries, crackles, pony hearts, diamond heads, lentil saucers, bells, spaghettis, star flakes, and cherries. The smallest wall display told me that when it came to needles, I could have had round eyes, long eyes, tapestry points, normal points, ball points, or glover's points. When had Ronald Reagan ever been able to offer that kind of variety to Oval Office visitors?

I could have browsed away hours in the store if Shari Glynn hadn't put me on a clock at our first meeting. The only time I was allowed to report to her was between noon and 12:30, when sister Christine was upstairs in their apartment fixing lunch and husband Marty was dealing with wholesalers over in Manhattan. This was Shari's way of ensuring I didn't exist for Christine or Marty. If either of them happened to enter the store while I was there, I was instructed, I was to start talking about buying a gift for my wife and leave the rest of the conversation to her.

I'd been recommended to Shari by a psychiatrist at Kings County, where sister Christine had spent as much time as the doctors and nurses. The general diagnosis was a bipolar disorder with psychotic episodes. Younger sister Shari and Marty had taken in Christine as much out of apprehension as family solidarity. The last time Christine had been on her own, she had used a broken beer bottle on an employer because, after one two-hour afternoon romp in a motel, he had refused to leave his wife for her. The cops had gotten involved, Christine had been hospitalized, and an assault charge had been shelved only because Shari and Marty had persuaded the employer he had enough trouble without bringing newspapers and TV cameras into it. Then John Wells had come along.

Wells had started off as a shopper for a costume designer at Beads, Beads, and More Beads, had graduated to regular schmoozer with Christine over the counter and had then begun taking her out. Shari and Marty had had no objections to any of this; in fact, they had been relieved Christine had found more to do with her evenings than take her meds and sit upstairs in her bedroom in front of a portable 16" black-and-white. But then Shari had begun hearing things about Wells. He had claimed to be an interior decorator, but the company he had boasted about working for knew him only as an odd-jobs man. He had claimed to be single with an apartment in Red Hook, but at least one friend of a friend of a friend had passed the word to the Glynns that there were two Wells children and a wife in Rockaway and that the Red Hook place looked like a very temporary shelter. Christine herself had joked about how the guy had paid for one of their dinners with a credit card not in his name and how he had explained it away by saying he had several names for staying ahead of collection agencies, but always paid off each card every month. In short, there were enough questions about John Wells that Shari had begun worrying about a repeat of the broken bottle scene at the motel. Marty Glynn's solution had been to confront the guy, make him tell Christine some of the more awkward facts he hadn't shared with her, and go from there. But Shari had enlisted Dr. Marian Freedman at Kings County for her alternative of spending a few dollars to find out how much truth there was in the stories about Wells. As she had said to me the first time in the store, "If this prick's leading Chris on, we'll have to deal with it. But first, let's make sure *I'm* not the one screwing up things for her."

I liked Shari Glynn and didn't mind the little game we had prepared for any interruption from Marty or Christine. I put her on my B client list—midway between the A's who reimbursed me for every drop of gas I used on a job and the C's who got my MetroCard rates. I guessed within five minutes of meeting her that, small and pert as she was, she had been the one to run with Marty's beads idea and turn it into a going business. Maybe it was a requisite for her trade, but her eyes didn't miss anything: It took her all of a half-second with our first handshake to notice my pleasant thumb scar from a store window shard of glass. I wouldn't have been surprised if Marty's dealings with Manhattan wholesalers were mainly an excuse for keeping him out of the store so he wouldn't gum up things.

Perched on a stool next to her cash register, her arms folded across her green blouse, Shari showed nothing while I told her what I had found out about John Wells. The gist of it was she had been right to be worried. The only John Wells I'd found who matched her description had also been John Walsh, Joseph Wells, and James Wells. As Joseph Wells, he had been married at St. Teresa of Avila church in 1989 to Rosanne Lucca, had fathered a boy and a girl, and had taken up residence in Rockaway Point, where the wife and children still lived. Johnny, Joey, Jimmy, or whatever his name was had in the meantime moved inland to pursue various careers having to do with living rooms. He had indeed worked for several companies as an interior decorator, for another as a house painter, and for himself as a burglar. In 1999, he had been sentenced to three years for breaking into a two-family house in the Morrisania section of the Bronx shortly after delivering shampooed rugs to the premises. He had done 11 months, then been paroled. His parole officer had had no complaints, had in fact been the one to put him into contact with his most recent employer—the costume designer who had wanted him to drop by Beads, Beads, and More Beads to price some merchandise. His Red Hook place belonged to an absentee landlord who rented it by the month. He had never officially separated from the wife in Rockaway Point. Bottom line: Would he eventually break Christine Sewell's heart and maybe more than that? Only an idiot would take money against it.

"That fuck." Shari Glynn said it calmly, trying to look interested in the thin gold bracelet shaped like a snake on her wrist. "The last few weeks, she's really looked happy."

"She's also helped him stiff people with those credit cards."

I didn't need to remind her of that. I didn't have to say another word at all. My job was done. But since she wasn't an A-list client, the kind I was only too glad to charge for services rendered and then forget about, it didn't feel right just to walk out with an announcement that my bill would be in the mail. "There's no way she's not going to be hurt. But there are ways and ways. Somebody could talk to him."

"And say what, Mr. Finley? Have him tell Chris he's going back to his wife? He's moving to Peru?"

I almost said it again: *"There are ways and ways."* But of course, there really weren't. Whether Christine got the news directly from Wells on a park bench, from Shari in the store, or from Dr. Freedman at Kings County, all the ways were going to end up back inside her rage.

"Well, that's not your problem," Shari said, unfolding her arms with a sigh and standing not nearly so much taller than the stool. "I appreciate what you've found out."

Like funeral directors, private investigators are trained to nod when told their work is "appreciated." Only the witless ones go beyond that. "You'll come off as a snooper to her," I insisted. "All in all, it might be better if he just disappeared from the scene. She'll hurt and she'll wonder, but she won't hold it against you. She'll never know for sure."

The iron came into her tiny jaw so fast I felt like I belonged in one of her bead bins. "You say that like it's something we should all strive for."

CHAPTER 4

Okay, so the day wasn't getting off to a glorious start. But there were still many hours to go for making everything worse, so I set off eagerly from Beads, Beads, and More Beads. Ralph Carey hadn't impressed the Dodgers even for an ability to run out the ground ball, but that much I could do.

I started by grabbing a couple of newspapers at Roger's candy store and taking them to Sal's luncheonette. No matter how ecstatic Dana was going to be just to hear my questions about Carey, I figured the smarter they were, the less chance of her ecstasy subsiding to normal elation. The *News* had it all over the front page (MURDER AT CITI FIELD), but hadn't regarded Carey as enough of a household name to mention him specifically before the page three story. I'm no newspaper editor, but that struck me as odd—missing the old Dodger connection with the victim. The *Times* had settled for the top of the fold of the Metro section, but at least had what the *News* had missed: FORMER DODGER SLAIN AT CITI FIELD.

I didn't find much in either paper the Professor hadn't told me. Carey had been in a press-level box waiting to go to dinner; an unknown intruder had gotten inside and killed him with a single bullet; the press-level guard, one Larry Grabowski, had heard and seen nothing; most of the reporters had already hurried downstairs for postgame interviews; the radio and television crews for both the Mets and the Cubs had been busy winding up their casts. Larry Grabowski's chief contribution to the investigation, according to the *News*, had been that "you wouldn't notice a shot so easy anyway because a lot of fans leaving like to pop beer cups on the ramp and that sounds like a shot sometimes." The *News* didn't say so, but I assumed (hoped) whoever had been asking the questions had immediately jumped on Larry Grabowski with that opening: "You saying you *did* hear something but thought it was just a beer cup, Larry?"

"A beaut, ain't it?"

Sal Reni nodded to the front page of the *News* from his regular standing post behind the register. Not counting muttered Hellos and Take Cares, the question just about doubled the number of words he had spared for me over the last year of daily coffees and a weekly burger. I never thought of Sal as unfriendly, particularly; just somebody who needed a reason to be friendly. Something Ralph Carey had apparently given him. "Remember him as a player?"

"Yeah. He was a bum."

He might have gotten that much from the *News* story, but then again, he had volunteered conversation and he had to be as old as the Professor. "What's your theory?"

He thought that was funny enough to merit a new toothpick from the basket next to the register. "Theory! I got no theory. Lunatics they got goin' to games these days, you're happy it's not happenin' every day. How's that for a theory?"

It wasn't from the great philosophers, but it hit me as so immaculately wrong, it amounted to wisdom. Whoever had chosen the time and place and been so thrifty and accurate, was anything *but* a lunatic. How could a scrub outfielder 50 years out of the game have attracted a professional shooter?

"I remember one game when he wasn't a bum. Probably his greatest game for the Dodgers."

"Oh, yeah?"

Suddenly, Sal Reni was digging for more than food particles between his lower teeth. It occurred to me I was probably the hundredth person sitting at his counter with the MURDER AT CITI FIELD headline since he had opened that morning. Had he weathered the other 99, but found me just one temptation too many for reliving some important moment?

"Must've been 1949 or 1950," he said. "Against the Braves. Shotton was the manager. The guy who didn't wear a uniform sat on the bench in a windbreaker. He sends Carey up as a pinch-hitter in the bottom of the ninth with Brooklyn behind by a run and runners on second and third. Only guy left, so Shotton had to use him. First pitch, guy hits a grounder to third. Goddamn ball goes right through the third baseman's legs, two runs score, Brooklyn wins. I remember that game like it was yesterday."

"Carey was safe on an error and that was his greatest moment??"

It was clearly my day. First Shari Glynn had wondered about my life's goals in the present-day world, now Sal Reni looked at me as though I hadn't appreciated much in the past, either. "Won the game, didn't it?"

Who could deny it? I even saw the score in neon circling the Times Tower or whatever the hell they called the latest monolith on Times Square. It said CAREY 1 FINLEY 0. And that was with him dead!

CHAPTER 5

I met Dana at the Italian restaurant in the Village that had willy-nilly become our public base. She thought Da Francesco was a fair midway meeting point because it was 20 miles away from my apartment on the other side of the East River, three blocks away from her apartment, and I had no sense of geography. I thought it was a good place because it gave me an excuse to get out of the apartment that doubled as an office for too many hours every day and because I had no sense of geography. In Brooklyn or Queens, the rose tablecloths, hanging wicker, and brownish lighting would have been the basics for a family restaurant in which nine-year-old Joeys were always demanding Chicken McNuggets instead of spaghetti. In the Village, they made for a date place where the only pastas ordered were those that didn't call for napkins over the chest and where the favorite dessert was grazing fingertips over espressos and sambucas.

Dana had more than one surprise for me. The first was the aqua blouse and black skirt I'd last seen on her the first time we'd met at Da Francesco. That night hadn't started off as a date at all; in fact, she had been only a go-between for me and a Midtown South cop for an investigation I'd been working on. But because the evening had *ended* as a date, I'd developed a special affection for that outfit, and had only refrained from asking her about it since because I'd wanted it to reappear on its own. When it did, I'd humored myself during long drives a couple of times, I might still be a fool when it came to geography but I would be very clear about how far both of us had or had not traveled in 11 months.

So, what was the answer? I had to postpone thinking about it when she sprang her second surprise—her announcement over our first wines that she was working the Ralph Carey case. Some kind of bureaucratic squeeze play over a lush who should have headed it and fears he wouldn't have been up to the media harassment over a killing that might not have been high-profile for the victim but that certainly was for its venue. Dana had gotten the job despite working at a Fresh Meadows precinct dubbed the Garden of Eden because of its fairly low crime rate. But rabbis she hadn't known she had apparently didn't think that was nearly as important as her Homicide background. And—surprise number three—she wasn't happy about it. She hadn't been involved in anything so loud in more than three years and even then when we had first met, she had been a sergeant seconded to the chief investigator. "I have a feeling someone's thrown me in the water to win a bet I'll drown."

She said it sardonically, but there was no humor in her eyes and her long face looked tired. She'd also combed her raven hair into one of those square dos Claudette Colbert and other actresses of the Forties had worn: the unmarried aunt who might wink here and there at the proprieties but who was eminently sensible. I hadn't realized before how much I'd counted on our being together to be the opposite of sensible. "Sure, it's not just because it reminds you of Bernie?"

She had been through that possibility with herself, and could now shrug it off as possible, probable, or irrelevant. Alan Bernstein, her superior, mentor, and secret love when I'd met her, had been killed during a case I'd been responsible for dumping on their laps. That had made it easy for her to accept two years of desk work at Police Plaza before moving on to the Garden of Eden and even easier to avoid good thoughts about me for a long while. "If that's the problem, I better get over it. I'm sure the Carey family wouldn't spend too much time being sympathetic."

"How's it going so far?"

She crinkled her small nose at the thought. "Ballparks are eerie when they're empty. The Ghost of Christmas-To-Come or something."

"Never been."

She nodded. She wanted business out of the way of our meal as much as I did. "You said Joe has some connection to this?"

I plunged in with the story of the Professor and his Brooklyn Dodger dinner and the invitation to Carey. She took it in as worn news. She had known about the banquet and had planned to talk to its organizers. Would the Professor know if anybody had been invited with Carey or, maybe more important, *instead of* Carey? I had no idea, but I would ask. What about the grumblers who hadn't wanted Carey as their guest—how seriously had they grumbled? I didn't know, but she was kidding, right? Did I think it would be productive to talk to the old man? I didn't know that, either. For sure, he would feel more involved if she spoke to him directly, and that might get him off my back. Shouldn't she consider that one of her priorities? She didn't say yes and she didn't say no.

"You've ruled out a random shooting?"

"I'd be surprised."

"And a nut?"

"No."

"Single shot? Right to the target? Careful about slipping in and out of the box . . .?"

She gazed at the wine in her hand more coyly; she didn't look like the good sport aunt anymore. Lieutenant McGill had a secret and you had to say Pretty Please to discover it. "He might not have been in the box at all."

"How's that possible? What I've read between the lines is you had powder burns establishing proximity."

"Maybe you shouldn't read between the lines so much."

"A feint? For what?"

She shook her head. "No, there were powder burns, all right."

"Then he had to be in the press box with Carey."

She wouldn't have minded our regular waiter Nello bringing a menu, and I didn't know if that was because she thought I was getting too close to the line or because she was simply hungry. "One of the nice things about this detail I inherited is a nerd named Herman Loschen," she said, sagging as Nello ignored her again. "Some people might say Herman has the personality of a dishrag, and from his sheets, the next time he qualifies on the range will be the first time. But he has more uncles with the right phone numbers than a Bush nephew. He's hidden away in the Garden of Eden, and who'll notice him? But Herman also has a saving grace that makes stashing him worth it every once in a while—he's got a brain. A handicap in the big picture, of course, but it's been a handy excuse for keeping him around. Now Herman, he gets this idea at the crime scene last night, but he keeps it to himself until the ME report comes in this morning. No doubt the bullet was fired at close range, but at a left-right angle that doesn't fit with somebody barging into Carey's box, getting him to look around in surprise, then dropping him. Something else Herman doesn't like is the guard not hearing or seeing anything even though he was standing outside Carey's box no more than 10 feet away."

"The guard sounds like he wouldn't notice a buffalo charging in."

"But why have the lowest common denominator for an explanation?"

I could hear her old boss Bernstein coming through her voice for that wisdom and went back to my glass before she saw I had heard it.

"So, this afternoon, Herman goes into the box next to the one where Carey was, leans out of it, and sees how much of a clear shot he would have had doing it that way."

"You're kidding."

She looked as proud for herself as for Loschen. "Not only that. The door to the adjoining box is on the far side of a big curve in the stadium that would have made it very easy for the shooter to get out without being seen by the guard. A few yards along, the shooter's out in a general traffic area, down a ramp, and out of the park."

"But what about the added risk? Anybody leaning out of one box to shoot into another one could be seen by anybody at all. All those people in the lower deck, for starters."

"The ballgame was over. The park was almost cleared out."

"I'm not talking about thousands. Just one. An usher picking up a dollar tip he dropped. Somebody back for a hat he left. A maintenance man sweeping up. And then you got the grounds-keepers out on the field laying down the tarpaulin. Anybody at all."

"I know. That's the one thing that bothers me about Herman's idea."

"So, you're still assuming the shot was fired from inside the box?"

"Oh, no. I think Loschen nailed it. That *is* the way it happened. What bothers me about the idea is that the shooter knew all the things you just said and still thought that was the best way of doing it. We're dealing with some serious North Pole blood here, Finley."

CHAPTER 6

I found out more about Ralph Carey over the next few days than I'd wanted to know. He had lived in Lincoln, Nebraska for more than 50 years, been married almost as long, had two sons and three grandchildren, been a pillar of the Methodist Church and the United Way, had chaired various committees for Reagan and the two Bushes, and had organized annual trips for underprivileged kids to Disneyworld or Colonial Williamsburg. In his 80-game career for the Dodgers and Pirates, he had batted .210 for 21 hits in exactly 100 at-bats, with two home runs, seven steals (he apparently did a lot of pinch-running), and five errors. In his career as an announcer for the Omaha Royals, he had been liked by listeners, players, and sponsors. Before retiring two years ago, he had been known as Mister Mike for never missing a Royals game in 32 years. Bottom line? If Ralph Carey had drawn the attention of a professional hitman, it had to be because he had swiped the guy's peanuts on the flight to New York.

The Professor called to tell me the banquet was going on as scheduled, with a commemoration of Carey in place of reminiscences about errors by Braves third basemen. He sounded elated when I passed along Loschen's theory about the lean-around execution. Only when I didn't see that tidbit in the next day's paper did it occur to me I might have blabbed something Dana wouldn't have liked. I reached for my phone without the slightest doubt I was too late. "Don't worry," he told me. "She and I have reached full agreement on what I should say and not say."

"What!!??"

"She's coming Wednesday night. You coming?"

It's bad enough feeling a fast one is being pulled right in front of your eyes, but I wasn't even sure who was pulling it. The old man because he wanted to impress his other salon guests with his personal pipeline to the NYPD or Dana because she wanted to be sure she wasn't overlooking some connection between the dinner and Carey's death? "Don't play games, Joe."

"What games! We need a little street talk to liven things up. The only street you know these days is Shore Road."

I didn't have time to work myself up further. Not only did he hang up, but the phone immediately rang. It was Shari Glynn. "I've thought about what you said, Mr. Finley," she said. "I've decided you're right about John Wells. Could you talk to him?"

There was a pleasant novelty in somebody saying I had been right about something. On the other hand, it hadn't been about a lottery number. "I really don't think that's my job, Shari."

"I'd pay you extra for your trouble."

It was undoubtedly my sour mood after talking to the Professor, but that hit me as taking back her compliment with interest. "It's not a question of money. You've got a family problem, and that's best kept in the family. Get your husband to talk to him."

Stupid me: That would have meant doing something sensible, such as telling her husband she had hired me to look into Wells in the first place. If I had lived off anything since leaving the Nassau County Department, it had been on people doing what *wasn't* sensible. For a minute or so, I listened to all her travels around that fact. She could have talked to Doctor Freedman, of course, but it was hardly Doctor Freedman's job to get directly involved with pond scum like Wells. She had thought about contacting Wells's parole officer, but that seemed like such an official step, she couldn't imagine it not coming back into Beads, Beads, and More Beads and not only angering husband Marty but fouling her relations with her sister for good. No, she had concluded, I was the only solution.

"And what about you, Shari?"

"Me?"

"You. You talk to him."

"But . . . what would I say?"

Since I had already decided Shari Glynn had never been conned by a wholesaler because she hadn't read a delivery order close enough, I wasn't taken with the startled belle in my ear. Clearly, the theme was that I was the hired help and could leave her free for belated regrets if any were needed down the road.

"It would only have to be one meeting," she said. "If that doesn't work out, Marty and I will just have to take care of it ourselves. I just don't want Chris hurt unnecessarily."

I decided I still liked Shari Glynn, but that her request and all the salad around it earned her a boost to my A-list. "One meeting. $510."

"$510??"

"$500 for the meeting and the other ten because I'm not going to leave my car on the street in his neighborhood. I'll need the garage I saw down there last week."

"I don't know if that's reasonable or not. I've never done anything like this before."

What was reasonable, I wanted to tell her, was that the $500 would do wonders for the phone and electricity bills staring up at me from my desk; I could make them disappear without having to touch the gag called Finley's Savings. "If you can find somebody cheaper, Shari, get him."

"Okay, okay. $510. When do you think you could see him? Chris just told me they're going out Thursday night."

What was Mr. Party Pooper to do? On the one hand, Christine Sewell could have one last night of illusion if Mr. Party Pooper didn't swing into action until Friday. Once Wells disappeared (to be optimistic), when would she be in condition for another one? On the other hand, if Wells was using her for some scam, Thursday night might have been trap-springing time. Did Mr. Party Pooper dare let her go ahead with the date in the name of romance, one final roll in the hay, or a last request to the warden?

Of course, he did. And being not only Mr. Party Pooper, but Mr. Keep Things Complicated When Possible, he also made up his mind to earn a few tens of Shari Glynn's $500 by checking in on the date, just in case Wells persuaded Christine over the restaurant candles to break into Beads, Beads, and More Beads.

CHAPTER 7

Fame can be fleeting, especially for old ballplayers nobody had heard of before they had been shot to death. Ralph Carey's body had barely been released for burial in Nebraska when the case slipped down to second place behind a subway shooting. The victim was a Chinese pastry chef named Michael Leong, who was going home from work after midnight. Leong might not have had Carey's even semi-celebrity, but subway station platforms touched a lot more nerves than Citi Field press-level boxes, especially with the shooter having apparently opened fire Buffalo Bill style from a train leaving the Canal Street station. Not that Carey was completely forgotten. He even provided a tasteless segue for the newsreader on my bathroom radio since he too had been taken down with a single shot. Or, as the moron couldn't resist cracking in the name of outrageous commentary: "Never let it be said New York doesn't have plenty of marksmen."

The moron wasn't only tasteless, he was wrong. As it turned out, there was only one marksman involved.

CHAPTER 8

I picked up Christine Sewell in front of Beads, Beads, and More Beads a little after 7:30. She was a bony blonde with pale skin, dressed in a blue suit that looked too staid for anything but a job interview. As she went down to the corner, she wobbled for more reasons than her black heels. But *why* had she needed to fortify herself for her date? I didn't like the answer I landed on. Since neither the shrink nor the sister had mentioned a drinking problem, I had a wormy feeling she had been hitting the Chablis for something special with Wells.

She stood on the corner of Fifth for almost a quarter-hour looking anxiously north and south. When she showed no interest in the empty cab that deliberately slowed for her, I worked it out scientifically that she was waiting for Wells. She didn't have my calm analytic mind. Three, four times she looked at her watch, each time dropping her wrist back down to her side angrily. Shari Glynn's sister was clearly not someone to be kept waiting.

Wells finally showed up in a blue Subaru. Christine gave him a rigid half-wave as she stepped into the car. All the body tension made me think too easily of the motel scene that had gotten her hospitalized. The value of $510 also seemed to shrink as I followed the Subaru down Fifth toward the Verrazano Bridge. I have no more against Staten Island than anybody else. It's there because a freaky gas fissure from the earth's crust put it there, and nothing's to be gained by pretending Nature doesn't occasionally work in perverse ways. But the bridge almost certainly meant some cut-rate Staten Island motel next to a Dunkin' Donuts, and that seemed to be *really* testing Christine's control over *déjà vu.*

Another trouble with the Verrazano Bridge is that it has too much horizon around it. Most of the other bridges in the city have an interior feel to them: You're over water for a couple of minutes, but you're never actually going anywhere outside. The wide roads of the Verrazano, on the other hand, insinuate big things—oceans, other states, other parts of the world. They hint at journeys taken and not taken, make you feel more vulnerable about both. The idea that I was collecting an easy $500, that I could give Christine and Wells a quick once-over and then go back home satisfied that I'd earned my extra money, suddenly seemed careless. Nothing was that simple, the bridge reminded me. Getting right down to it, I might have been a lot safer helping the Professor track down Ralph Carey's killer.

And then surprise surprise. The Subaru's destination wasn't a motel at all, but a lodge house two blocks up a hilly street off Hylan Boulevard. An Irish flag hung over the entrance, and a sign proclaimed THE EMERALD CLUB. Music was playing inside, and middle-aged couples were going in for what looked like some kind of racket. I was so confused processing this development—Wells as an ethnic militant? —that I almost rear-ended the Subaru. Christine got out of the car, looked peeved to be told she couldn't help with the parking and stalked over to the sidewalk. If Wells had anything like a brain, I told myself, he would find his parking space somewhere west of Philadelphia.

But of course, if Wells had a brain, he wouldn't have done time, picked out Christine Sewell as his next mark, or blithely waved me out of his way so he could back up into a space around the corner. By the time I found my own niche another block away, I had visions of him beating it back to the Emerald Club, telling Christine his plans for breaking into Beads, Beads, and More Beads, and getting a broken glass in his jugular for having used her. But why get stuck on grim views of humanity all the time? I remained a Finley, and if a Finley didn't have a friend named O'Connor or Callaghan somewhere, he didn't deserve to be a Finley. Luckily, the woman at the club door agreed with me. For twenty bucks, she urged me to wait for my friend O'Connor inside and "meet your neighbors."

The turnout was for a combination dance and recruitment drive. The one big room, more like a converted meeting hall, was a sea of trestle tables with beer pitchers holding down paper coverings. A heavily amped quintet of kids was in a platformed corner playing something that didn't sound remotely Irish; at least it was upbeat enough for a graying couple to revive their lindy days. Since I had absolutely no idea what I was supposed to do next, I dropped down on the first empty folding chair that didn't belong to a family gathering. A beaming guy in a Navy T-shirt and anchor tattoos running down both arms immediately introduced himself as Arty and "the Missus" as Joan and poured a beer into one of the Styrofoam cups he had stacked in front of him as though they were personal possessions. While I went through some rigmarole about friends who hadn't shown up yet, I zeroed in on Wells and Christine.

They were seated with two thirtyish couples right off the bandstand. Wells couldn't possibly hear what the brunette across the table was saying to him in the din, but he kept nodding genially, encouraging her to keep going. He was a slight, balding guy with frameless glasses, more accountant at leisure than con man in rehearsal. I had seen a thousand John Wellses on subways and at ballgames without thinking they were hatching a scheme that would set off an unbalanced mark. Call it the effects of the first beer I'd drunk in months, but I started wondering if I was charging Shari Glynn for nothing more than tailing her sister and Wells on a cheap date.

Arty and Joan were new to Staten Island and had seen a notice for the beer party in the newspaper. They saw no reason not to join the club, and I understood their attitude. They were glad to have my understanding, but then fell silent and looked at me expectantly. It was my turn. I got it into gear to tell them about my old school buddy O'Connor, as late tonight as he had always been for physics class, and they had known enough O'Connors in their own lives to laugh appreciatively. I decided I liked Arty and Joan—as long as they kept their heads apart so I could have a clear view of Christine. She had lost some of her edginess from the street, but not all of it. The way she sat hunched over at her place at the end of the table, her hands on the bag on her lap, trying to find the brunette as entertaining as Wells apparently did, told me she had a timer on her cordiality.

Arty was an exterminator, Joan a computer web designer. They had decided to move from Rahway, New Jersey to Staten Island because he had been offered a partnership in an exterminator business and he figured there were more termites, rodents, and lice in New York than in New Jersey. ("Just a joke.") Joan was three months pregnant because they had agreed "new beginnings should mean beginnings all around." ("Only kidding—sort of.") What did I do for a living? Oh, I was a researcher. Old documents, gravestones, that kind of thing. They found that interesting. Arty himself had always had "that family tree bug." Could I suggest some place where he might get a start looking up his ancestors?

I had barely mentioned the Mormons when Christine jumped up from her chair and did another of her stalking marches toward the back of the hall. I assumed she was heading for the Ladies, but her style in doing so cast an immediate pall over Wells and his friends. He looked more like a bumbling husband than a con man as he stood up, said something apologetic, and tried not to act frantic about hurrying after her. There was a lot of eye rolling at the table—a reaction I imagined Arty and Joan copied when I also got to my feet, promising more about Brigham Young after I made sure Christine wasn't about to start hacking away at the Sewell family tree in ways the Mormons would have never endorsed.

The rear of the hall was a narrow corridor with wooden paneling and a century's worth of beer fumes. There were three doors— a Men's Room, a Ladies Room, and the usual heavy emergency exit with an iron slide bar. The exit door's tongue had been left loosely off the lock and the voices outside told me who had left it like that. The first words I heard were Christine's: "I've changed my mind! I don't like those people!"

"You barely met them, Chris!"

"I know people!"

I would have felt better about snickering at that claim if I had known what I was supposed to do next: retreat to my table, just go on standing behind the door, or go out into the alley or yard or whatever it was and look astonished I hadn't walked into a room of urinals. A flush from one of the bathrooms hinted I make up my mind fast.

"Let's just leave, Johnny!" she said again.

"Okay, okay. But let's get them to cash your check first."

"I told you I changed my mind. We'll cash it with somebody else."

"Why? They said they'd do it. What difference who cashes it?"

A small drop of nasty fluid dropped out of my lungs into my stomach. I hadn't needed to hear about checks. Weren't there banks for those things? What could possibly be good about Christine Sewell—in the company of John Wells—going all the way to Staten Island to meet strangers so she could cash one of them? Nothing occurred to me. What did, on the other hand, was the likelihood that the check had something to do with Beads, Beads, and More Beads.

An elderly pixie-sized woman with thick glasses came out of the Ladies Room, joggled her lenses, and took me in as a fire violation. "You should quit, young man. It's a nasty habit and it'll kill you. There's a reason they've banned smoking, you know."

It was as good an idea as any I'd had, and fortunately, there was a two-week-old pack of Marlboro Lights in my pocket. I had a cigarette in my hand a second before Wells and Christine came in from the alley. The old lady didn't notice they were more put out than she was. "What's going outside supposed to prove?" she demanded of them. "You're just putting all that nicotine in the air. They should ban that, too."

Wells went from suspicion to bewilderment as the woman toddled off. I gave him a shrug about the strange ways of old people, and he seemed appeased. Christine wasn't so sure. She had been living on the edge for a long time, she had been up to something sneaky with a check, and now somebody had been lurking near her conversation in the alley. Not even the Marlboro in my hand seemed to convince her completely. But whatever was on her mind died behind her thin lips when Wells took her by the elbow and led her back to the hall. I told myself it didn't matter that she had gotten a good look at me, that I would be seeing only Wells one more time, not her, to earn my $500. I wanted to believe that more than she was ready to believe I had been in the corridor for a cigarette.

When I returned to my table, I found Arty and Joan with another couple. The guy worked at something in Manhattan and the woman worked at two or three kids, and both had more fascinating things than lame gambits about the Mormons to say to Arty and Joan. I smiled along without taking my eyes off the Wells table. It seemed to have taken only half the night, but I finally focused on the people who were being primed for cashing Christine's check. Maybe it was just the fact that they were at least acquaintances of John Wells, but they didn't strike me as innocuous as Arty and Joan or the new couple now talking about traffic on the Belt Parkway. One of the guys in particular—a redhead with sharper's eyes, a laugh that didn't quit when somebody was looking directly at him, and a laugh that vanished instantly when nobody was looking at him—wouldn't have been out of place on a police computer screen. The word *accomplice* started digging a hole in my brain. As long as I already had Christine swiping money from the profits of Beads, Beads, and More Beads, why not add a few curlicues to that inspiration by deciding that Wells and the redhead were setting her up for something even worse than hitting the till?

When the transaction took place 15 minutes later, I almost missed it. Having a clear view of Wells and Christine didn't help much when the food came out of the kitchen behind the bandstand and was laid out between our two tables. The buffet line for the ziti and the chicken formed quickly, blocking me off from whatever I was supposed to be watching. I'd already eaten, but a chicken wing didn't seem like much of a diet splurge for being able to keep my eyes on the front table. I was still looking for the end of the food line when the sharpie took out a clip of bills and peeled off a few. Christine wasn't watching because she was busy endorsing her check. I lost whatever appetite I'd had for the chicken wing.

Figuring Wells and Christine had accomplished what they had come to accomplish and would be leaving sooner than later,

I cut out with a wave to Arty, Joan, and the rest of the gang. The hilly one-way street where the lodge was made it impossible to hover over Wells's Subaru without being conspicuous, but I still needed a head start to retrieve my car. I had underestimated their haste. I was still descending toward Hylan Boulevard at stall-speed wondering about the best place for positioning myself when the Subaru cut me off and started down to the big avenue. Obviously, there had been no social niceties with the sharpie and the others about sticking around for another round. Cashing the check *had* been the sole purpose of their get-together, so why pretend otherwise?

Wells went straight back to Brooklyn, to a Flatbush Avenue apartment above an art supplies store on the edge of Park Slope. He fumbled with the keys long enough at the street door to persuade me he was borrowing the place for the evening; he certainly convinced Christine, who finally yanked the keys from his hand and got the lock on the first try. I had dealt with hustlers before and I had dealt with marks before, but I had never dealt with people who had such feeble holds on their roles.

As soon as the lights went on on the second floor, I got out from behind the wheel and crossed Flatbush to check the bells. The second floor said MONAGHAN, and that didn't exactly rule out the redhead at the Irish racket. The ferrets I kept tied to my nerve endings as pets immediately announced they wanted to chew on something. They also wanted to know why Wells couldn't have gone to his own Red Hook place with Christine—a question I took back to the car. The answer I liked least was about Wells and Monaghan pulling an ever-tighter net around Christine. Compromise her with a check. Compromise her with Monaghan's cash. Compromise her as somebody who knew Monaghan well enough to screw in his apartment. Compromise her . . . with what next? Whatever it was, Beads, Beads, and More Beads seemed sure to be in the middle of it.

The next three hours were tolerable, but barely. The minus side was that I dipped into my ancient Marlboros twice—not only giving myself incurable diseases but forcing myself to pretend I wasn't smoking nicotine mold. I wouldn't have minded some music for company; instead, I had the lyrics of how fast I had talked Dana out of buying me an iPod for Christmas. Turning on the car radio was out for any number of reasons—frying my battery, waking up somebody in the brownstones around me, and, especially, drawing attention from the cops moving in and out of the 76th precinct diagonally across from where I was parked. As it was, it seemed a small marvel none of them gave me a second look. Two uniforms even walked past me on their way to foot patrol. One reason that came to mind—from the bad old days in Nassau County—was that they *had* seen me, but had also assumed I was from Internal Affairs doing a surveillance on one of theirs. That notion did nothing at all for my ego.

But the three hours also had a plus side. In the middle of trying to picture the furniture in the second-floor apartment, I had an epiphany: *I knew exactly what I was going to do as soon as Wells and Christine left the place.* Wells had done me a favor by bringing her to Monaghan's. The most diplomatic way of getting him out of her life, or whatever it was I had promised Shari Glynn to do, was to forget about both and lean on Monaghan. The rest would be falling dominoes: Monaghan telling Wells, Wells taking the hint and moving on as fast as he could, and Christine resigning herself to having to strike up new conversations in the beads store. She would never see my fingerprints, her sister's, or her brother-in-law's. The key to heading off another bloody Christine Sewell scene, in other words, was in moving even further away from her.

That was the answer to everything!

CHAPTER 9

I didn't worry about the speck in my inspiration—the possibility that the redheaded sharpie with the check and Monaghan weren't the same person. Why be negative when all the stars in the sky are shining up there specifically for you? When the lights went off on the second floor, I saw myself as one of those pudgy straw-hatted Dominicans in Sunset Park setting up his dominoes on a sidewalk table ready to clean up Fourth Avenue. I told myself it was neither here nor there that Christine came down with her arm around Wells's waist, looking contented for their interlude. I couldn't have been more confident watching them as they strolled up to St. Mark's Place for his car. Granted the next half-hour could have gone faster while I stayed put waiting for Monaghan and granted I didn't need the thought of Wells and Christine meeting up with him at Beads, Beads, and More Beads to pull off their job then and there in Bay Ridge while I hummed George Harrison songs to myself on Flatbush Avenue. But, as I said, I was in a positive frame of mind, and as any Born Again will tell you, faith is its own reward.

And Jesus was good again. A green Honda finally pulled up in front of the art supplies store, delivering the redhead. The driver was the chatty brunette from the Staten Island table, and she wasted little time hitting the gas when Monaghan slammed his door closed. I had apparently missed his first bad scene on the evening. I waited until the lights went back on on the second floor, then walked over. I didn't know what I was going to say until he answered the bell. A mumbled "Beer delivery from the Emerald Club" wasn't exactly "When in the Course of Human Events," but it was enough for Monaghan to buzz me in.

The stairs seemed to be made of flakeboard, but I took them quickly and lightly enough not to go through them. I was only a few feet away from the door on the second-floor landing when Monaghan, still in his suit jacket, opened it. He looked surprised for all of about two seconds. But by the time the yard rat came into his eyes I was nudging him back into his apartment with my favorite two fingers in his chest. "You have something of mine."

"Who the fuck are you??!!"

"Christine's banker. She said she gave you a check by mistake."

Say this for Monaghan: He'd had more ethnic right to be at the Staten Island racket than anybody else there. The red hair and pale blue eyes came with an actual brogue. "You're talkin' to the wrong party, lad. Must have me mixed up with someone else."

There were probably a hundred reasons for belting him. I didn't like what he and Wells were plotting (whatever it was). I didn't like having to shoot my gas on a drive to Staten Island. I didn't like having to sit in my car for almost four hours. I didn't like brogues. I didn't like the results of the last presidential election. Down to it, though, I just liked reaching the jut of his jaw with the back of my hand and watching him try to propel himself over a front room table without going down. He almost made it, using the rim of the table to stop his ass. But then he overcompensated, taking an extra step forward and losing his balance altogether. I caught him just before he finished his dive. There were drug stores that didn't have as much Old Spice in stock as he had over him.

"Very simple. You give me the check and I leave. How's that?"

"I don't know what . . .!"

"You're Monaghan, he's Wells, and you're not doing any shopping in a beads store. You following me here?"

He didn't struggle all that much to get out of my hold, and his legs were safely under him where they couldn't be troublesome. He looked more bullshit Irish than pub brawl Irish, anyway. If he had worked out in the last year, it had probably been only to get close to a mark in a gym. "And you'll give me back my money?"

I wouldn't call it regret exactly, but I actually felt a tiny caving in at the thought that he was going to wind up short of whatever he had given Christine for the check. At least I didn't promise to give him Shari's $500 to help tide him over. "The check."

I hadn't really thought about what amount I expected to see, so the sum of $2,000 on the Bank of New York check he finger-pincered out of his shirt pocket and waved at me wasn't all that surprising. But what caught me off-guard was that Christine had not only swiped the check from the store but had forged sister Shari's name. Wells and Monaghan would have been able to work their pigeon in their sleep.

"All right, where's my cash?"

Up to that moment, I guess I had never really seen blood in the eye. At least in Monaghan's version, it was one part rising rage and one part leak from some punctured side of his personality. "I've got something better than cash for you. I'm going to help you and your friend stay out of harm's way. You'll phone Wells and tell him he's never going to bother the lady again. If he has to buy a machine to screen his calls from her, that's what he'll do. But if he's smart, he'll move altogether. And since she knows about this place, you might do the same. Is that clear?"

He didn't waste a second working out the odds of ever getting his money back from Wells, and they were gloomy enough for him to try wresting his right arm from my hold. "You're not listening, Monaghan. The lady has a background of not reacting well to disappointment."

"Yeah, sure."

"Okay, I'm making it up. And you're not setting her up for anything. You just helped her out by cashing a check. So why don't we go downstairs to the station house to file a complaint against me?"

It wasn't completely Bluff Poker; forged checks rarely got sorted out to anybody's satisfaction. Still, I was relieved when he went limp again, his darker thoughts looking trained beyond me to whatever fool had talked him into his bind. "Right. Take it up with Wells. He's probably spending your two thou right now."

I didn't know how much he was taking in, but I resisted the idea of spelling out Christine's potential in more colorful detail. The doofus boys were only too capable of capping a bad Chinese meal one night by deciding an emotionally unstable Christine might be even more exploitable for a few bucks than a love-starved Christine. But I still had to do something to be sure Monaghan relayed my message to Wells, so I dug out my old Nassau County ID and flashed it just long enough for him to see the badge but not the name or date. "We'll be watching. You understand me?"

I drove home replaying his miserable nod. In the vein of the still-to-be-done, there was the call to Shari Glynn to tell her not to worry about a missing check. In the vein of the I-don't-want-to-know-about-it, there was the if and how she would confront Christine. Was she smart enough to confront her without mentioning Wells or should attempted robbery have made that a minor consideration? In the vein of the what-have-I-accomplished-on-this-mission-of-mercy, I counted $510 as income and niggling things as expenses. Showing my old badge always bothered me. Same thing for clipping Monaghan. New Finley didn't like resorting to Old Finley, even if that promised a shortcut. Neither move represented progress on my evolutionary chart. And then there was my whole tactic in tackling Monaghan in the first place. I knew it was sound in theory. I knew that if Monaghan, Wells, and Shari all did what they were supposed to do, Christine would have nobody in her sights for avenging her misadventure. But maybe because of Rennie Miller and some Valley Stream bank robbers, or because of all the people I had flown over in the century since then, there seemed something too good to be true about finding an ideal solution in the creation of an even greater distance between me and Christine Sewell. Was it P.T. Barnum or Aristotle who said that when things looked too good to be true, they weren't?

CHAPTER 10

The Professor's Wednesday gathering was close to SRO. Even though I'd made it at least once a month since he had turned cordial weekly host, half the 20-odd people spread out over the living room, hallway, and kitchen were new to me. There were teachers, students, neighbors, what looked like the odd kidnap victim from the LIRR station. Why did I have a picture of the old man going around Garden City with a staple gun and posters to tell every tree in town that his special guest for the evening was the chief investigator in the Ralph Carey killing?

Dana was ensconced with a glass of red wine at the edge of the couch next to the Professor's good right ear. She was amused to see me amused by the sight of her listening to an argument between him and two academic types about the significance of the European student revolts in the sixties. I took her relaxation to mean she had carried off whatever pretext there had been for her presence by asking a few official questions about the Dodger banquet. For his part, Joe was doing his best not to acknowledge my arrival. If he had been in uniform, I would have been expected simply to admire the medals on his chest.

I went into the kitchen to get a plate for the taleggio I'd brought. There was a first of sorts in Dana's presence, and it hadn't really hit me until I'd seen her pinching at the knee of her gray slacks and the old man trying to be sly about noticing it. She was, in fact, the first woman I'd been with since Jenny's death who had sat in the old man's living room. I hadn't gone out of my way to bring that about, and maybe it wasn't even 100-100 percent true since I'd dated somebody I'd met there originally. But it was enough of a first to make the house feel different, as though I was as much an outsider as Dana and would be going home with all the other visiting teams at the end of the evening. I was surprised that fact should have teethed on me even a little.

"So, what'd you find out?"

It was the kind of bark I'd grown used to from Joe Carroll. Except, as I discovered looking around from the plate closet, he was still outside in his recliner talking about France and Italy. The barker this time was a knobby little guy closer to 80 than 70 in an old Brooklyn Dodger cap and wielding a cigar as big as any bat Roy Campanella had ever hefted. He seemed to have gotten his high-pitched voice from a tailor press. I didn't have much doubt about where he had been recruited.

"You're the son-in-law, aren't you? The one supposed to find out what happened to Carey?"

"And you would be . . .?"

"Vince Galassi. Joe never mention me?"

"No, Vince. Sorry."

Galassi needed a second to take that in; then again, his shrug said, he shouldn't have expected any better from Joe Carroll. "I run the goddamn banquet, that's all. When Carey got killed, I started gettin' the calls 24 hours a day. That's not good for my ticker, son-in-law. And now I'm supposed to write some damn eulogy or somethin' for the dinner."

"What can I tell you?"

"That's not your problem, that's mine. I don't need your input on that. Your problem is to come up with some answers. I got the eulogy, then I got those rubes out there in Nebraska. I need a little more to tell 'em than we got rotten apples in the barrel here like any other burg, but it don't reflect on the city as a whole and sure as hell not on our organization. You hear what I'm sayin' to you?"

I had never been particularly good at unwrapping cheese; unless it had a hard rind like edam, too much of it ended up sticking to the paper. But with Vince Galassi and his stinking cigar as inspiration, I concentrated on the melting taleggio the way a surgeon did on a naughty brain. If I left the smallest trace of it on the paper in moving it to the plate, I warned myself, it would mean the patient had been closed up again with some of his vital thinking matter left outside.

"The one inside, she any good at her job?"

"Who's that?"

"The cop in pants. Who else?"

"The best."

"I got nothin' against woman cops. Got a niece in uniform. I could do without seein' her clompin' around in those clodhopper shoes all the time, but she seems to take care of herself. But a woman in charge of the whole case? You don't even see that on TV, for Christ sake!"

"Hey, Vince!"

"What?"

"You a member of the Carey family?"

"No . . ."

"You have something useful to tell the cops? You know anything about police work? Or we just talking here about how the banquet's shrimp cocktails might get delayed a few minutes?"

He wasn't the Professor; he turned mushy too fast. "You don't have to get your drawers in a knot."

"Yeah, Vince, I do. Because right now you're breaking my balls, and I don't even know who the fuck you are. So, go get a beer and enjoy yourself."

So, he was 105 years old. When you're hot, you're hot. I not only got rid of Vince and his cigar, but I couldn't detect the smallest trace of cheese on the paper. And who better to show it off to than Dana?

Except she came into the kitchen not to admire my catering skills, but to use the cellphone in her hand. "What is it—some kind of brie?"

"No, it's not brie. And you know it."

She smiled and punched out her number. "I think I made him feel helpful. He had more questions than I did."

"Frankly, my dear . . ."

"Yeah, I can see that. You must've had a charming day." She got her connection. "This is McGill."

Actually, the day hadn't been bad at all. I had snagged a malpractice job from my main insurance company supplier, had made appointments for two people who sounded serious about becoming clients, had received my check for $510 from Shari Glynn, and had done my laundry without losing a single quarter on the washer or dryer. If the charm had worn off, it had only been with Vince Galassi bugging me.

Or not.

I looked over at the window where Dana had taken her phone for what had become more than a routine check-in call. Had I been kidding myself about seeing her in a Carroll family setting? Maybe being a little too precious about how natural it should have been? Christ knew that if it had been Jenny standing there on the phone, she would have looked much leggier in her slacks and would have been flexing the fingers of her free hand to ward off some new arthritis twinge. And for sure she wouldn't have been consulting her watch to make an appointment for midnight in the city.

"We could have a match," she said when she clicked off the phone. "The TV cameras at Citi Field picked up somebody who might—let's say it again, *might*—be the same person the Canal Street station monitor picked up the night Leong was shot there."

I must have looked as dumbfounded as I felt because she took pity on me right away. "Oh, I didn't tell you. That Chinese cook shot on the Canal Street subway station was killed by the same .40-caliber Glock as Carey. We established that this afternoon."

I didn't like looking *or* feeling dumb.

"What're the odds a baseball announcer from Nebraska and a Chinese cook in New York have the same enemy? I think we're dealing with random targets. Your average sociopath with Annie Oakley's aim."

I finally got something out. "Don't jump, Dana. I've had Ballistics tell me things they couldn't possibly . . ."

I shut up before she told me to. I might as well have had Vince Galassi back to recount some of *his* adventures in Homicide.

"In any case," she said, coming back for another look at the cheese, "they have a tentative ID on some guy and I've got to check it out. Where's Joe keep the knives?"

I went to the drawer myself before she saw more disapproval. *Tentative ID*? Grainy subway station monitors gearing people into action within hours? The rush smelled. Worse, any objective person not named Finley might have said the odor was coming from somebody trying to make a quick impression on her first major investigation.

"I thought this Leong guy was shot from a train leaving the station," I said, handing her a knife.

"What about it?"

"Well, if he's already on the train, how does he get himself seen on the station surveillance camera?"

She thought I was being funny. "Duh! How about, he got on the train there and fired as he was leaving the station?"

"He'd have to do a lot more than get on. The car itself would have to be completely empty. If not, somebody sees him pulling this fabulous trick of going right to one of those windows sealed with 30 years of grime, yanking it open, and then doing his imitation of Annie Oakley. All within, what, twenty seconds? Or maybe the window was already open against regulations and you've got witnesses who saw the guy?"

"Who said he shot from a window? Maybe it was from the door."

"But still an empty car."

She cut off the tip of the cheese and put it in her mouth with the knife. "What's your point, Finley?"

"I think I just made it."

"The other one."

"They used to have it in my first-grade classroom. A big sign over the blackboard: HASTE MAKES WASTE."

"Good cheese. Some of your favorite taleggio, right?"

"It just sounds all a little too frantic to me, that's all."

"Don't confuse speed with haste," she said, walking the knife over to the sink and turning on the water. "I've got a lot of manpower on this thing, and most of them know their little areas inside out."

"Okay, okay. Who's the guy?"

She told me about some Arthur Thaler, a Desert Storm veteran who had brought his war home with him in various assaults and one shooting incident. She had sucked in a few more facts like that on the phone, but I was more interested in her reaction to hearing herself repeat them aloud. I assumed it was because she knew what I was up to that she not only washed the knife she had eaten from but kept her back to me as she wiped it cleaner than Lady Macbeth would have. "They have a Queens address on him. Parsons Boulevard. We're picking him up tonight."

"Can't all this manpower you have handle it?"

"While I'm partying here? I don't think so."

"No, I suppose not. So, what'd you just hear?"

"Hear?"

"When you were telling me about Arthur Thaler."

She smiled at her blush. "Was I supposed to hear something?"

"One thing, maybe. If Ballistics is right and you got this sharpshooter running around the city, how does crazy Arthur fit in? He sounds like somebody who would've tried to blow up Citi Field, not have the patience to fire one shot against one target."

"Doesn't quite fit, does it."

"No, Dana, it doesn't."

"But he's the one we have on two cameras."

"Maybe."

"Maybe. I'll call you tomorrow."

She kissed me on the cheek and walked out of the kitchen. A *party* she had called the gathering? Then where was my festive air? Why did I feel surrounded by Wrong? She was going off on a wild goose chase, and that was Wrong. There was nothing to gain from going except tangling with some psycho after midnight, and that was Wrong. There was no way I could object further to her doing her job without sinking fatally into Wrong. There were too many possessive notes about her in my skull, and that was Wrong. And all of them had swelled into the Wrong Symphony by trying to make a philosophical statement about her in a Carroll house, and that was Wrong. Even the taleggio tasted a little Wrong.

Joe was returning from the front door when I went into the living room with the cheese. I couldn't remember the last person he had seen out personally. "That's a bright woman there, Finley," he said, needing some new grievance. "Try not to fuck it up with your nonsense."

"And what would that be, Joe?"

"Being yourself. What else?"

CHAPTER 11

I devoted the rest of the night to doing stupid things. I drank too much. I talked too much about Greeks and Turks with firm opinions I made up as I went along. I enjoyed my own cheese too much. If I earned any points at all, it was for keeping my mouth shut about the serial killer theory apparently working its way through the NYPD. It wasn't just a matter of not betraying a confidence from Dana. A Ralph Carey who was merely one of who-knew-how-many victims, some totally random casualty, wouldn't have done much for the Professor's shaky grip on self-esteem. Sure, he could be obnoxious about it. But how did that make him any different from actors who thanked their grandmothers for Oscars and ballplayers who attributed their bunt single to God? Let him have his moment, let the caravan move on, and let the dog bark or something. As it was, he was having a tough enough time trying to keep his head above the way Vince Galassi was sitting in a corner chair smoking another Louisville Slugger, sipping seltzer, and daring someone to ask why he was sulking. The more rings Galassi blew into the air with a loud pucker, the more Joe looked like he wanted to wrap them around his neck. I thought he could wait until the morning paper to have the relevance of his privileged access to Ralph Carey punctured.

Not that I was ready to wait that long for the scoop on Arthur Thaler. Even though it wasn't midnight yet, I rode home with my radio tuned to the all-news station. I didn't know what I expected to hear: Maybe just enough noise to block out the big NO I'd once given one of the regulars at my neighborhood dive who had offered to set me up with a police band. As soon as I got home, I activated the Finley Entertainment Center: the radio on the all-news station, the television on the local news channel I never watched outside my dentist's office, and the telephone in the middle of my desk blotter where it might ring for a change instead of giving off its usual prissy trill. I was so plugged in I should have been on a magazine cover with one of those skinny models in a thong and six-inch gold heels.

Needless to say, there was plenty of madness to the method. A few minutes before one, or just about the time anything ugly in Arthur Thaler's neighborhood would have started being reported, I got bored leafing through a book on the Greek-Turkish wars the Professor had given me, deactivated my TV link to the universe, and went to bed. Since I wouldn't have heard it anyway, I switched off the all-news station in favor of B.B. King. I nodded off thinking about the Balkan Entente of 1934. The Professor had been severely critical of it.

About two minutes after falling asleep, I was awake listening to Sarah Vaughan aching through "Misty." For some stupid reason, she needed my doorbell for accompaniment. Okay, it wasn't two minutes, it was seven-thirty in the morning, and I had slept the sleep of the oak log. And why not? Thursday mornings were my in-week break when I didn't schedule appointments and even my neighbor Mrs. Chalian knew better than to bother me for keeping the hall littered with Chinese menus.

And then the sadist at the bell reminded me of what I had been so worried about before going to bed.

I was relieved before all my neurons lined up to tell me I should have been relieved. Dana gave me a smirk from Hell and left me to close the door after her. She was pallid and sweaty and she had a smudge of dirt near her left ear. "I was expecting the coffee to be on," she said, "but as long as it isn't, I'll do the honors."

"It wasn't a great bust."

She shook her head as she tossed her jacket and weapon on the couch, and wobbled on her boots out to the kitchen. I didn't want any goddamn coffee. "Come back here!"

It seemed to take forever for her to reappear in the doorway. I took the stain—catsup, tomato sauce—around the second top button of her blouse as a good sign: Somewhere during the night, she had found the room to eat something. But then she spoiled that thought by putting her hand on the kitchen door jamb; it was trembling. "The son of a bitch shot Ronnie Hersh and killed a cop named Locatella. Bronx kid. Father, two uncles on the job."

I didn't know who Ronnie Hersh or Locatella were, but my ignorance felt like skates getting over to her. She didn't fall easily; there were still centers of resistance in her shoulders and in her legs to giving up anything to anybody. Her cheek and ear were so cold it might have been January outside. "I think you better do something really really distracting," she said.

I walked her into the bedroom and undressed her. There was a large black-and-blue splotch on her right arm that hadn't been there four nights before. "I smashed it against the car door when Ronnie lost control," she said. It was the only thing she said. There was lovemaking, there was fucking, there was therapy, and she wanted them all at once, one second demanding what a hundred mes couldn't give her, the next seeming to want nothing more than my forearm for staring at and caressing. None of it was supposed to be for me, and that made it just more urgent to take it all for me. I wouldn't have minded if she broke my neck with her ankles: I wanted to be discarded empty and broken somewhere even faster than she did.

Absolutely everything had gone wrong in Queens. The first stakeout team on the scene had failed to notice Thaler leaving his apartment to go to a tavern a couple of blocks away on Hillside Avenue. The raid on the apartment had accomplished nothing more than waking up an infant across the hall, this bringing out an irate father who had almost been taken in for obstruction. Scene Two had been everybody back in street positions waiting for Thaler to come home. Dana had been in a car with her boy genius Loschen and Ronnie Hersh when a spotter radioed that Thaler had just turned onto Parsons. The net should have closed and that should have been that—except some kid from a house across the street had flung open a window, yelled out "Cops! Cops!" then had slammed the window closed again. The panicked Thaler had pulled a gun, fired into the uniforms behind him to kill Locatella, and managed to get through Locatella's partner back to Hillside. Hersh had made a U-turn with too much help from a parked car, banged up Dana's arm, and gone after Thaler. They had finally taken him down a block short of Sutphin Boulevard, but not before he had gotten off another shot that had slashed Hersh in the jaw. To cap off things, Dana had had to talk down Locatella's partner from evening the score against the handcuffed Thaler right there on the street. Through it all, three detectives had sat in Thaler's apartment and on the stairs of his building with their thumbs up their asses. One of them had complained his radio hadn't been working; the other two hadn't said anything. And, oh by the way, there was absolutely no resemblance between Arthur Thaler and anyone on the Canal Street platform camera.

"The ranting," she said, shuddering with it into my chest. "He never stopped. Hitler and oil wells and terrorists and the CIA. Kept screaming it as he was running along Hillside. Hitler, oil wells, terrorists, and the CIA. He never stopped. He was still yelling it back in the house."

"That's what ranters do."

"So why was I trying to make sense of it?"

I put the blanket higher over her. I mainly wanted to look away from her eyes, which needed a more serious answer than I was capable of giving her. "Maybe you just needed to make sense of *something* on the night," I said anyway, "and that seemed a little safer than other things."

She was waiting for me to look back at her. "You have your moments, Finley. Now count the ways I screwed up tonight."

"The guy's a wack job."

"That's his excuse. What's mine?"

"For what? The first team didn't see him leaving the apartment. The kid at the window wasn't on your radar. You weren't the one who passed Hersh at Driving School. I don't see all this beating yourself up."

"I could've deployed my people better. But most of all, none of it should've gone down in the first place. You were right. That loon never fired a single shot at anybody in his life—here, in Iraq, or in his dreams."

"I was guessing. You were working."

"Sure."

It took me a second to recognize the stare that shied off from landing on anything in particular. I could have done without the reminder. "Is there some kind of epidemic going around I don't know about? The other day I have Joe in the kitchen telling me he's responsible for Carey because he was the one who invited him to the banquet. I'll ask you the same thing I asked him. If you hadn't taken Thaler down tonight, would you be beating yourself up next week or next month because some cops got killed trying to collar him for something else altogether?"

"Very philosophical."

"Fuck it is!"

"See how it plays in Locatella's family."

I stopped myself from saying it: I didn't care about Locatella's family. They were probably wonderful people going through the pains of hell at that moment, but every apartment in my building and every building on the street had a reason for crying, and I wasn't Irish enough to try to be a mourner for everybody.

"The commissioner came by with half of Police Plaza," she said.

"A cop was killed. That's what he does."

"He went to Queens General with the mayor for that part. He came to my office for my part."

"And you told him what you thought about Thaler."

"I was in the minority."

I suppose I could have taken it as a compliment: She wanted my reassurance she was thinking clearly. But I didn't take it as a compliment. It felt more like an assignment I hadn't asked for. "You told them Thaler wasn't their guy for Carey and Leong or you told them he was good for it so the city can feel warm and cuddly again. Whatever. Your call."

She immediately threw off the blanket and sat up on the edge of the bed. A tiny mole under her shoulder blade didn't like me, either. "Maybe you want me to take a loyalty oath or something," she snapped.

"Not to me."

"He killed one cop and almost killed another!"

"And he confessed to Carey and Leong?"

"He tried."

"Oh, isn't that nice! What'd he get wrong—the ballpark?"

For a second, there was nothing. Then her back started shaking in a weird up and down motion. I told myself I should have been surprised the tears hadn't come sooner. Then I told myself—for the hundredth time in 24 hours—to shut up. When she turned around, she was laughing so hard she was jiggling. "You're a real fuck. You know that, don't you?"

That I could accept as a compliment, I thought, as she came back down on me harder than I had expected.

CHAPTER 12

The first day was all about the street shooting and the blue named Thomas Locatella. Only the *Post* labeled Thaler "the number one suspect" in the Carey and Leong killings, and it milked Police Plaza's cutesy no comments so hard it practically gave the "high-ranking officials" making the claim the Pulitzer Prize. In the *Post* and everywhere else, though, there was definitely one cat out of the bag: the link between Carey and Leong. What the *News* had finally come around to calling the Brooklyn Dodger Murder was now just part of the work of a "serial sniper." I was traditionalist enough to think that wasn't quite accurate, that snipers were on rooftops with telescopic sights, but nobody was paying me to edit the *Daily News*.

Not that what I was getting paid for didn't have its impurities, too. But hey, how many of us lived in Zion? For a few hours Thursday, I managed to forget about the serial sniper; even about my admiration for Dana for having stood up to Police Plaza. Maybe they weren't as lethal as the Arthur Thalers or the serial snipers of the world, but there were still all those hustlers in white coats out there, and who better to take them on than the head of Finley Investigations? Francis Forte, D.D.S., to name just one, had met his match.

It was a little after six when I found a parking spot along Grand Army Plaza and marched my report on Dr. Forte down a block to the Great American Insurance building. With Shari Glynn, I could show up at Beads, Beads, and More Beads only between noon and 12:30. With Great American Insurance, the window was between six and six-thirty because they didn't want me bumping into some policyholder I might one day be investigating. Lunch hours, after-office hours—I could imagine my next client insisting we meet only under the Brooklyn Bridge at three in the morning.

I was about to enter the pocket office building off Seventh Avenue when a car door slammed behind me and somebody called out my name. I recognized him because the Claims office file had included a photograph of Francis Forte, D.D.S. What I had not paid too much attention to was that his broad face and beady eyes were on top of a good six feet and 230 pounds. "You're Finley, right? The one bothering my patients?"

At least his hairy hands were empty. "Do I know you?"

"Quit the horseshit. You've been bothering my patients, getting them to tell lies about me so they can collect."

I considered saying something like "Collect what?" thought that would have insulted the man's intelligence, then said: "Collect what?"

Give this to Forte: Anybody who put himself into the ape's dental chair deserved what he got. He didn't have hands, he had paws. It was a miracle he had been pulling only the wrong teeth and not whole jaws. "You don't want to fuck with my practice, Finley. You really don't."

"You seem to have a beef with somebody, pal. It isn't me."

One of the other disadvantages of toting my reports down to Great American Insurance after six o'clock was that the doorman on duty during the day was either in the back changing into his jeans or already on his way home. This made for one less obstacle for Forte in getting over to the glass door to cut me off. "It's with you," he said, reeking of onions. "Two of my patients told me you had a hundred questions. You want to know something about my practice, ask me."

That had been a gamble on my part, and I had obviously lost it. There were three patients suing Forte, and the three had been recommended to him by two others who had no gripes. Evidently, the referral patients had also felt a loyalty to him. "Work it out with Great American, okay? Now get the hell out of my way."

In my bender days, I would have been counting on my belligerence to decide the issue, to provide the final push for the lug of the occasion to swing into action. But that had been another life. Forte himself also suddenly looked out of snarls. Apparently, he had programmed me for seeing the desperation beneath his threats, then happily tearing up my report while the two of us locked arms and went dancing down the street together. "Accidents happen, Finley," he said, his plea louder. "That doesn't mean you ruin a practice it's taken years to build up."

I didn't think he'd get it if I told him that, based on my experience, accidents were the best of all possible reasons for wanting to ruin someone's practice. "Could you get out of the way, Doctor?"

I was so fast to assume he had taken the same cure I had for boorish barroom behavior that I was already reaching for other aggravations with the door. How long had he been waiting for me outside? What fun person at Great American Insurance had told him when I might be dropping by? Had he really hoped to accomplish anything? The answer to the last question, at least, was yes. He had hoped to accomplish the sledgehammer punch that hit me in the back of the head and that, in the glass door, left me gaping like one of those painted clown faces in a Coney Island tunnel of love. ("Let's go through one more time, Randy!")

There are sillier feelings than falling down in front of a glass door, watching yourself every inch down, but then and there I couldn't think of any. I was down to tightening my grip on the manila envelope, making sure it fell under me. I didn't think of that as a professional instinct, just as a suddenly vital need not to let Francis Forte have something he wanted.

And he didn't get it. Not because of me, but because the sight of me on the ground must have made him the second most shaken person on the block. While I was warning my head not to start pounding, promising it I would do nothing if it would stay numb, Forte was already running back to his car. It was the click of his door that I really hated. That was the one sound too many, the one that woke up the numbness behind my right ear. *Gratuitous*—that was a pet word of the Professor's and that's what Forte had been. He had slugged me for the envelope, then hadn't made a single grab for it. What kind of a dentist did that make for? A *gratuitous* one!

I rolled around just in time to see his gray Honda screech away from the curb down toward Seventh. The man clearly wasn't getting rich by being inconspicuous, he was satisfied just being incompetent. Then somebody came running from inside the lobby, and I told myself it was my idea to black out.

The doorman, still in his rug of a coat with epaulets, was just bending down when I opened my eyes again. As blackouts went, it lacked a little something. "What happened, fella?"

"Ice in front of the door."

He let me climb all the way up to a knee before he stopped scanning the pavement. "There hasn't been snow since . . ."

"Never mind, never mind. Give me a hand here."

He didn't like my idea of humor, but he did it, offering a firm hold to my elbow. "What was it—a mugger?"

I made the mistake of nodding and barely beat off another run into black sheets. At least that made him less reluctant about walking me inside to the marble lobby bench. Once he was sure I wouldn't roll over onto the floor, he also remembered what office I had asked for last time. As he went over to the lobby phone to call upstairs, I told myself the best way to stay awake was to collect the two or three spasms that passed for thoughts. One was that I hadn't been hit on the head in years—a junkie in the men's room of a Mineola bar who had crowned me with a metal toilet paper holder. Another was the ex-jock Jake Early upstairs, who usually gave me 10 minutes for a new assignment and half of that for going over my report. A good spasm pictured Early getting the doorman's call, grunting he had to get up from behind his desk, walking out to the elevator bank, waiting for a car to arrive, riding down, and recoiling in horror at the sight of me—not because I might have already grown Quasimodo's hump over my ear, but because I was sitting in plain sight of the street.

That was when I blew. One second I was thinking about Jake Early worrying about the riffraff in the lobby of his office building, the next I hated Jake Early more than Francis Forte. I'd had it. I didn't want any more looking-down-their-noses insurance people, scabby dentists, cheating spouses, or the other slag that made up Finley Investigations. There had to be a million other ways of not paying bills, waiting for double bills to consider paying one, and piecing out a dollar here and a dollar there for paying that one. When had something I would be "good at," as somebody had once pitched investigative work to me, turned into something that was bad at me? And why hadn't I been watching for the change? We were all beads in one of Shari Glynn's trays? Fine, but that didn't mean we had to be the cheapest plastic kind. Dana was torn up because she had lost somebody on a detail, but she had also taken a psycho off the streets and made the suits admit there was still another one out there. That wasn't a cheap plastic bead; that was at least an opal. How could she have listened to me for a second, let alone thought I had been right about something?

Head or no head, I jumped up off the lobby bench and went over to the desk. The doorman shied back as though Boris Karloff had returned. "Give this envelope to Early when he comes down," I said, telling myself I was shouting only because my head was clogged up. "I don't want to mess up his fucking lobby."

I knew I was going to the Green Fox or something like it before I hit the street, but it was more interesting not to think I was. There were much grander possibilities, such as leaving New York, weren't there? How about some little town in Tennessee where they needed a deputy, or even better, a *constable*? I could sit in a main street office with my feet up on the desk and fine people for fishing without a license, be a regular Andy Griffith. Or forget about leaving the city. What about just leaving any trade that worried about good and bad, right and wrong, wise guy and victim? No badges, weapons, and reports. No checking up on, skulking around, or trailing after. Something where people walked up to you, said hello, and asked did you have . . .? Did I have what? Name it. Ice cream? No. Cashmere sweaters? No. But what about opening a beads store around the corner from Beads, Beads, and

More Beads? Not only could I drive Shari Glynn out of business, but I could drive her, her ticking-bomb sister, and her phantom husband—all of them—to Dr. Marian Freedman. If Dr. Freedman decided they were lucid enough, I could give them a subcontract for beading blouses in the loony bin and make even more money from those sales. Paul Finley would be celebrated as just another name for outsourcing entrepreneur.

CHAPTER 13

The drive back to the Green Fox was too long. By the time I got there and found a parking space, coherent thoughts were threatening to slink back. The sight of Johnny Yeager and the other skels lumped together around the Fox's short arm next to the door came none too soon. Blanche Walsh was holding forth on how the weather patterns had changed since she had been a kid and Yeager was doing his best to interrupt her with his usual contemptuous waves and "You're nuts" drone. I got down to Cynthia at the end of the bar with the shortest of high signs and with responses from nobody. Cynthia had cut her hair to a duck tail, but it didn't look so much cut as grown back, the way French women had grown back hair after the underground had shaved them for screwing German soldiers. Where had that tidbit come from? Did I have the Professor or Paramount to thank for it? It seemed like six of one and half a dozen of the other.

Cynthia wanted to know what I was doing there at such an odd hour. I told her it was because I wanted a Dewar's on the rocks and had the money to pay for it. From there we went swimming. She told me how lousy business was. I told her my business *was* lousiness. She said she was thinking of letting the second day man Peter go because he was asking for a raise. I told her I was thinking of letting me go from Finley Investigations because it was one downer after another. She told me I was full of shit. I waited until I had filled up on my third Dewar's to tell her I was serious. She closed the paperback novel about fathers and daughters she had been scanning during all our mumbling and took a more thoroughly skeptical look at me. "Our Paulie feeling rejected these days?"

I started to toss off the yes she wanted to hear, but couldn't get it out. She was wrong; rejection covered nothing. Just the opposite, it had been a week for making friends and influencing people. From Dana to Shari Glynn, from Monaghan to Arty and Joan at the Emerald Club, everybody had been impressed by me. For all his wheedling white-collar ideas about who was respectable and who wasn't, even Jake Early was probably in a snit at that very second because Indispensable Finley hadn't taken his hand to lead him through the report on Francis Forte. Besides, I would have recognized rejection just from Cynthia. We had our own experiences in it, in rejecting each other. When I had moved to the neighborhood, she had been my first friend and I had been that novelty customer at the Green Fox who didn't have to take out his dentures to chomp at the olives. We had given it a few months before coming to the identical conclusion that gratitude shouldn't make more of us than we were. And even that mutual rejection—totally civil, friendly, and logical—had nothing to do with the mood I had carried back to Bay Ridge from the Great American Insurance Company.

"Then just the opposite," she brightened malevolently. "Paulie's afraid he's being accepted too much. Who we running from? The lady cop?"

"I'm talking about this shit called work."

"You say so."

It took her forever to sashay down to the front of the bar to settle up with Blanche; every rise and fall of her ass in her jeans could have been a jeer. Running from Dana? That was so trite it wasn't worthy even of me. So what if I had bought the track shoes and the shorts and was looking around for my marked lane? That didn't necessarily mean I was going to run, did it? I could have just been going to . . . what? Anything!

The night refused to die. One reason was that it had started so early. As Cynthia had said, I wasn't used to the Green Fox in those twilight hours when the matinee skels were beginning to crawl out and the night crowd was still finishing off Chunky Soup suppers at home. Another reason was that she refused to abandon me, even insisting I share the Spanish omelet she had made in the back. "I didn't collaborate with any fucking Nazis," she reassured me at one point. "I just got tired of looking at the same broken ends every morning. This is my Demi Moore look."

"I haven't seen her in years."

"You haven't seen me, either. Maybe you're the one out of step."

She said it only for the record, and I kissed the back of her hand in accepted drunk fashion, both of us knowing I wasn't *that* lit up yet. But it was also a line in the sand we owed each other: She didn't want to hear about Dana. So, I went back to talking about the groundball I had been running out in the name of Finley Investigations. She looked relieved to hear something so entertaining.

CHAPTER 14

Just as I was beginning to feel like a ringer to myself, the Professor asked me to be one for him. He went so far as to use the scary word *favor*. That should have warned me he was sucking it up to lead me somewhere I didn't want to go. But I didn't want to be warned. In my surly frame of mind, I preferred hearing about how tickets to the Dodger banquet had hardly been moving when Ralph Carey had been alive but had then become a hot item after he had been shot. But now that he was back to being a random corpse? Not good for the box office. There had even been cancellations. The serial sniper might not have realized it, but his third victim had been Joe Carroll. Who knew if the association would ever recover from such a mishmash? "Forget Seward's Folly," he snorted. "Now you have Carroll's Debacle."

"So, we'll end up bragging about Carroll's Debacle, too?"

"You coming or not!!??"

In the cosmic picture there was probably a choice, in the social family one there wasn't. Besides, a few hours of Brooklyn relics remembering their most thrilling double play from Ebbets Field meant a few hours away from my couch and the answering machine. Jake Early hadn't been alone in being disappointed in me. I seemed to have made promises to half the city to deliver reports, send checks, or just stay within arm's length of my phone 24 hours a day. Too bad I'd made the promises in another life.

I skipped the pre-dinner drinks for no better reason than asserting my principles as a whimsical creature. When I arrived at the Brooklyn Heights hotel, I found Joe pacing outside the entrance. He seemed to have been rehearsing a speech for explaining my absence. "I told you I'd come!"

"Yeah, right" was all I got for a reply as he urged me through the revolving door, and it wasn't even that high on the Carroll Sarcasm Scale. A distracted Professor wasn't always the best Professor. More than once, that had meant I was essential to the agenda, in turn causing him to question the planet's priorities. I wanted to spare him his suffering; I didn't want to be essential to the agenda, either.

The hotel had seen better days but had enough hopes for holding on to its chandeliers, cream walls, and green satin chairs. I presumed that was why the festivities had been shoved into the lesser banquet room while the main one, an indoor ballpark called the Roebling Room, remained closed off by a frayed velvet rope. Who knew when an incensed mob might come storming into the place at the last minute and demand the bigger space for a cotillion? As for the Whitman Room where the Professor led me with all the gravity of approaching a sacred temple, it had probably once been as big as the Roebling Room, but had long been sliced in two by a plywood board that ran up to a few feet short of the peeling ceiling and cut off all but two of the windows. I knew the board had been there for a while because some wit had dated it with a red Magic Marker; the hotel had done its best to plaster the surface with the old blue-and-white Dodger logo, but REAGAN SUCKS still peeked out between all the Bs.

The old man paused dramatically in the entrance of the Whitman Room as I picked up a program. As he waved here and there into the din of people already moving to their dinner places, he had finally found something that relaxed him: his diplomatic table setup. Because there would be no former players on hand, he had argued for the elimination of the usual dais. To hear him, that had cost an ulcer attack when Vince Galassi had fumed about organization officers being denied their one opportunity a year to eat above the herd. But he had persisted, winning a majority to his point of view. "For Christ sake, I told them, you want to emphasize how Five-and-Dime this'll be? There are people sleeping over in McDonald's who have more of a right to put up a dais!"

"You didn't say that to them."

"I was thinking it, Finley. I was thinking it."

The tradeoff for the no dais, he pointed out proudly, was an extra chair at each of the three most prestigious tables at the front of the room. Together with another half-dozen tables, it added up to between 80 and 100 people. And players or no players, my program still threatened a lot of speeches—what it called Remarks. "You build up for something all year," he said over another smile to somebody, finally moving inside, "you want a little more than 'and now here comes the dessert.'"

It was cluttered moving. Not only wasn't everybody yet seated but all over the place there were camera bugs backing up into bodies and whacking waiters with their elbows while they recorded the evening. A couple of them didn't look so amateur wielding their movie cams, either; I had no trouble imagining Paul Finley and his fellow stiffs ending up on some local news program for all of two-and-a-half seconds. No great surprise that most of the association members looked like fugitives from a senior home or that too many of them sat painfully erect in shining blue suits and pearl dresses that looked like they had just come out of storage. What I wasn't expecting were the 30ish and 40ish baseball geeks who had shown up in bleacher ware—baseball caps, windbreakers, sweatshirts, corduroys. From the door down to our table, I counted five of them in total absorption with the laptops in front of them. "You told me to a wear a suit!" I whined.

"The price you pay for fresh blood. They cough up their dues, I don't care if they sleep in their clothes."

"Sleeping may be the least of it."

"Do me a favor, Finley . . . Never mind. Just make an effort."

I made an effort. There were six people with us at the center table in the first row, and, naturally, one of them was Vince Galassi. He had doffed his Dodger cap for the occasion in favor of an Ebbets Field tie and a sports jacket that had been borrowed from a burlesque comic, but his trusty cigar was still in his hand. Even better for emphysema forces, he had an accomplice in one of the laptop geeks, who raised his head from his screen only to check how his cigar ash was doing. Galassi introduced the guy as "Gary, a serious student of the game," and who could doubt it? Gary, who had black nails, a boulder of a head, and a mustache that threatened to cover his nostrils, had a hard time justifying a hello if it meant losing track of whatever the hell he was looking up.

I made up my mind to direct my sparkling conversation away from Galassi and Gary as much as possible. That meant the 60 Games Club—four organization members who could boast they had attended at least 60 home games during an Ebbets Field season. How had they managed that when they must have been in their twenties and thirties with jobs, I asked, sounding like a representative of If They Don't Work for a Living, Let Them Die in the Gutter. A bright-eyed, chubby woman named Dorothy giggled at what had apparently become her favorite question. "I was selling cosmetics door to door," she said. "I just made sure the doors were near the ballpark." Her husband Ben, who looked like he was wearing somebody else's hair, nodded in confirmation. "That's how we met. We used to stand behind first base. I was supposed to be selling insurance. So, you had a lot of people in those days who looked like hell and died without coverage!"

Ben and Dorothy roared at their practiced line, which would have been funny enough even without Gary taking it upon himself to translate for me. "They played 77 home games in those days," he glanced up from his screen to tell me solemnly. "If you went to at least 60 of them, you were there for approximately 78 percent of the home games. You don't get percentages like that too often today even with season-ticket holders."

I looked at the Professor, who was suddenly relieved to sit back in his chair and stare down at his chest so the waiter could deposit our cocktails. I knew I was being tested, but I still wasn't sure what circle of Hell I could skip if I passed. Then Galassi abruptly ended the suspense. "So, you gonna do it or not?" he asked.

Not only was my pal Vince staring at me, but so were Dorothy, Ben, and a brother-sister couple named Tuohy. "Do what?"

"Something we'll talk about later," the Professor said, diving into his Bloody Mary. "A little idea we had."

"*You* had," Galassi objected.

"We all had it, Vince," Gary ruled tonelessly as he tapped another key.

Galassi and the Professor went back and forth a couple of more times while Dorothy and Ben kept their attention glued to me, waiting for some reaction they had apparently been told to expect. The Tuohys just looked embarrassed by the bickering. I wondered how much more embarrassed they would be to see me stand and toss my napkin on the table and stalk off like a diva. But I had already played that scene in the lobby of Great American Insurance. How much self-righteousness did I have left in the tank? "How about you just tell me what's going on, Joe?"

He couldn't possibly have told me anything I wanted to hear, of course. But even for presumptuousness, he had gone the extra mile. And it was all so coordinated that he was still getting through his warped proposal when Ben removed an envelope from his inside jacket pocket and handed it to him. "This is about $700 . . ."

"$725," Dorothy corrected cheerily.

"$725. We collected it from all the members. We want you to look into who killed Ralph Carey."

I went from face to face because I refused to believe they had all heard what I had. Tuohy Sister blushed I was even looking at her, while Tuohy Brother gave me a nervous grin. Gary returned my stare as though I should have been grateful for the springing of a surprise party with me as the guest of honor. "In case you people haven't been following the news the last few days . . ."

"We don't trust that woman in charge," Galassi growled.

"That's not why!" Joe thundered. Tuohy Sister almost did a back somersault over her chair. She had plenty of company. Half the table behind her was gaping at us. "The thing is this, Paul," the old man continued more calmly. "We have a special responsibility here to the Carey family. Hold on. Forget our past conversations. We're not talking about self-importance. You were right about that. But as a gesture to the Carey family . . ."

"In their grief," Dorothy prodded.

"In their grief. We want them to know . . ."

"The Brooklyn Dodger family," Ben put in helpfully.

Joe was on the verge of exploding, but then so what? He had to stand in line. "A personal gesture is what we're after here."

"A gesture."

He finally hit me with both fish eyes. "How's it going to hurt? And you can do things the cops can't."

"Name one."

Galassi wanted that answer, too. I figured he had thrown at least two dollars into the pot—probably in nickels. "A personal symbol," Dorothy said. "Let the family know we don't just invite people to the city and then wash our hands of what happens to them."

Was a symbol more or less than a gesture? It sounded like more, but maybe that was just because it was Dorothy pushing it. Galassi, meanwhile, was still waiting for his answer. "You still gotta convince me he can do more than the cops. He know more madmen? That the difference?"

"We agreed on this, Vince," the Professor said, addressing the tablecloth. "Why don't we let Paul talk?"

I could have agreed with Galassi and ended everything right there; among other things, he happened to be right. But I had to be me, and that meant, even in the middle of feeling manipulated, maneuvered, and all those other things people never wanted to feel, giving a thought to how I actually might have been doing things differently from the way Dana had been doing them. And bad sign: the fact that I couldn't think of anything specific irritated me only as lack of industry by my brain.

"What it comes down is just something personal we can write to the family," Tuohy Sister said. "Let them know we care."

"I'd be stealing your money." Galassi looked vindicated. "At best, I'd get the cops to tell me what they're up to, then pass it on to you. If the Careys waited another day, they'd read the same things in the paper."

The Tuohys looked disappointed, but Dorothy and Ben didn't. If anything, Dorothy seemed on the verge of adopting me. "If that's the kind of honesty we can expect from your work, I'd say it's money well invested," she pronounced. "Don't you agree, Ben?"

"Absolutely."

"Just think it over," the Professor said, pocketing the envelope. "We don't need an answer until the salad comes."

Dorothy and Ben thought that was funny. Gary snickered, too, but not because of anything to do with me or the serial sniper. "They always overlook the fact that Reese stole 35 more bases than Robinson in his career," he declared, happy with his reading of the laptop screen.

Tuohy Brother finally had something to say. "Yeah, but look at how many more years he played!"

I defied the Professor to take another swallow of his Bloody Mary without gagging on it. Needless to say, the son of a bitch managed it.

CHAPTER 15

By the time the waiter was clearing away the salad plates for the roast beef and the table had reached a consensus on the height of the right-field screen in Ebbets Field, I figured I had gone through all the permutations. The nastiest thought was Dana and the Professor: For all his declared admiration of her, she was still with Finley the way his daughter had once been, so why not create some conflict between her and Finley? Another was his hating the idea that anything associated with that renowned historian and purveyor of reason Joseph Carroll—for example, a dead Ralph Carey—could come down to the psycho the newspapers and television were talking about. Then there was the way he liked hovering over Finley Investigations—something I'd exploited more than once over the years in asking him to do a little research or to reach out to somebody for me. It was only after running up and down all those staircases that I also landed on Joe Carroll, Brooklyn Dodger Association member who still felt personally responsible for Carey and who wouldn't have minded me helping him shut up Vince Galassi. If there was some motive I'd overlooked, I was open to that, too. The main thing was to zero in on him when he got up to hit the head.

The trouble was, he was so determined to avoid me cornering him in the john for a one-on-one that he pretended not to have a bladder. When I had to go for real and stood up in surrender, he practically toasted me on my way with his second Bloody Mary, then went back to the Tuohys to debate some fine point about Carl Furillo.

I went into the Men's Room fantasizing about my conversation with Dana when I told her about my $725 hijacking. I envisioned her laughing, me still being annoyed, then her too realizing there was nothing to laugh about. Before I could see her working herself into a tirade, though, I almost stumbled over one of the laptop nerds bending down over somebody on the tile floor. The one on the floor was Vince Galassi. "I just found him!" the geek said, sounding on the edge of hysteria. "He looks out!"

Galassi looked more than out; the sweat glistening off his forehead and his pasty color were a pretty good imitation of heart attack symptoms. "Get out to the front desk! They must have a doctor around somewhere!"

At least I didn't have to repeat myself: The guy was gone in a flash. On the other hand, I didn't like the spit burbling out of the corner of Galassi's mouth. "Vince, you got pills? Heart things?"

I found them in his shirt pocket before he got his eyes open and took me in. "Yeah, right, you're in Heaven, and I'm the official greeter," I said, relieved there were still a couple of pills in the bottle. "How's them apples? Hold on. I'll get some water."

The road to Hell, etc., etc. The closest thing to a glass in the place was the liquid soap dispenser. I went back down on the floor, propped the old man up against my thigh, and applied dimly remembered swallowing techniques from three hours of first-aid class in Nassau County several lives ago. Vince had too much tongue for my taste, but the damn pill finally went down. "They're getting a doctor," I said, not ready to bet on it.

He nodded to humor me, but then slowly found more space in his lungs, especially after I remembered to loosen his tie. A final, liberated exhale came with a "You better do it, wise guy. It's important."

I thought about swinging my leg open to conk his head down on the tile, but remembered I was more lovable than that. "Why's that, Vince?"

He pitied my obtuseness so much he had to close his rheumy eyes for the strength to shake his head. "Because nobody should die like it's some fuckin' joke, that's why! What do you think? Think those cop friends of yours give a shit about Carey? All they're worried about is this nuthouse who killed him. If and when they ever get him and don't put your life savin's on that one."

"I think they're the same thing, Vince."

"Bullshit! Me and your father-in-law and those other mummies out there, we're not responsible for this nuthouse, but Carey wouldn't have been in the city if not for us!"

"Calm down, man. We can talk about it later."

"Yeah, it's always later. *Mañana, amigo.*"

"Think about Duke Snider home runs."

"That supposed to be funny?"

"No, Vince. That's supposed to shut you up."

"I know what you and Carroll talked about. He told me because he thought you might've been right. Well, you're not, Finley. I don't want to hear about how Carey might've gotten run over by a tractor if he'd stayed out in goddamn Omaha. The fact is, he *didn't* get run over by no tractor. Nothin's ever the same thing as what really happened."

"I'll remember that."

"Better do more than that. Get to this nuthouse before the cops do. They just want the headlines to go away."

The geek had not only found a doctor, but what looked like a nurse, a manager, and half the population of Brooklyn Heights. The doctor, a rail as white as Galassi, listened to what I'd done, then had to listen to Galassi's protests that he hadn't written a eulogy for Carey so he could take it to a hospital with him. Then it was the nurse's turn to play mediator, suggesting Vince lie down for a few minutes in the hotel office. I made my way through a lot of eyes waiting for me to shake my head at the tragedy of it all. When I got back to the hall, the Professor and Dorothy were just arriving at the head of a Whitman Room contingent. "Good thing you didn't spring your surprise on him," I pouted, coming ever so close to reaching into his pocket for the envelope. "We'll talk. And we *will* talk, Joe."

I kept going to the front door. I would miss the entree and the speeches, but the salad lettuce had been gristly and I'd heard enough speeches from Vince Galassi, anyway.

CHAPTER 16

What could I do that Dana and 38,000 other NYPD cops hadn't already done? One possibility actually occurred to me in the shower the next morning. If the Carey and Leong shootings had anything in common besides the marksman, it was bravado. And people long on bravado rarely liked doing their numbers and then running into a cave to leave the reviews to others. So, Bobby Qualls seemed worth a call.

Qualls worked in the news department of Channel 11, the station that also happened to televise Mets games. I'd known him since my Long Island days when he had been working freelance for outfits not up to paying a staff reporter to attend police press conferences. There had been a few beers and coffees together along the way, and a couple of times I had put him on to somebody in Mineola for deep background information. Bobby was the first to admit he was a cop groupie; you couldn't spend five minutes with him before he started lamenting how his 280 pounds and three chins had blocked his way into the Academy and to what he called "the only job worth having." If you wanted something from him, you encouraged him to keep thinking about a diet and taking steps to realize his dream (he was already well past 40). Your reward was an eventual "whattya need?" and, as often as not, what you needed.

This time, though, even Bobby Qualls sounded dubious. "We sent all that footage to the cops, Paul. They were on us for it right away."

"You sent them the interviews you didn't televise, too? Not just the stuff you put on the air?"

"What's her name? McGill? She was emphatic about that."

Good for Dana and bad for Finley's unique contribution. But then he added: "Hold on a second. I may have something else here . . ."

I listened to him tossing things around on his desk, telling myself the call was my freebie for the Professor, Vince Galassi, and the other dreamers who thought I could really accomplish something the cops couldn't. I would have felt better if I hadn't also pictured Dorothy's downcast expression for such a modest effort.

"Here it is," Qualls said, coming back. "Guy named Owen Bronsard. How's that for Yuppiedom? Anyway, he came in here the other day with some footage from Citi Field that night. He couldn't peddle it anywhere else, so he thought we might be able to use it as filler since we were likely to be more interested in Mets things than other stations."

"What's on it?"

"Interviews at the park that night, he said. Beyond that, you got me. He left it on consignment, and I haven't had time to look at it. Now that this thing seems to be about more than Ralph Carey, I don't see us ever using it. I think we were Bronsard's last shot. Gloomy kind of guy. Reminded me of me in my freelance days."

I laughed with him. And he heard the eager-to-please as much as I did. "You want a peek, right?"

"I promised somebody I'd see if there was anything the cops were skipping over. What can I tell you, Bobby?"

"You sound ready for a career change."

I could have done without that crack, or with the idea that I was wearing a sandwich board advertising my sulks. "What's your schedule like today? Can you squeeze me in somewhere?"

He gave me a choice of right before or after lunch, and I took after; I didn't need career counseling during the three or four bourbons he would have considered lunch. Having made that commitment for the day, I felt less timid about doing other manly things, such as resolving to get back eventually to Jake Early and the others who had been clogging up my answering machine. That might not have been the same thing as actually getting back to them, but, whatever Dorothy and Ben thought, I'd never re-garded myself as a miracle worker, anyway.

Qualls's office was on East 42nd Street, which meant the subway. If I took the car, I would have needed the Professor's envelope just to manage the midday parking charges. As the R line did its customary hiccoughing run through Bay Ridge whole inches at a time, I caught up on the latest developments around the serial sniper. To judge by the *News*, there weren't enough of them to get me from 86th Street to 77th Street. The one new note was Dana doing her own talking to say that Arthur Thaler was not—rpt not—being looked at for the Carey and Leong shootings. I was disappointed to see she was wearing the aqua and black outfit. Did that mean there had been other occasions when she had worn it in the months between the two times I had seen it? Well, if she was going to be that unfaithful to me, what loyalty did I owe her about poking into the serial sniper?

What was I looking for from Owen Bronsard? Qualls took it for granted he was the first to ask, but he hadn't been eavesdrop-ping on me in the R train. The automatic answer, of course, was that I would know what it was when I saw it. Ba-da-dum. That satisfied Qualls's preconceptions about cops and ex-cops, but it rang a little tinny to the congress convened in my brain. I hoped I looked confident as he slipped the cassette into his machine and, assuming I wanted to be left alone, practically tiptoed out of his office and closed the door behind him. Sometimes the fat man's deference was a pain in the ass. Stick around, Bobby, I wanted to yell after him, *you* tell me what I'm looking for! He didn't listen.

What came on the screen was the usual parade of the shocked, stunned, and dismayed—all of them taped near Gate B at Citi Field after the Mets-Cubs game. The first woman, in her twenties, had never heard of Ralph Carey, but it was terrifying to think *anyone* could be shot in a ballpark. Two bozos with matching guts and black polo shirts said it was a terrible, terrible thing, then asked if they could wave to their cronies back in their home saloon. A tall slightly stooped guy with a gray fuzz cut and the look of a priest hadn't heard about the shooting and wanted Bronsard to furnish more details; he became pretty unpleasant about it. A couple with a four- or five-year-old who couldn't keep his eyes open were mainly curious about all the police running in and out. It wasn't until the sixth or seventh interview that Bronsard had found somebody who had heard of Carey: a black guy with a billiard ball head who must have been pushing 80. "That old outfielder? You kiddin' me? Shot right here? What the hell was he doin' out here anyways?"

I told Bronsard to put the guy in touch with the Professor for an answer, but he didn't hear me. So, I was feeling crabby again. And Owen Bronsard certainly wasn't helping. He seemed to have only two questions in his knapsack— "Have you heard Ralph Carey has been shot?" and "What do you think of it?" I had a bad feeling none of the interviewees to come were going to say, "Who gives a shit?" and "Great news!" My eyes began wandering. Qualls's office was a dimly-lighted warehouse of cassettes and DVDs; the only books I saw were telephone directories and dictionary-looking things on a shelf above the computer. The desk in the middle of the room looked too small for its chair. For a second, I imagined hearing Qualls denying he was so fat that they had to order a special chair for him. But the familiar voice wasn't in my head, it was on the TV screen. It was another Citi Field fan shocked, stunned, and dismayed to hear of Ralph Carey's death. Only this one was Gary, the laptop geek from the dinner. A "serious student of the game," as Vince Galassi had introduced him.

CHAPTER 17

No *Little House on the Prairie* farm girl ever did more skipping around in her bedroom over starting her hope chest. I was piling it up. I had the copy of the Bronsard tape Bobby Qualls had made for me. I had the banquet program listing Gary Stein as the Dodger association's "official statistician." I had Gary Stein's peculiar silence to me about having been at the game at which Carey had been shot. Still better, since at least one of them would have made a passing remark otherwise, I had Gary Stein's even more suspicious silence to the other association members about having been at Citi Field that night. The one minor thing holding off the Wedding March was not knowing what a shred of it meant, let alone connecting any of it to Carey and Leong. But that was a mere detail. Who could expect to have everything with one discovery? That was why the teenage girls on "Little House on the Prairie" always had more mooning to do before their ideal buckboard driver came along.

In the meantime, I felt reinvigorated. And pending further revelations about Gary Stein, I received definite signs I should honor that rally by getting back to my humdrum activities. The first omen was waking up to my favorite song—Ruth Etting singing "Ten Cents a Dance." I heard that on the radio about once a decade, and though I couldn't recall any of the rich particulars, I was pretty sure the last time had launched a tremendously fertile period in my life. The second sign was Dana phoning to say she needed a "normal evening" and inviting me to her place for dinner. To celebrate, I immediately blurted out the events at the Dodger banquet to her. What that got me was a "just what I need—another free-lance expert." Being the constitutionally weak but dogged person I am, this only inspired me to impress her by giving away my secret stash of the Gary Stein interview. For about 30 seconds, she listened with what I took for fascination. And it was—in what new idiocies *I* happened to be fascinated by. As for Stein, he just "sounds like a dweeb." So much for that attempt to be complex and interesting.

Still, I felt so perversely liberated by her dismissal (and by having still another reason not to accept the Professor's $725) that I immediately called Jake Early, ignored his cool hello, and told him about my encounter with Dr. Forte. I heard him explode in indignation, heard his indignation drop down to sympathy for me, and heard his sympathy for me drop down to resignation that policy-holder Forte clearly was a high-risk character. I would have been content to cut it off there, but Early kept going down, next stop the suggestion—not a request, he stressed—that the little karate chop stay in the Great American Insurance family. In fact, if I needed a medical checkup, I should feel free to list that on my expense sheet, no questions asked. In the meantime, he would take care of Dr. Francis Forte personally. How did that sound?

I said goodbye before I ruined our renewed friendship by telling him how it sounded. But his appeal to the Great American Insurance family emboldened me to break my days-old silence with my real almost-family. The Professor picked up the phone before the second ring. "Oh," he stumbled. "I thought it was that jerk Greg Zev. He's got some paper he's delivering on Swiss neutrality. Like I give a goddamn . . ."

"How's Galassi?"

"How should he be? He's an old man with a bad heart. Turns out that wasn't the first spell he took."

"Looked like more than a spell."

"You're a doctor now? He remembers to put the pills in his pocket but never remembers to take them out when he ought to.

The way some countries find it easy to go into others, but don't get out again until they're being ridden out on a rail."

"That's cute. Why, Joe?"

At least he didn't go into an act. "Galassi said he told you why."

"I'm asking you."

He walked his phone near a dead zone. I couldn't believe he was going to resort to such a lame trick. But then he came back on even stronger than before. "That dinner you skipped out on the other night," he said, "if that's not the last one, you'll fool me. The old stars that aren't dead are just bored with the whole thing or getting around with walkers. You saw that crowd we had. They're more rickety than the players. Ralph Carey talking to people like Gary Stein, that's what it's come down to, Finley. Only we don't even get Carey."

It wasn't the moment to talk about Owen Bronsard's tape. "That still doesn't explain your little envelope."

"Then you're not listening," he sighed. "If we're drying up, then we dry up. Everything does eventually. But I don't think we should go out with a whimper like we did last time."

"What last time?"

"1957! When they moved to Los Angeles! What the hell do you think I'm talking about?"

I almost went for it; at bottom, he was just another old man waxing nostalgic about his youth, wasn't he? But Joe Carroll also wasn't Vince Galassi or Ben the insurance man. "And?"

It took him forever to stop looking at the birds or traffic outside his window. "You make it personal," he said finally. "I'm sorry, Paul. Dana's a nice lady and all, but . . . it's not personal with her. She's just doing her job. You're our proxy into something closer."

"What the hell's a proxy into something closer?"

"Figure it out. Anything else?"

Where did I start? If Joe Carroll had gone to Rennie Miller's memorial service on Central Park West, he would have claimed to be her rabbi, father, lover, and all her friends rolled into one. Especially after my conversation with Dana, the Bronsard tape with Gary Stein on my desk looked like the drivel it was. "Just one thing," I said. "The real world. Like I've been trying to tell you, there's nothing I can do Dana and the cops haven't already done."

"Then get out of the goddamn real world and be useful!"

It wasn't the first time he had left me holding a dead receiver in my hand; it just felt like it was.

CHAPTER 18

The third shooting came while Dana and I were sitting on her couch watching my favorite scene from *The Towering Inferno*. It's the one where fire chief Steve McQueen is trying to rescue the people trapped in an elevator that runs up and down the facade of the burning skyscraper. To save them, he has to disconnect a broken cable that's left the car dangling over Los Angeles and replace it with another cable being swung down from a wind-blown helicopter. I would've found that hard enough to do on the 61st floor, but McQueen has to do it from the 62nd floor with the people in the elevator shrieking and one of his own firemen clinging desperately to the roof of the car not to go plunging into the night. It even impressed Dana. For a whole minute, she had stopped the cracks at my taste in old movies and had ignored the fitness reports she had brought home from work.

"I can't believe you never saw this."

"It's always on. I just don't like fire movies."

"And there've been so many of them!"

"Yeah, there have. You don't count them because they don't bother you. I count them because they do . . . No way anybody could do that. You know how much those cables weigh? And he's holding on to an elevator at the same time?"

"It's a movie. And it's Steve McQueen."

"So, in the next scene, Paul Newman must do something heroic, right? You can't have one star more of a star than the other."

"You're taking me out of the moment."

"Ah, golly!"

"Why does fire spook you so much?"

She went back to her fitness reports. "Why else? It's uncontrollable. You don't know what it's going to do."

"Plus, it's hot."

"Plus, it's hot. This is really going to piss them off." She checked off a couple of boxes. I saw the name of LOSCHEN, HERMAN at the top. "Some people want to put him behind a desk so he doesn't get in harm's way. Most of them want to just get rid of him. So, I think a hearty endorsement of his field work's in order, don't you?"

"He's not cut out for anything else."

"And you know it without even meeting him!"

I didn't want her losing her merriment. She had been catching up with a week's worth of the light, lighter, and lightest since I'd walked in and smelled her meatloaf in the oven. For a few hours anyway, she had been able to shelve her dead ends with the serial sniper. That was why I knew as soon as her phone rang that it wasn't bringing good news. Nothing at all from the outside world could have.

She nodded through what she was told as Steve McQueen and the helicopter brought the elevator to a safe landing. For once, it wasn't an especially exciting sequence. "A woman on the West Side Highway," she said when she hung up. "Apparently just driving along when somebody going by in the opposite lane fired one shot and got her. Somehow she managed to stop the car without smashing up."

"So? That's Manhattan, that's not you."

"There are enough resemblances to Carey and Leong for now. They want me to go see. Look, I put my car in the garage for the night. Stupid optimism. Could you drive me over?"

Once I had gotten my car, it was less than 10 minutes over to the Hudson. That was long enough. Every second seemed to peel away another piece of Dana's casualness. By the time we came to the road flares, she had completely forgotten about meatloaf and *The Towering Inferno*. She fished her badge out of her jacket so hard she could have torn the pocket, then yanked open the door as if evening an old score with my car.

I was ready to sit until she was ready to go back home or go on to work, but, as she went over to where the plainclothes were huddling, she told the blues locking down the area I was with her. I got out from behind the wheel before they forgot what she had said. They both nodded to me as if I were there representing the Intergalactic Police Department.

A gray Honda was parked zigzag on the shoulder of the lane going north. I pictured Francis Forte, D.D.S. slumped over the wheel; he had learned the hard way not to mess with Finley Investigations. But it was a different gray Honda, and the body was of an auburn-haired woman somewhere in her thirties or forties (or maybe twenties or sixties). Two Crime Scene technicians were finishing up on the car. One of the EMS people was smoking until he got the signal to move in for the body; his partner was talking on a cellphone. I knew nothing about the woman in the car or even all that much about how she had been shot, but there was something familiar about the scene besides the possibility of another bullseye for the serial sniper. Nothing on the sleeping Hudson piers or across the river in Jersey told me what it was. The blinking beacon lights on the George Washington Bridge taunted me to figure it out for myself.

There were three detectives, a uniformed captain, and a uniformed sergeant in the huddle with Dana. She and the captain were doing most of the talking, and it didn't sound all that friendly. The only word I could make out was *witness*. I decided the sandy-haired string bean picking his nose was her pet Herman Loschen; he looked more interested in the rubberneckers going uptown than in what was being said in front of him. Now that I'd seen him, I would have put him behind a desk, too.

And even that didn't seem like enough. Suddenly, I was working on a snit at Herman Loschen for more than forgetting his mother's instructions about using a handkerchief. Because he looked so flimsy, Dana did, too. If she was leaning on people like that, how did she expect to get anywhere? What was the other genius's name, the Indy 500 driver who had given her the black-and-blue mark on her arm—Hersh? And then there had been the Kojaks who had been babysitting Arthur Thaler's apartment while happy Arthur had been turning Hillside Avenue into Dodge City. Had she actually asked for those people? Or had they saddled her with them to win the kind of bureaucratic button game she had suspected from the beginning? Either way, she was flying with one wing.

I had my old Marlboros as punishment for my airs. The cigarette tasted agreeably rotten, even worse than when I had been waiting for Christine Sewell and John Wells outside Monaghan's apartment. Since leaving Nassau County, I couldn't remember a stronger urge to be back in the mix, to have the hack captain direct some of his official petulance at me. I was being so transparent it was laughable. Finley the protector of the damsel in distress in the vicinity of a car that had been through a bad time. When last heard from a few years back, that Finley had been collapsing in a drunken heap on the Professor's couch Christmas night, doing nothing to prevent Jenny from driving Susan home on icy roads. His real specialty was waking up when state patrolmen came around to announce he had no more wife and no more daughter.

The thought had descended so brazenly I wondered if Marlboros *did* change composition with age. I hadn't had an attack of those guilts in ages. Why now? Why should that beast suddenly come roaring back to life standing in the middle of a sealed-off patch of midtown highway? Just because it would always come back whenever it felt like it?

"I'm going to need a few hours' sleep while they're doing the bullet," she said next to me. "Tomorrow is shaping up like a real treat. What's the matter? You all right?"

"Fine. Let's go."

I half-listened on the way back to her place. The testiness had been over a witness the Captain had allowed to leave the scene because of kids in the car with him. "Sure, he'll come in tomorrow and give a formal statement. But by then we'll have a few imaginative extras and maybe a big hole or two in his memory.

What's the great sacrifice? The kids would've been excited to be in a police station, wouldn't they?"

I didn't want to get into that. "What did this guy say?"

"He couldn't identify the shooter's car. Only that it was red."

"Red? Doesn't sound shy, does he?"

"The witness was going uptown about 40 yards behind Rosen—Karen Rosen, that's her name—when this red car coming downtown just drew abreast, one shot, boom. He didn't know how Rosen managed it, but she got over to the shoulder before she collapsed. He was too busy watching her so he didn't pile up, but he assumed the red car just kept going downtown. I mean, even if he didn't get anything on the shooter's car, he might remember something about the vehicles behind it. One of *them* must've seen something. A partial plate. Just where the shooter turned off. But that'll be gone tomorrow."

I wasn't in the mood for hard-ass; in fact, I wasn't in the mood for much of anything involving Karen Rosen.

"What's that face mean? You agree with Wendell? The captain?"

She was trying not to make it sound like an accusation; she could have tried harder. "How old were the kids?"

"I didn't ask."

"Six-year-olds might find a station house an adventure. A three-year-old might just need sleep more."

"You mean *does* need it more."

"Okay. Does need it more."

"So, say that."

"We getting a little frazzled here, Lieutenant?"

"Yes, we are, Mr. Finley."

"Rosen's number three, all right."

"What makes you so sure?"

So much for turning off Karen Rosen. "Not just the single shot, although that's a pretty good start. There was something else back there on that highway. Something familiar."

"What?"

"If I knew, Dana, I'd tell you!"

So, I could be as cross as she could, and we called it a draw. When I pulled up in front of her building, I knew I was going home. We both needed a little room. "I forgot to turn out the damn light," she said, buying another couple of seconds with a nod up to her second-floor window. "Well, at least I made Con Ed happy tonight."

My ferrets jumped. They weren't chewing, just cavorting. They were as struck by the living room light as I was. "I know what it was."

"What what was?"

"What was so familiar about that highway," I said, knowing I was right. "Think a second. The West Side Highway late at night. Citi Field after a game. The Canal Street subway stop at midnight."

"He likes deserted places. What do you expect? Fifth and 57th in the middle of the afternoon?"

"Not just deserted places or empty places. *Emptied* places, Dana. Places that are busy, then aren't."

She wanted to see it, to be as sure as I was, but her frown wouldn't let her. "Is there a difference?"

Of course, she couldn't have known, I realized. She had never walked into a house after a funeral for a wife and a daughter. "I think so," I said, hating the serial sniper more than I had ever hated anyone in my life.

CHAPTER 19

I didn't go straight home. First, wandering east toward the Midtown Tunnel seemed like a good idea. When you drove into a tunnel, you could always reemerge from one, too. Then, once I found myself on the Grand Central Parkway, I felt old gears locking into place. When Jenny and I had been dating before getting married, I had gone into the city on my day off almost every week to pick her up from her office to go to dinner and a show. Then we had driven back to the Island, always between eleven and midnight, almost as often promising each other to throw out our money next time on a crap game instead of on the latest musical based on a movie that had been based on a novel—none of which had been based on anything to care about. How long ago had that been? Passing LaGuardia, I thought of the slew of airline companies that had bitten the dust in the years since. On the other hand, wasn't it also possible scores of people still working in the terminals—porters, maintenance men, cab dispatchers—had seen us speeding past? Sometimes time raced, other times it crawled, but the real trick was how it seemed to manage both simultaneously.

What was there to see on Lakeview Avenue except what I couldn't see anymore? Nothing. And so what? That was still a familiarity I could control, that couldn't sandbag me standing in the middle of a crime scene on the West Side Highway. I knew the roads to get where it had suddenly seemed like a good idea to go. I knew Valley Stream and Lynbrook and Malverne. I even knew the mysterious number 7 painted over a fire hydrant at the mouth of the street. Only when I took the right into Lakeview did I remember how conspicuous it was to be driving past the quiet one- and two-family homes so late. I didn't dare slow down, let alone pull over to the curb because my engine would have been twice as loud as whatever some lawyer was declaiming on a "Law and Order" rerun. When I saw the solid white frame of #53 approaching on the left, I wanted to raise my foot from the gas so gently not even my toes would realize what was happening until it was too late. It should have been the natural, instinctive reaction. But I couldn't do it. There was a black plastic bag with some kind of garbage on the top step of the stoop. There were lights on upstairs in what had once been Susan's bedroom, but no more Dr. Seuss decals on the window. There was a green Skylark parked in front of the garage. Did it belong to the accountant named Wister who had been so quick to buy the house from me, making me feel even in my worst hangovers that I had lost track of the pea under the shells? How many owners ago had Wister been? All I could see from my rearview mirror was that the kitchen lights on the side of the house were off. Nobody was making black raspberry jam sandwiches for a late-night snack. It was probably a grape jelly house by now.

And then the block was over, and I had to make another left or right. I hadn't had time to hit anybody, least of all an absolute stranger. The sniper would have jeered at me.

CHAPTER 20

Since the sniper didn't have a name or identifiable breeding line, the media ignored people and pinned the killings on things—video games, crime shows, the parole system, whatever else had been invisible until the first bullet had been fired. The indignation came mixed with lurid warnings that the killer was probably taking aim at that very moment at every nursing home and school bus in the five boroughs. Nobody should panic, went the advice, but if you're in the mood to go screaming down the street or cowering under your bed, here's why you might.

I left a message for Dana at home, just to let her know I was there, but she didn't return it. Every couple of hours, I managed to be philosophical about her silence: In her place, I wouldn't have called back, either, unless I had half a day to vent, and I knew she didn't have that kind of time. One *Post* gossip columnist was already carrying water for "authoritative Police Plaza sources" supposedly "disappointed by the pace and thoroughness of the investigation." If she hadn't been set up by somebody, it was a reasonable facsimile. What I couldn't fathom was why. It took plenty of long-fuse malice to help boost someone into a visible position that, with the arrest of a suspect, could have just as easily exploded bad intentions. She claimed not to have an enemy in the department like that, and I had no reason to doubt her. But what did that leave?

Mainly a lot of idle thoughts until Shari Glynn called. "She's gone, Mr. Finley," she announced without ceremony.

When I figured out she was talking about sister Christine, I decided it was my theme for the week: The past was never dead, it just played hide-and-seek sometimes.

"She wasn't in her bed this morning. She took all her medicine with her. Her underwear and blouses are gone. Just about everything in the dresser is. The valise I gave her . . ."

She checked off the inventory as she might have for one of her bauble suppliers. I heard that and I heard the effort not to sound panicked, but what I didn't hear one way or the other was if she was blaming my Monaghan Strategy for Christine's disappearance. "Did you have a fight? Maybe you said something about the check?"

"I never mentioned it. Not directly."

"What's that mean, Shari?"

She had already been through that with herself and hadn't liked the answer she had come up with. "I made a joke when we were having lunch yesterday," she said, more rattled. "I said my hands were getting shaky, maybe I needed some of her pills. I couldn't even write a check lately without messing up one and throwing it away . . . She's my sister, Mr. Finley! We said those things to each other all the time!"

I should have been relieved: It was about the Joke, not about the Monaghan Strategy. "And what did she say?"

"Nothing. She just kept eating. Why would I believe anything she said anyway? She's always been a liar. Likes to be interesting."

The curtness caught me off guard. I seemed to have missed that Christine Sewell attribute—and that kind of unqualified dismissal from big sister. "Let's keep our eye on the ball, Shari. The joke that wasn't a joke."

"Okay, I just wanted her to know . . ."

"You knew?"

"If you want to put it that way."

I didn't want to put it anyway, and I didn't like the caginess I heard behind her embarrassment. Still, it had been her two thousand and her forged name. "That was your right, Shari."

"Yes, I know. But . . ."

"What does Marty say?" Silence. "You haven't told him."

"No. I just . . ."

Wanted it to boil inside, and what else was new in the world of sports? "Well, if you're sure she's really . . ."

"I told you—she's gone!"

"I don't know what to say, Shari. Christine's an adult, she's no teenager running away from home."

"You know it's not that simple, Mr. Finley!"

"Yes, it is. If you think she's in danger or might be having another episode, you've got to call the police."

"That's what Marty would say."

As curses went, there probably wasn't a Bedouin in the desert who could have topped her. "And he would be right," I said anyway. "These characters she's been hanging around with are bad news. If she's run to Wells, you don't want to wait."

I suppose it was a big tell that, even as she was insisting I was the only person in the industrialized world who could help her, I was tapping into the Switchboard on my computer to look up Monaghan. Why was this necessary? It wasn't on any level whatsoever except for the tiny fact that I had been in the guy's apartment, slapped him around, and threatened him, but had never bothered to learn his first name. When the Switchboard told me it was Dennis, I felt more what they call up to speed.

"I feel so guilty, Mr. Finley! If I'd only kept my mouth shut . . ."

I didn't want to drag it on for either of us. "What are you asking, Shari? Just ask it."

"Well, if this friend of Wells feels cheated because you brought me back the check and . . ."

There was the Monaghan Strategy. And the trouble was, she might not have been completely wrong. Christine was not supposed to have been around when Monaghan went back to Wells for the money. "All right, all right. I'll drop around to Wells's place and see if she's there. But I've got to tell you I don't know what that's going to accomplish . . ."

"Anything, Mr. Finley."

It sounded like a specialization: *Anything Mr. Finley.* Some private investigators were good at divorce cases, some at malpractice suits, and Mr. Finley was good at Anything. I should have had business cards made out to advertise myself. The Yellow Pages could have listed me first, under A. Pending those moves, I tramped into my bedroom to the bureau for my .38. I had caught Monaghan off-guard, but if Wells had even a piece of brain, he would have been expecting somebody to drop by. And that was without counting Christine, who might have taken her medication that morning or who might not have and who was now running around Wells's apartment with a knife in her hand. If there was one thing specialists in Anything were good at, it was deluding themselves they were prepared for Everything.

I drove down to Red Hook determined to think positive things. I was out of the house with more to ponder than the sniper and the bureaucrats who had Dana in their sights, wasn't I? It wasn't raining, was it?

That took care of my positive thoughts.

Wells lived in one of those deteriorating rowhouses that some real estate operator 30 years ago had decided would look gentrified by being coated in lime green paint. The whole block, in fact, was out of an old Crayola box—reds, blues, oranges, greens. What the colors hadn't covered up were the great chunks of torn up asphalt on both the sidewalks and in the gutter and the sulfur-marinated fish odors wafting up from the Gowanus Canal. At least I didn't have to hunt for a parking space. I had apparently just missed the police tow away trucks that had cleared the street.

A middle-aged Latino in a striped polo shirt with enough belly to cover his belt buckle was sitting on the stoop of Wells's place. He watched me every step of the way from the car as he went at some figs from a bag next to him. "Hi. I'm looking for Johnny Wells."

The guy thought that was funny, but slurped up some more fig before saying, "You're an hour late. Gone."

"Today?"

He had to think about whether anybody connecting an hour earlier to the same day was harmless; he came down on my side. "Him and his friend. Took off. Luggage and everythin'. He owe you money?"

I didn't know if I had just heard good news or bad news. A living Wells who hadn't infuriated Christine was probably better than a dead one who had pressed her buttons, but a living one also sounded like somebody with ongoing plans for her. "Smallish blonde? Thin?"

"Her," he nodded. "Your wife?"

He thought that was worth showing me a gold-toothed laugh, and maybe it was. "So, he was going for good, not coming back?"

"I don't take no luggage to buy a newspaper. You? Too bad, too."

"You liked him?"

He shrugged. "Johnny was all right. I knew who he was. Before he moved in, they were rentin' out his place to somebody new every mont'. Never knew who was livin' in there. You like to know who's downstairs, know what I'm sayin'?"

I looked up at the front door, thinking it would have been nice to get inside for a look around. But nobody put aside his figs to jump up with a key. "No idea where he was going?"

"He didn't even say goodbye. Fuck him."

"Right."

I stood there staring off at the elevated Gowanus Expressway waiting for a truck to fall off with a good idea. I should have had more in mind than a call to Shari Glynn saying I'd been too late, but I didn't.

"She got a temper," my friend said, dipping into the bag for another fig. "The blonde. He don't put the bags in the car the way she wants, she's gonna chop his head off."

I shook my head at the wonder of it all. What I was really wondering was why Pete Piccolo, the Long Island insurance claims man who had once told me I would be good at investigative work, had forgotten to warn me there would be times when it wasn't all that clear who exactly it was I was supposed to be trying to help.

CHAPTER 21

I sat in my car in front of Wells's house for a few minutes consulting my manual on correct procedures for private investigators at a dead end. The most obvious move was to go over to Monaghan's to hear what he could tell me about the whereabouts of Wells and Christine. Drawback: If the guy held down anything like a job, I would be in for another long stint in front of his place, not to mention in front of the 76th precinct. The next most obvious move was to report in to Shari, urging her again to alert the cops. Drawback: Shari didn't think there was any problem afflicting mankind that couldn't be solved by keeping husband Marty and the forces of law and order in the dark while Finley Investigations went stumbling through the city. There was even a third logical move: Dumping it all in the lap of Dr. Marian Freedman, at the very least so the doctor could persuade Shari to do what she should be doing. Drawback: I was supposed to be Marian Freedman's solution, not the other way around, and I didn't want to have the doctor questioning why she steered clients to me every once in a while.

All that heavy thinking made me hungry watching my friend on the stoop continue to go through his figs. It also made me careless when a black Hyundai slowed next to me in the middle of the street. The driver seemed to be waiting for me to pull away from the only patch of curb on the whole deserted block he found acceptable for parking. Or was I supposed to roll down my window because he wanted directions? I was about to go for this saner explanation when my passenger door came open with a hard tug on the handle. Monaghan shoved himself inside in full Old Spice splendor. "And here we are again, lad!" he said, looking more confident with his hand in his jacket pocket. "Guess what I have in here?"

He was a con man, not a thug, so that should have made the answer his hand. But even with the odds 3-1 in my favor, they seemed a little long. "I was just thinking about you, Dennis."

"And me you, mate. You owe me two thousand bucks."

"No, Wells does."

"I'll start with you. How's that?"

"Sorry. Fresh out."

So much for the theory of if-your-enemy-is-my-enemy-you're-my-friend. He nodded at the Hyundai, which had started up again and was now rolling slowly down toward the Canal. "Just follow him."

I did it telling myself what he was telling himself: I was the one with the edge. Assuming, of course, he didn't get over liking himself so much that he remembered to frisk me for the .38 in my belt.

"Funny how the world is so interconnected," he said. "You're here, I'm here. Both of us after the same thing. Funny, don't you think, Finley? . . . How do I know your name? Oh, these eyes may be baby blue, but they've never missed an ace being palmed at a table. So, you flash your little badge at me the other night like I'm supposed to be overwhelmed by seeing something like that for the first time. A word of caution, lad: They print the names much too big. And the Nassau County shield . . . Well, let's just say I've seen it before. How many seconds you think I need for a little read like that? . . . But wait a tick! I stand bloody corrected! It *was* the first time I ever saw a badge like that! At least from someone who shouldn't be carrying it around. That's what the nice woman in Mineola told me. She didn't lie to me, did she?"

It was the best argument yet for the New Finley disposing of the Old Finley once and for all. I *deserved* having to follow the Hyundai deeper into the shadows under the Expressway. "If you put half as much effort into checking up on your marks, you might not be in the spot you're in now."

The redhead had definite limits to his good humor. "I don't need your advice. What I want is some satisfaction."

"Don't we all!"

He still didn't take out whatever he had in his pocket. Second tell: He couldn't escalate his threats because he had nothing to escalate them with. His real edge was the driver of the Hyundai. Too bad I hadn't gotten a closer look at the guy. It would have been nice to know if I was dealing with a muscleman or just another blowhard Dennis Monaghan. "I think they went off to Niagara Falls on their honeymoon."

"You don't say."

"Probably using your money to buy some trinkets."

At least he tried to think that was funny. "Minus your piece?"

"My piece?"

"You mean you were just doing Johnny a favor the other night? Out of the pureness of your heart? What was it worth to him? A coupla hundred? You've fallen on lean days, Finley."

The suggestion of working for Johnny Wells was so galling I almost saw heat waves. I counted to three, reminding myself that Dennis Monaghan was a small-timer and small-timers had to come to the kind of conclusion he had. "I'm not interested in you or Wells, Monaghan. My job is to make sure the lady doesn't do something stupid. *Capisc'?*"

He seemed to consider it as a genuine possibility. "And who is it who gave you this great job?"

"None of your business."

"Right, you people never tell your sources."

"What people?"

"Never mind. You go on playing it close to the vest and I'll go on thinking Wells screwed you over, too. How's that?"

There were certain people you didn't engage in conversation because the best that could happen was you ended up sounding like Archie Bunker dealing with Edith. Monaghan was definitely an Edith Bunker. "Repeat: I don't care about you and Wells."

"Yeah, well," he sighed, "sometimes that's not important. All those interconnections again. We're all just dots on the big grid."

"The what?"

"The big grid. Air controller talk. A pal says it all the time."

There were more comforting thoughts than a Dennis Monaghan friend directing air traffic over Kennedy Airport. One of them was getting a better look at the Hyundai driver at the corner light: Through the rear window, he resembled the other guy from the Emerald Club. No bruiser, just another 35ish suit. What it came down to was being able to get out from behind the wheel without either of them spotting my weapon.

The Hyundai kept going past foundries and oil storage depots, toward what I imagined was the source of the stench in the air. Monaghan looked around a little more nervously; the area seemed to be strange to him. "I guess this is your friend's old neighborhood, huh?"

"He don't think much of you, either."

"More of that interconnection thing."

"You got it. Now shut up."

"Just one thing I'm curious about. Was the check your only role in this? Or were you setting up Christine for something really ambitious?"

"I guess we'll never know, will we?"

The Hyundai took a left into a cobblestone street, then abruptly stopped next to a high metal fence; sealed warehouses took up the opposite side. I didn't like the way the driver reached over into his back seat for some object. "Out," Monaghan prodded.

If there was one thing more ragged than a Finley Production, it was a Monaghan Production. His friend had passed up any number of desolate pocket areas to park on a street that practically guaranteed driver witnesses by running long three blocks in either direction. The friend, a wavy-haired once-upon-a-time quarterback on the high school intramural team, tried to look gleeful as he came out of his car tapping an iron bar in his palm. But then he ruined the thug effect by giving Monaghan an anxious glance for a signal. And Monaghan gave it to him: removing his hand from his pocket to show not a gun, but a smaller, knobbier iron pipe. "You weren't polite the other night, Finley," he said. "I owe you for that."

"Find Johnny and your money, Dennis. You'll be happier."

Call it a vibration in the air, but a second before he raised his hand to point, I could sense the Hyundai guy taking a harder look at my buttoned jacket. "You didn't pat him down!"

Monaghan took a long time to process the accusation, then to look at me with some unspeakable complaint. That was time enough to show both of them the gun. Monaghan turned whiter than he had the night in his apartment. Hyundai didn't know where to start with his fury. "You stupid fuck! How can you forget something like that!!??"

I was expecting one of them at least to fling their pipes, but Hyundai was too disgusted and Monaghan was too busy trying to deny his mistake to himself. When he finally accepted it, he looked across the roof of my car at me as though I had become an honorary burden in his life. "I take it neither of you can give me a clue where Wells might have gone."

The red hair finally seeped down into his face and he finally did throw his pipe, but down on the ground, and so angrily it bounced back up and almost cost him a whack in the knee. "Fuck you, Finley!" And with that, he started marching toward the Hyundai.

"I asked you a question before, Dennis."

"Screw your questions!"

I took a chance on the echo and let a shot go in the air. It was louder than any of us expected. Just the pigeons fluttering up from the warehouses took something out of my stomach. Hyundai staggered back a step and Monaghan froze. I almost did both. "What was the idea with Christine?" I got out, praying one of the sealed doors across the street wouldn't turn out to be not so sealed.

Hyundai didn't like the idea that he was suddenly closer to me on our side of the cars than Monaghan was. "It was Wells's idea," he said quickly.

"What was?"

"He's Don Juan. He was going to smooth-talk her into letting us into her store some night. Take what there was to take."

The guy looked serious, which seemed to be the only serious part of what I was hearing. "Take what? A bunch of beads?"

Now it was Monaghan who was looking less than pleased with his partner. "Why don't you tell him everything, Kitty? Just in case he has a wire on him and somebody's listening."

"He could have fucking P.C. Richard under that jacket and you wouldn't spot it!"

I let them fume at each other for what Monaghan called a tick. One question was how any adult went around with the name Kitty. Another was whether Shari was dense enough to keep cash in the store overnight or whether Wells hadn't been selling a bill of goods to the two doofuses as much as to Christine Sewell. I really liked the scam possibility. "Hey, guys, pipe down. Has it ever occurred to you that your friend Johnny's conned you? That all he was in this for was the two grand he's already got from you? No store, just the check?"

Monaghan had been ready to believe I would have worked for Wells for a couple of hundred, but he had higher expectations where Wells and two thousand dollars were concerned: Apparently, that wasn't even worth thinking about, just more crap out of my mouth. Kitty, though, wasn't so sure. "Tell him that's a crock of shit, Dennis. Tell him your friend Wells is too big-time for that kind of shit."

With both of us staring him down, Monaghan had to think some more, and he didn't like his thoughts. I was doing a pretty good job of convincing myself, as well. Wells thinking only about scamming a quick two thousand sounded a lot more like him than some elaborate scheme for bedding down Christine Sewell and breaking into a store with a burglar alarm and a safe with a combination.

"Anything else, Finley?" Monaghan asked, not quite as much sneer in the question as he would have liked.

"Yeah. Next time don't count on all those interconnections so much. Sometimes they mean less than they seem to."

They threw themselves into the Hyundai as if bent on shaking the chassis off the frame. Giving the car the key, Kitty was already launched into a lecture on Monaghan's "*quote sure thing unquote.*" I watched to make sure they didn't have a Hail Mary play still in them, but the last thing in their heads was something like backing up the Hyundai on me. Their bickering continued as they bumped over an especially high cobblestone and rumbled on down the street. I still wanted to know where Kitty had picked up his nickname. But I settled for watching the pigeons returning to the ledges of the warehouses. They too seemed to recognize small-timers when they saw them.

CHAPTER 22

Shari Glynn bristled at seeing me walk in the door after three o'clock. Not only had I ignored her schedule, but she had two customers in the store, making it impossible for her to scold me. She had little choice but to suppress her scowl for the guy standing at the register while I drifted over to the beads tables. I had seen her little wadded ball of tension before: on sister Christine while she had been waiting on the corner for Wells to pick her up for the drive to Staten Island. The Sewell girls probably hadn't grown up in a cotton candy household.

The customer at the register wanted a birthday gift for his wife but was having second thoughts about maybe buying her a yacht instead. The more Shari went through her too cheerful explanation of the differences among ropes, bibs, lariats, and operas, the more distracted the guy's nods. The other customer was a teenager with turquoise hoop earrings checking out the bins. I thought she had the right idea in putting her hand in one tray after another, then feeling the beads trickle through her fingers. It felt good when I did it, too; until I came to the shells, anyway. Tiger shells, bonnet shells, trochus shells, cowries, corals—they ganged up to give me a good slit between my third and fourth fingers. I caught Shari looking over her customer's shoulder and smiling as I inspected my punctured skin. Shari Glynn expected people who broke her house rules to be punished.

The husband finally left with a lariat, and a minute later the teenager followed him out without anything but a couple of sensations for her time. Shari maintained her look of silent disapproval through the tale of Monaghan and Kitty, finding a half-dozen ways to log and file the single American Express slip left from her sale. I had expected her to be unhappy about where I had gone after getting rid of Monaghan and Kitty, and she was. "You went where??!!"

"Wells's parole officer. If he's climbing into cars with valises, that's probably a sign he's not going to be at his registered address."

"This was supposed to . . ."

"What it was supposed to be was a mission to find Christine. You *were* worried about her being in danger because of the money, right? Wells's friend feeling ripped off?"

"Well, yes, but . . ."

"One way of doing that is to have interested parties find Wells."

"You could've . . ."

As much as I liked her steaming, I had to cut it off by telling her the whole story. "Relax, Shari. A very impatient woman named Robinson didn't want me there any more than you did. And she had more reason. Wells's parole ran out last week. He's a full citizen again. They don't care if he and Christine have gone to Japan."

Her eruption over going to the parole office I had foreseen; her relief over leaving it again without help I hadn't. I had an unpleasant stirring that I had missed more than her curfew on store visits. "But just in case they haven't gone to Japan, do you keep money in here overnight?"

She looked almost perky pointing to the credit card machine. "This count? Any currency goes upstairs with me. So, no, her boyfriend or his friends have no reason to break in here."

"Wells won't have to break in if he has a key."

Her eyes went instantly to the door, and without any sense of triumph. I knew the locksmith down the street was about to make a few bucks. "You're glad she's gone, aren't you?"

"That's silly."

"Is it?"

She gathered up the neck pieces the husband hadn't bought and began returning them to the wall case behind the counter. "I don't think you'd understand, Mr. Finley."

That seemed like a given. "Like maybe what's a new lock compared to the expense of having your sister upstairs with you?"

Her spidery hands were meticulous about laying out the operas and matinees on the shelves so every bauble could be displayed. "You're the one who said it, Mr. Finley. Chris isn't a teenager anymore. And between you and me, my home, my business, my marriage, none of them have gotten better since we took her in."

I thought of the trip to Staten Island, the stakeout outside Monaghan's place, the visit to Wells's place. I thought of having to take out my .38 and having to fire it in the air. I even thought of the goddamn pigeons. What was it the Professor had said? A gesture. Looking into Ralph Carey's killing was a gesture. Or, in Dorothy's view, a symbol. The gesturing symbol had struck again! "This has all been some kind of game to you??!!"

She whirled back with more indignation, but this time she was in full control of it. "I don't think you've been underpaid for your services, do you? I think it's time we all acted like adults and stopped trying to protect what can't be protected. If she wants that lowlife for company, that's her choice. If she wants to lie about it, that's hers, too."

"Lie? So, you *have* talked to her about Wells?"

She didn't like being caught in contradictions. "Don't take me so literally. The point I'm trying to make is that I would just like to get on with my life. And so would my husband."

"You could've done that a lot cheaper. You didn't have to go through this game of mirrors with me."

"Please stop calling it a game. I *do* feel responsible for Chris. She's my baby sister. That's why I was glad to get her out of that hospital. She needed to know her family was there for her when she was going through the worst. But that doesn't mean I'm going to dedicate my whole life to her and nothing else. You do what you can, and thanks to you, I have to accept now that there's not much more Marty and I can do. You call that a game? I don't.

You've made us realize just how far we can go. You promised a service and you delivered it. I can sell beads in here, Mr. Finley, but I can't guarantee the person wearing them is beautiful or they'll look good on the garment they're sewn on. We have to know our limitations."

She looked so courageous saying it, too.

CHAPTER 23

I went home thinking thin lips. Jenny had always said don't trust people with thin lips, they were self-obsessed and takers. I had no idea where she had gleaned that wisdom and I wondered if the craze among self-obsessed models and actresses for blowing up their mouths into collagen balloons would have changed her mind, but there was no doubt that both Sewell sisters had thin lips. Come to think of it, so did Dennis Monaghan and Mrs. Robinson at the parole office and Sal Reni at the luncheonette. Clearly, I had to tighten up my trust standards.

Back in the apartment, the first message I fielded from the machine was from Dana. The traffic noises in the background said she was calling from her cell on the street, but she was even more cryptic than when she phoned from her office. "I'll be out of town for a day or so. You'll be getting a call from Loschen. It'll help. Talk to you when I get back."

At least the suspense was brief. After a wrong number, the next message was from the scarecrow cop. "Mr. Finley, my name is Detective Herman Loschen and I'm working with Lieutenant Dana McGill on an investigation I believe you know about. The Lieutenant mentioned you had a videotape that might be of interest to us in the investigation. We would appreciate it very much if you could bring it around to the 107 precinct sometime tomorrow. Of course, if this is difficult for you, we could dispatch somebody to pick it up at your apartment. Please let me know at what time it would be convenient for you to drop by the station. Thank you."

I needed a Sprite to think that one over, or maybe just to belch out the gasses suddenly circulating inside me. *"Out of town?"* Where was out of town in the middle of an investigation as pressing as the sniper? The Himalayas for getting the insights of a holy man? Dana hadn't just been cryptic, she had sounded like someone aware her calls were being monitored; worse, like someone aware her every administrative move was being recorded, so better one of her assistants call me the way he would have called anybody else who happened to have the Bronsard tape. Personal was a no-no. And Loschen had played it the same way. He might have been dude ranch material to some, but he had enough sense of his authority to insinuate I would have been better off dropping by the tape than waiting for some patrol car to come by to pick it up.

And all for what? When I had coughed up my factoid about Gary Stein being on the Bronsard tape, Dana had written him off as a dweeb. Granted I'd mentioned it as casually as I could have, giving her little reason for dropping all her other leads for Stein, but to go from that total indifference to what was close to an air of urgency? There seemed to be only two possibilities: Either she had uncovered another Gary Stein connection independently or she had reached the bottom of the barrel and was scratching up anything at all to appease her superiors. I really didn't believe in the first possibility and resented the second one.

The beginning of clarity turned out to be only a finger away. I zapped on the TV to see if I had missed anything during my crusading adventures on behalf of Shari Glynn. I certainly had. Channel 1 had something to say about stock market prices, then about the Yankees, and then about what it termed the "involvement" of the Homeland Security Department in the sniper case. If I had been a TV show, I would have started humming the "Twilight Zone" theme. The justification for the Federal interest, according to the tomb-eyed news anchor, was that the shootings might have had a "terrorist component" aimed at "creating panic among city residents." The guy didn't laugh, either; he just kept staring at his teleprompter until it ran out of words and a Delta commercial came on. If the teleprompter had said *he* had been identified as one of those terrorist components, he probably wouldn't have noticed until he finished reading and they came on the set to drag him away.

I zapped off the TV. The Sprite was good for belching, but not much else. A practical person would have found something positive in the arrival of the Feds; didn't that make it all the less likely Finley Investigations would be able to earn it's $725 in the name of Ralph Carey's family? That practical person would have grabbed the phone and called the Professor to say gee, I'm sorry, I would've liked to help, but there are so many cops of all kinds around, we'd just be tripping over one another. But that would have been a practical person. The longer I sat on the couch listening to the Fagans screaming at one another across the courtyard about his boozing, the more the burn-cut between my fingers from Shari Glynn's shells made me comfortable in my normal state of irritation. As I had found out more than once, Homeland Security didn't "involve" itself in something half-way; if it was in, Dana was already fetching coffee and Xeroxing pictures of Yemeni students with A averages at Columbia. Wherever "out of town" was, it was sure to have conference rooms where suits talked a lot about national security. And that, ladies and gentlemen, was not the shortest route to giving Ralph Carey's family or Michael Leong's family or Karen Rosen's family any of that famous closure.

I knew I had to drop off the tape in the morning if just to spare Dana complications. The details I could get from her when she got back from her mysterious trip. But that didn't mean I had to empty my hope chest, either. If there was one thing Jeffrey Chalian, my neighbor's sluggish son, had been good for, it had been pulling me into the high-tech era. Not only had he set up my computer and taught me the buttons on my VCR, but he had enough electronic equipment in his bedroom to eavesdrop on the Klingons. In Mrs. Chalian's words, Jeffrey was "looking for his own niche in this terribly complicated world." Some might have said that, at an age closer to 30 than 20, Jeffrey had already found that niche in his bedroom. But what I said when the yawning hulk answered his door was "Jeffrey, can you make me a copy of this tape?" The kid gave me one of his grunts that had more meanings than *aloha* but then showed his charm by refusing to use my tape of *Face Off* for the copying, volunteering a blank tape of his own. I was so happy about that and about Mrs. Chalian being out while he did the copying that I gave him twenty bucks when he had finished. "I don't need that," he said, as though possession of currency was illegal in his bedroom. "Take it," I insisted. "Go out tonight and get a couple of beers."

I pretended not to hear him protesting "I don't drink beer" as I scuttled back to my apartment and closed the door. I gave it a few seconds until I heard him close his door, then got down to seeing what the copy of Bobby Qualls's copy of the Bronsard tape looked like. It looked like the original copy. After downplaying Gary Stein's importance to myself for a couple of days, I suppose I should have been content not to find anything that would force me to change my mind back again. Stein might have omitted mention of the Carey game to the other members of his auld lang syne club, but there was no noticeable dissembling in front of Bronsard's video cam. Yes, he knew who Ralph Carey had been; he even looked smug at recalling that the guy had played for Pittsburgh as well as Brooklyn. And what was he to think about the killing except that it was a horrible thing? He grimaced—genuinely enough to me—to hear about the press box shooting. There was no way he belonged in my hope chest.

I was also struck again by the blandness of the questions. Compared to Owen Bronsard, Larry King was a Salem judge hunting witches. You were on your own to figure out if anybody talking had a pulse. At least Fagan across the alley shouting he'd had "just one fuckin' beer" was alive; maybe not to everybody's liking, but alive. If anyone stood out from the pack on the tape, it wasn't Stein, but the priest-looking guy who kept pressing Bronsard for more particulars. There was an eerie gleam in the priest's eyes that Stein would have reserved for a Hank Aaron home run overlooked by baseball historians. He also had a tote bag of some kind, but Bronsard had held his camera manically steady, never dipping below the bag straps around the priest's wrist for helping me make out a label or trademark. I decided Bronsard had done that deliberately to piss me off.

Since it was already after four and I wasn't in the mood for any of the other epic investigations on my desk, I decided to eliminate Gary Stein from my fantasy life altogether. Through the wonders of the Switchboard link, Jeffrey Chalian had shown me, I tracked down Stein's address, telephone number, and e-mail in Bayside. This, I hoped, would make me sound like less of a pain in the ass when I called up my contact at Motor Vehicles, Jimmy Heyer, to ask for a make on Stein's car. It worked—sort of. Heyer had already started a countdown to the end of his working day and really didn't want to be doing me any favors before morning. But when I told him I had all the address information, he couldn't disguise his pity. "I don't need his blood type, Finley. You give me a name, spell it reasonably right, and I click my own buttons. We've got a very sophisticated operation down here. I'll call you when I'm leaving. Half-hour."

To fill up the wait, I mused about what I would have done if I had been working the case with Dana. She was out of town, right? She wouldn't have heard me. One thought was shooting ranges. What were the odds a lethal marksman like the sniper didn't keep in practice? Too long to be dismissed, so I made a note to ask Dana if she had visited the city's ranges. Add to them the hunting clubs where Big Ed in the lumberjack shirt and cartridge vest probably had targets out back with the old tires and discarded refrigerators. Who knew when it might be profitable to visit them and show a photo of, say, Gary Stein? If there was any flaw in this inspiration, it was that the sniper could have also been keeping sharp by shooting lemons in some woods in Pennsylvania. But why be negative, especially since it would have been Herman Loschen, not me, going on that wild goose chase?

Then Jimmy Heyer called back and fouled up the evening. Gary Stein drove a Mercury that wasn't blue, black, gray or any of the other drab colors of the spectrum, but flaming red! I thanked Jimmy Heyer. He didn't think I meant it, and he was right.

CHAPTER 24

Herman Loschen gave a tight nod of approval when he saw I had put the cassette in a paper bag; he didn't want our business becoming the business of every uniform buzzing around the 107's booking desk, either. Up close, he was beakier than he had seemed on the West Side Highway—sharp nose and jutting chin, one of those people who seemed to have grown up from his elbows and knees. "Thanks for coming by," he said, making no move to take the bag. "Got a second?"

I had counted on giving him more than a second. Whether it took small talk or official talk, I wanted more of a feel for the pressures Dana had come under. I got the first feel when, instead of leading me into an office, he ambled into the roll call room a few yards away from the desk: We were aboveboard, nothing secretive, in full public view. That seemed to be the theory, anyway. Too bad for the theory there was a uniform in the sun-bright place, banging the juice machine for his swallowed-up money. Loschen's frown said staying public should have somehow guaranteed him privacy, and for a second he looked seriously gangled up, not somebody who would score high in intuitive response tests. Even when he recovered to tease the irate uniform about losing his dollar to the machine, the jibes came out awkwardly, in a flat monotone that described anti-funny. I sank back into my gloom from the Rosen crime scene that Dana had surrounded herself with Department rejects. Finally, though, he went over to give the bill dispenser a shove of his own. Whatever he did worked; a bottle of apple juice immediately came thumping down the chute. The uniform walked out with a jab about how even machines were impressed by detective shields.

The only chairs in the room were those white wooden classroom seats that came with a desk attached. Loschen slid into his as if still back taking high school algebra. While I tucked and squeezed, he pretended interest in the bulletin board circulars and precinct sector maps. I realized he wasn't just being polite when a toilet flushed from behind the door at the end of the room. He gave me a shy smile, I caught on and asked him if he was a Mets or Yankees fan, he looked insulted I could even suggest he had any Yankee blue in his veins and lamented the state of the Mets pitching. It took a couple of years, but the uniform in the john eventually ran out of water faucets and towel dispensers and had to emerge. He walked the length of the room and out crooning to himself.

"The Lieutenant says you were on the job," Loschen said as if picking up from something we had already been talking about. "Out on the Island did she say?"

"Ancient history."

"And you know someone in the Carey family or something?"

"Extended family. I'm sure she's told you the connection."

"Yeah. Maybe I'm just a little foggy this morning."

That seemed like a half-truth a couple of times over. One because he wasn't foggy just that morning, but probably every morning, afternoon, and evening on the calendar. Two because his fogginess was such a natural condition it had long ago ceased affecting his thinking. "Well, she certainly talks you up. She seems to trust you a lot."

He relaxed a little, letting his long legs sprawl out from under the desk. Thirty years old or not, NYPD detective or not, he acted dirt-kicking, bumpkin timid. I wondered how much of that came from the family juice Dana said he had in the Department—the junior nephew who had never been completely convinced he had earned adult company. "I like working with her," he said.

"She says the same thing about you."

He smiled, truly flattered. Before we went on in that vein for another hour, I put the tape on his desk. "As I said to the

Lieutenant, I don't think this will help too much. Just an odd coincidence that struck me when I first saw it. But, obviously, feel free to talk to the guy."

There was a glint in his soft eyes: Like he had been waiting for my permission to talk to Gary Stein! "Thank you."

"No problem. Whatever happened with your witness—the one who was driving behind Rosen?"

"Nothing useful."

"Too bad."

"Some people see less than you hope they'll see."

"You can say that again."

"The way it goes, I suppose."

"Nobody ever said it would be easy."

"You got that right."

I had a few hundred more of them and I was positive he did, but we were probably only a few hours away from the next tour reporting and a sergeant coming in to muster it out. "The Lieutenant around?"

"No, she's not in today."

"Right! She was going out of town, she said." I threw the dice. "Some kind of conference in Washington?"

Bullseye. "You've worked with these people?"

"Oh, yeah. They're always the home team. They don't know squat about the places they parachute into and you've always got to go to them. Don't take them away from their flagpoles and big wall eagles. They get a bad case of separation anxiety."

He laughed with an odd twitter, then fell abruptly silent. For a second I thought I had missed something, that I was supposed to be the one talking. But then he said: "With them coming in, I advised the Lieutenant to dot all her I's and cross all her t's. She'd told me about this tape, so I thought it was best to get it on the record, too."

"Good thinking."

He nodded, welcoming another compliment, and seemed on the verge of another nap. But then: "It was the ballplayer. This Ralph Carey."

"What was?"

"Homeland Security's interest. Carey had friends in Nebraska real big in the Republicans. The scuttlebutt is some of them even made calls to the White House. That may be bull, but sure as hell, the snowball's been rolling down the hill. And I don't think it was because of Leong or Rosen."

Being so anti-funny, he couldn't pat himself on the back when he *was* funny. "No, I'd guess not. And this so-called . . .?"

"The 'terrorist component?' The only components we have are three corpses of people with nothing in common between them. In fact, they're so different in absolutely everything—gender, ethnicity, demographics, name it—the Lieutenant has half an idea that might be the key. Somebody trying to show the world how random random can be."

Dana hadn't tried out that conjecture with me, and I didn't think it was half-bad—or wouldn't have been if the sniper had known a Jewish bookkeeper named Rosen had been coming toward him at 40 miles an hour. "Sounds like a point worth exploring."

He shook his head. "No. He couldn't have known who Rosen was. How can you know who's driving toward you on a highway?"

"Right."

"You have any thoughts along those lines?" Suddenly he was interested in seeing what a video cassette inside a bag looked like. "You must've speculated a little. I mean, since you know the Lieutenant and you've probably talked about the case."

"I'm sure you guys have it covered."

"Whatever. Never hurts to have another voice."

It didn't? Outside of as a tactic for warming up an interrogation, I had never heard that from a cop before. And who didn't know what a cassette in a paper bag looked like? It looked just like a cassette with brown paper around it. But he suddenly couldn't get over his fascination with it. "I guess I had one thought," I said, curious if we were going anywhere in particular. "This guy must keep in practice somewhere."

"Yeah?"

"Shooting ranges. Someplace where he doesn't lose his eye. You don't go three-for-three just remembering how good you were in the Army or Marines 10 years ago."

He didn't fall down in front of me in awe; in fact, he closed the bag over the tape as though accepting he had wasted his money on a bad bootleg movie. "Probably not," he nodded. "We've looked into that a little."

"Oh?"

"Some private ranges too. You know, the guys from the bowling alley and one of them has targets, that kind of thing?"

"Sure."

"Of course, there're probably thousands of those people, but we're really not equipped to go into every house in the city. Not even Homeland Security would give us that kind of manpower."

"No, of course not," I said, wondering what I would look like inside the bill slot in the juice machine.

"And we're not really sold he's been three-for-three, either."

"Excuse me?"

It was nod time again, and this time he had the odd sight of his fingers splayed on the chair-desk as a more immediate concern. How was it, he looked to be asking himself, his hand had only five fingers? "We've got at least three other shootings you might call suspicious," he muttered finally. "Two were complete misses. The night before Rosen, though, there was another drive by on the QBE. Shattered the back window of the vic. The driver reported it, but it was filed under . . . I don't know. I forget." He raised his eyes to see if it was okay to come out. "I guess I had the same thought as you about the shooter being so perfect. So, I just ran a couple of patterns through the computer to see if there were any other matches. Three so far, and I wouldn't be surprised I find more."

If I had ever doubted Loschen's version of how Carey had been shot on the press box level, I didn't anymore. I also didn't know how Dana worked with such an unnerving cricket. I would have taken Jeffrey Chalian as a roommate first. "The QBE. Late at night?"

"Yeah."

"And the two misses?"

"Also, both at night. A maintenance man catching a smoke in front of a Wall Street brokerage firm and a bartender closing up a saloon. Neither saw the shooter. The maintenance man wasn't even sure it was a shot at first. Thought the glass door had just given way."

"Who thinks bullets on Wall Street?"

"Who thinks *Glock .40-caliber* bullets?"

"The same?"

"Yup."

Yup. That was what the comedians had always said for their imitation of Gary Cooper. Why didn't Loschen make me think Gary Cooper, make me believe that what he knew was equal to what he had under control?

"I like what you said about the emptied places . . . Yeah, the Lieutenant mentioned it. All these misses fit that pattern, too."

"Some people might not see such a great difference . . ."

"With empty places? Oh, no, there's a difference. I knew exactly what you meant as soon as the Lieutenant said it."

"Speaking from personal experience?"

He nodded quickly as if to get rid of the memory. "My father had a bad cancer when I was a kid," he said, eyes again glued to his long, hairy fingers. "Sometimes when he was really bad, my mother would ask me to stay home from school because she couldn't afford to miss work and my sisters were too young. This one day I was home with him alone and he asked me to go buy him a malted at the store. When I came back with the malted, he wasn't in bed. He'd crawled out to the garage and turned on the engine to end it."

"Jesus!"

He shook his head with an old hurt. "Whenever I went into that bedroom afterward, I remembered the hospital bed he was lying in the last time before I went to the store. I couldn't let go of the idea that bed had been taken out of its natural place. And that's stupid, yeah? It shouldn't have been there in the first place. But even after my mother redid the whole bedroom, it seemed emptier because that hospital bed was gone. Sort of what like you're saying about these crime scenes."

"Sounds like you blamed yourself for going to the store."

He braved another look at me, this time with a wan smile. "It's not always in the past. Know what I mean?"

I didn't even have to say I did. He could read it on my every pore.

CHAPTER 25

I spent a good part of the rest of the day trying to figure out how Loschen had gotten more out of me than I had out of him. I hadn't actually *told* him anything, but I had felt so outflanked sitting in my little desk-chair I might as well have been back in Mr. Rakosi's biology class. Then too guessing right every once in a while about what others appeared to know by heart had been as close as I'd gotten to learning something.

I took it out on Sanford Lefkowitz. According to Mrs. Lefkowitz (and a big box of an ad in the Yellow Pages), Sanford had a thriving physical therapy business for people sent home from the hospital with artificial hips and knees. But also, according to Mrs. Lefkowitz, he had been providing massages and supervising exercises for one of his charges long after she should have been primed for the three-minute mile. Confirming this came down to sitting across from the Crown Heights apartment building of Ida Fleischer. It was really nothing more than a clocking job, but especially after my morning session with Loschen, the clock moved as fast as a sundial.

When the third hour approached with no sign of Sanford, I decided Mrs. Lefkowitz had been right and headed home. The really bad news for Sanford was that he had wilted not just me, but the driver of a black Saab halfway down the block. I played with that fancy for a few blocks, picturing Mrs. Lefkowitz hiring an army of private investigators, all of them staking out Ida Fleischer's place while Ida plowed away with Sanford in between questions about how long she would need a cane. The fancy evaporated, but not the Saab. And that was only the first of bad awarenesses.

The second was that I seemed to have spawned my own little army of potential tails. And I had never even seen Ida Fleischer! The list got longer with every second of thought I gave to it. Even before Homeland Security had become Homeland Security, I hadn't exactly ingratiated myself with the FBI as either a cop on the Island or a private investigator. I had called it following my nose, they had called it trespassing on government land. Frank Vincent, Brian Seldes, John Cicut, Mary Bellini—the names went on of bad-sport Feds who wouldn't be on hand for my next surprise birthday party. Then there was my friend Loschen, who behind his attacks of narcolepsy, dandruff-in-the-brain, or whatever was ailing him might have decided *I* was the sniper. And why stop there? Francis Forte, D.D.S., was still roaming around, wasn't he? Maybe he had developed a bloodlust for shots to the back of the head. And let's not forget the Shari Glynn clan—Christine, Wells, Monaghan, Kitty. If there was somebody in the city who *didn't* have a reason for shadowing me with bad intentions, I just hadn't gotten around yet to pissing him off!

I told myself to calm down. Thinking finally kicked in. I'd been quick to sneer at Loschen for being rattled by the cop banging the juice machine, but I seemed to have grown a little rusty myself in the response department. A few years before, I would have simply waited for a red light, gotten out of the car, and gone back to the tail. Now I was whinging, making up an enemies list. I'd seen slowed down reflexes in older cops on the Island, but they had been in their forties with college kids and mortgages. What homestead was the aging Paul Finley protecting?

I finally hit a red light at Fourth and 54th. I got a freebie, too: There were no other cars. I got out from behind the wheel so fast I caught my hand on the belt buckle still sliding back into the seat. El Speedo. In fact, I was so quick I got a full view of the Saab turning off at 53rd Street.

I made out two guys in front. That seemed to eliminate Christine Sewell. Francis Forte, too, unless he had made an alliance with another serial yanker. Too bad it left in too many others.

CHAPTER 26

Dana checked in near eight. She had been back from Washington since early afternoon but had gone straight to her office. She hoped my meeting with Loschen had gone well. She hoped I hadn't minded throwing the Bronsard tape into the pot. She hoped we could meet at Da Francesco for dinner the next night. I hoped I wouldn't be spending the next 24 hours guessing about what she really wanted to say.

I needn't have worried. The wake-up shows were still on the radio the next morning when I opened my door to find the Professor standing in the hall with Gary Stein in tow. The old man was working on a stroke, while Stein had the wobbly look of somebody who had taken a very hard punch.

". . . So, they invade the man's home! His mother and father are sitting there in their bathrobes like they've opened the door to a tornado! Could he account for his whereabouts on such-and-such a day? Did he have any witnesses to verify that? What did he do for a living? Why did he drive a red car instead of a blue one and how often did he go into Manhattan?"

"Why don't you let Gary tell it, Joe?"

Propped up on the high middle cushion of my couch, Stein didn't look like he could tell the time. I hadn't noticed before how his big head was the top part of a fire hydrant of a body—like those two paleolithic rocks that sat atop one another in deserts. Hadn't I even seen a movie where the things had come alive and stalked around like monsters? "Gary?"

He eventually got it out. Two Feds had knocked on the door of the Bayside house where he lived with his parents around 11:00 the night before. They had asked him about the Citi Field game, the interview with Owen Bronsard, and the fact that he hadn't mentioned any of it to anybody. They had asked him a lot about his car, too, and whether he had been on the West Side Highway recently. In short, they had drilled him in all the curiosities I had put into their heads through Dana and Loschen.

"*You* started all this?" the Professor asked when I told them.

"I saw the interviews. You wanted me to find things the cops weren't doing, didn't you? Well, they weren't looking at that tape."

"But it's Gary, for Christ sake! He's our statistician!"

"Oh, excuse me!"

"The man is all baseball. If it doesn't have a number with it, he won't look at it a second time."

"And not only that, Joe, he's sitting right here, where he probably doesn't like being talked about in the third person."

The old man shook his head in wonder at one of us—at me for passing along the tape or at himself for passing along me. "But it wasn't any secret!" Stein said, close to whining. "I'm a season ticket holder! I go to all the games! Sure, I was there. When am I *not* there? Everybody who knows me knows that. But so were a lot of other people sitting in my section. Maury Slagel, the kook sisters . . ."

"Tell me this is being helpful," the Professor said, shooting gamma rays at me from next to Stein. "Tell me having these fascists running around with their desperate agendas . . ."

"All right, all right."

"There's nothing all right about it, Finley! They wouldn't leave until Gary gave them the names of the other people in his section."

Stein nodded with a dab at his mustache; he wasn't proud of it, either. "They wanted to know names. I told them there were twenty thousand people there. Did they want all of them? They didn't think that was funny. Just the people I knew, they said."

"So now they're banging on more doors and flashing their badges," the Professor interpreted. "People who have nothing to do with anything except the numbers of visits these dangerous cretins can say they've made in the name of keeping America safe!"

I had no answer for that except to go into the kitchen for the coffee I had put on. The percolating might have been the sound of debts piling up: what I owed Stein, what Dana owed me, what Stein owed "Maury Slagel and the kook sisters," whoever they were. Too much of the serial sniper had been reduced to People Behaving Badly. Vince Galassi was beginning to look like the class of the league. At least he had been clear from the start that I might not be such a great help.

I brought the coffee back to the living room just in time to see Stein lighting a cigar. The Professor shook his head at me, but he wasn't going to be in the apartment all day. "Could you save that for later, Gary?"

"No problem. I'll just take a couple of puffs."

Obviously, that answered that. I was about to dump his coffee into his lap when the Professor said, "Tell Paul what you told me about those interviews. The other guy there."

"Yeah," Stein said, looking closer to recovery with his first puff, "there was this weird guy there. Had a crazy look in his eye."

I knew right away he meant the stooped character with the gray fuzz cut and the tote bag. "Could've been a priest?"

"I didn't see any collar."

"I don't mean . . . Never mind. What about him?"

Stein shrugged, more concerned about not seeing an ashtray on the coffee table. "Nothing. He was just there. He said the one with the camera had asked him the same questions he'd asked me. Think he was lying?"

"I don't know, Gary. Go ahead."

"What's to say? He started asking me a slew of questions like I'd know something he hadn't learned from Bronsard."

"But . . ." the Professor nudged.

"Yeah. When he was pushing me, it was like he already knew what I could've said, but he wanted to hear it anyway. You know, like that'd make it real or something for him?"

"He had a tote bag. You notice what the logo was?"

"He had a tote bag? You say so."

"I wasn't there, Gary. You were."

He paused to give it more reflection, if only for my sake. "Now that you mention it, he did keep one of his hands to his side. Yeah, he might have been holding something with it."

"People always keep their hands to their sides," the Professor spat. "It's called having arms."

"Talk to Finley," Stein said, becoming more comfortable with every puff. "He's the one that wants him with a tote bag. I didn't say I saw one."

"What else, Gary? The other people Bronsard interviewed—any of them say or do something that stuck out?"

"Like what?"

"Like anything. Something that stuck out."

He made a sour face at the taste of his coffee; any second he'd be criticizing the furniture. "Nothing. Me and this guy you say is a priest, we just kind of hung around to see if some of the other channels wanted to interview us, too. But when they got there, none of them did. Must've been my CUBS SUCK shirt. That didn't bother Bronsard, but these local channels get all uptight about something like that."

The Professor was staring at me as if to say he had supplied all the ingredients, so why was I taking so long to bake the cake? "You tell all this to the Feds?"

"Tell them what? I didn't even know that guy was a priest!"

"So, what do you think, Paul?"

"About Gary having his couple of puffs and now putting out that damn thing? You mean that?"

Stein relented—in a way. Since my coffee wasn't up to his jet-set standards anyway, he simply dumped the cigar into it. "I can take a hint. But what about these FBI guys? They're not gonna queer my Unemployment, are they? That's all my parents have to hear. You gotta talk to them."

"To say what?"

"Whatever they want to hear. They wouldn't be climbing the wall if you hadn't sent the FBI around to the house. C'mon. A one-minute call."

The Professor started to object, but it was my turn to shake my head. The fact was, Gary Stein, social lion, was more right than wrong.

CHAPTER 27

As soon as I got rid of them and tossed Stein's soggy cigar into the garbage, I looked around for a couple of dogs to kick. Once again, I had to settle for Sanford Lefkowitz, calling in my report to his wife. She sounded disappointed, and I welcomed her gleefully to the club.

I arrived at Da Francesco 40 minutes before my appointment with Dana. That was time enough for a couple of merlots to get me in some kind of mood—friendly, unfriendly, whatever the grapes dictated. They didn't say one way or the other while the waiter Nello asked what was new in the exciting world of private investigation and, minus the names, I told him about Ida Fleischer and Sanford Lefkowitz. He said physical therapists had a leg up on woman patients—wink, wink—and I gave him his laugh. There was a joke in there somewhere. I might have laughed harder if the crack didn't also ring some distant bell in my brain. But then the merlot was doing a pretty fast job of turning my head into a mission tower anyway.

When Dana showed up, she was wearing a tan suit and matching tan shoes, not her aqua outfit, and I took that as an appropriate sign. She wanted to be tired, hungry, and friendly. The grapes finally announced their decision: I didn't want to be any of those things. For a few minutes, she tried to ignore the me across the table for her trip to Washington: The two of us were just little people united against bureaucratic and political machinery in an overwhelming universe. Was I supposed to feel more intimate, more human listening to her? I resisted the invitation, thought picky things about the way she looked. Why didn't she do something about that tiny zit on her chin? And at bottom, I really didn't like her square Claudette Colbert do. She had been much sexier when I had first met her and she had been working with Bernstein. She hadn't been responsible for things then. She'd also had short hair, not all that different from the way Cynthia at the Green Fox was wearing it now. And say this for Cynthia: She hadn't had any part in forcing Gary Stein's parents to sit around in their robes listening to how their son might have been doing Osama bin-Laden's bidding in between calculating how many National League batters hit .250 with two strikes on them.

". . . Carey seems to have been super-connected. The least of it is a brother who runs anything with an elephant on it in Nebraska. Not once, not twice, but three times, somebody sidled over to me to say, 'Lieutenant, you should know people here are giving the *highest importance* to resolving this case.' I said, so am I. They looked at me like I was deaf, didn't hear a word they said."

"You don't recognize a terrorist component when you see one."

She made a dismissive sound. "They don't believe that crap. One of them said as much. That's why they're still just 'assisting,' not moving in as part of an official task force. But if there's a remote chance . . ."

"Whoa, whoa. They put something in your water down there?"

"I said it was bull, didn't I?"

"But I'm hearing a *but*."

Sometimes Finley required a sigh from the depths of her diaphragm. "All I'm saying is, they have their directives for getting into things. Today it's terrorism, yesterday it was, what, a Communist plot or an anarchist plot or whatever. It was usually garbage then and it's garbage now. It's annoying, maybe worse than that sometimes. But let's also keep our eye on the ball here, folks. There's a killer running around out there and he doesn't work for Homeland Security."

"That you know about."

"That supposed to be funny?"

"Just humorless. First, you're worried about somebody in Police Plaza throwing you in the water so you'll drown, now you have these Feds coming in and holding your head under water and it's all right."

She finally had more color than the reflection from the table candle. "I don't think I said anything like that. In fact, I said the opposite: The case is ours. They're on the sidelines. Besides, there's always somebody looking over your shoulder. You know that."

"But they're not always barging into Gary Stein's house at night."

She conceded a nod. "Yes, I heard about that this morning."

"They're just *assisting*. So, what's wrong with this picture?"

She was able to smile at Nello for bringing her wine instead of having to look at me. "I'm still waiting for an answer on that one," she said after he had gone again. "I don't think I should hold my breath."

"Mind telling me how Stein graduated so fast from a harmless dweeb not worth a second thought to a suspected terrorist?"

She was still a couple of steps behind me: She had yet to accept she should have been smarting instead of giving me another benefit of the doubt. "Anybody ever tell you you have a curious way of asking one question for a dozen of them? Where'd you learn that? C'mon. Fess up. I'll feel part of the process."

The wine made her lipstick smell stronger. The candle made her silver bracelet glisten when she put her hand across the table to touch mine. But there was suddenly too much *stuff* between us—whole closets and cabinets and trunks of things I didn't know, she might have volunteered to tell me but hadn't, and I might have volunteered to tell her but hadn't. "When you called to tell me Loschen would be getting in touch, it sounded like somebody had a gun at your head."

She withdrew her hand. "I couldn't help that. Captain Wendell from the Rosen crime scene? He made you that night."

"I never saw the guy before in my life."

"Then he ran your plate. I left him pissed off, remember."

"All right, you left him pissed off. So what?"

"I get a call next day from downtown asking what you're contributing to the investigation. You could hear the smarminess through the receiver. I just wanted to shut it off, so I mentioned the video, said it might be of interest. That's when Herman thought it might be a good idea to throw in the tape so I wouldn't get any more phone calls like that. He meant well."

"You could've told me that on the phone."

"Yes, I could have."

Her stare was so stony not even I deserved it. But a trap on her line? "Oh, Jesus, Dana! No!"

She leaned down to nudge her chair closer to the table. "Why not?" she said as if reaching for a fallen napkin. "Maybe they didn't. But why say something on the phone for entertaining the boys wearing the headphones in the back room?"

"And these are the scumbags you're working with."

She came back up still trying to look casual; I thought she managed it a little too well. "If you've called me as a heavy breather any time since this has started, Finley, you're a cooked goose."

She wanted me to smile with her, and for a second I couldn't think of any reason not to. But then I remembered the Saab. "And when Loschen finished with the video, he did what with it?"

It was one question too many. "Made a copy and sent it where he was told to," she said evenly. "Along with everything else in the file. Did I do something wrong, Detective?" Nello came out of the kitchen with huge platters of clams and mussels for the next table. The bell started ringing in my head again, and that seemed like another reason to be irritated. "Any second now you're going to tell me what's really bothering you, right?"

Right. And down to it, it wasn't just the Saab or neurotic Herman Loschen or all the tan colors she was wearing. "Everything."

"Could you break that down a little?"

I blamed it on the grapes, of course. It wasn't enough they squeezed themselves, they suddenly wanted to squeeze me, too. "You. Me. Us."

"Okay. With you so far. What about you, me, and us?"

There should have been other choices, and maybe there would have been if I'd taken the time to look for them, but just saying what burbled up in my brain seemed fastest. "Lately, I'm spending all my time disapproving of you, making excuses for you, protecting you when you don't need protection, and sometimes just being scared for you. I want to help you, I want to compete with you, I want to beat you, I want us to finish in a flat-footed tie. I want you to nail this fuck who's turning the city into a bullseye, and I want you to screw these other bastards who think the bullseye's just a noisy opportunity for them to go on with their rotten games."

She smiled; she didn't know what else to do. "That's all?"

"No. But I have to get through these things first."

"And where are we now? At the disapproval part?"

"Maybe. How far you going to bend over backward before these terrorist experts don't come out as maybe so expert?"

"I still have to cover my ass. Remember that part of the job?"

"Fine. But don't buy into it for yourself and talk to me like it might be a reasonable possibility."

"Maybe I'm just a hypocrite."

"We're all hypocrites. We wouldn't know what to do if we weren't. But bullshitting ourselves, that's where it gets fatal."

She gave it a nod and a sip of wine. "Okay," she said, still wanting to be amused more than angry. "I guess that's clear."

"No, it's failure. Failure and a pretty big fear about failing again. The other night after I left you, I drove out to my old house on the Island. I had this sudden need to see what I had left behind or what had left me behind. I still don't know which it is."

"It left you. And by now maybe you should have left it."

She pronounced it so unapologetically, a rule of law, that it sounded like a sentence. And of course, she wasn't the first one. "Friend of mine says I'm running from you. I'm afraid of you."

"Are you?"

"Maybe. Maybe that's why I want you perfect before I stop running. I don't want you making mistakes with your genius Loschen and the other stiffs they've saddled you with. I don't want you buying into these hustlers who'll say anything to keep their government pensions."

"Because that wouldn't be you."

"Because that wouldn't be me."

"And for you to stop running I'd have to be you."

"Does sound like I'm saying that, doesn't it?"

"Yes, it does, Paul."

Suddenly I felt tired. And hungry.

And for some reason, she still wanted to be friendly.

CHAPTER 28

I woke up thinking of Sanford Lefkowitz and Ida Fleischer. There wasn't a sound from the street and the clock on Dana's bedtable said 4:10, but Sanford Lefkowitz and Ida Fleischer might as well have been partying in the bedroom. I told myself to feel privileged, that there wasn't another soul in the country aside from Mrs. Lefkowitz lying awake thinking of them at that moment. Dana's breathing came so smoothly I knew she certainly wasn't. What about Sanford himself? Did he have waking dreams about Ida? Could he have been serious about her? Without ever talking to the guy, I didn't think so. There was something about that prominent ad in the Yellow Pages that said Sanford Lefkowitz wanted the stability of his wife and his business, that anything else was just a little adventure.

Then I did remember someone else who might be thinking of Sanford and Ida—Nello, the waiter from Da Francesco. He had never met them, either, but he had made his little joke about having a leg up. It wasn't all that funny, but it still seemed accurate in some agitating way, still ignited all those mission church bells in my head. Sanford had Ida's leg up because he was massaging it or rolling it or doing some other thing to make it more flexible before he fell down on top of her. And the reason he was able to do that was he had gained entry to the Fleischer home as a physical therapist. He had been invited in as *a professional!*

And then the dominoes began tumbling—the way they were supposed to have, but didn't, with my Monaghan Strategy.

Dana didn't want to come awake. Even when I got her eyes open, she clutched at her pillow, ready to put it over her head. "It's always the first one with these sociopaths," I reminded her. "What you have to check is if there were any more misses before Carey at Citi Field. Pray there weren't. Pray Carey was first."

"I don't know what the hell you're talking about."

"You don't just walk into the press box level of a major league stadium, that's what I'm saying! You either have one of those luxury boxes that gets you in that area or you work for the media."

"We had that covered the first hour. But thanks anyway for the thought. Now drop dead."

"How much did you have it covered? This Ronnie Hersh and the rest of the Three Stooges? Let me guess. They checked the credentials of all the sportswriters, radio-TV people, and photographers, then they did a little sweep of the luxury boxes, asking if one of the ticket holders had a special guest for the evening, somebody who came along with a gun."

"You're really pissing me off, Finley."

"Did anybody shake the dust out of the guards up there? That klutz, who was he? Grabowski or something? Did anybody make doubly sure some so-called free-lancer didn't impress Grabowski with a lot of fast talk and gain access to the level?"

"Of course they did," she said, becoming suspicious.

"No problem, then. You just triple check when you go in that nobody walked up to one of the guards, flashed some facsimile ID, and was let in because . . . why? He had a video cam, maybe?"

She sat up, her hair wild and without her pillow. "You're talking about this Owen Bronsard?"

It sounded so much more possible coming from her. "We've all been looking at who's on the tape, not who shot it. And Stein said something else. He said he and this other guy waited around in case one of the other stations wanted to hear their pearls of wisdom all over again. In other words, the other channels sent their teams in *long after* Bronsard had already done his interviews. I mean, talk about Johnny-on-the-Spot!"

I said something else, but she had stopped listening to grab her cellphone and tap out a number. I didn't feel sorry for Herman Loschen; he seemed to sleep enough during the day anyway.

CHAPTER 29

Cop groupie or not, Bobby Qualls sounded mainly like a news hound when I asked for Owen Bronsard's address. "Find something useful on the tape, Paul? Something an old friend in the trenches should know about?"

Dana read my expression from the other side of her desk and held out her hand imperiously for the receiver. I figured I owed Qualls a little more than that. "You'll be the first to hear if I do."

"That sounds a little weaselly."

"Let's be helpful, Bobby."

Loschen came into the office with a cassette; he looked like he had slept in his white shirt and gray suit. He waved the cassette at Dana, but she was too busy working on her impatience with Qualls. "Okay, okay," Qualls said. "Bronsard's half-expecting to hear from you anyway."

"Excuse me?"

"He called yesterday afternoon to ask if there was any chance we'd air the interviews. I told him probably not, but maybe somebody else was interested. I didn't give him your name, don't worry."

"Hey, there's something!"

"It just felt better than giving him a no and hanging up."

Where had I come across this philosophy of life before? Too many people, from the Professor to Shari Glynn, pushed their way into my skull. "And stringing him along is going to make him feel better??!!"

I understood Dana's curious look. Owen Bronsard's emotional well-being and its relationship to Paul Finley's self-esteem had not been the purpose of my call. "I've been there, Paul," the voice in my ear said. "Nobody knows that better than you. A free-lancer lives on hope, on the next phone call. So, let him hope for a few days a producer like Paul Finley's going to call him. You let him down easier that way. By the time he gets the message you won't be calling, he'll be on to something else."

"But I'm *not* a producer, Bobby."

"He doesn't know that."

It seemed worth remembering that even if the telephone had had an old-fashioned cord, I wouldn't have been close enough to Qualls to wrap it around his neck and pull tight. "I'd really appreciate that address, Bobby," I said, admiring my calm.

"Okay, okay. But what goes around comes around. Remind Bronsard of that if something good comes out of this."

"Count on it."

He dropped the receiver to find the address. Dana seemed to be expecting me to pass along what I had just heard in some intelligible way. "He told Bronsard I might be calling because I'll need talent like his for my new television show on Channel Four."

She appraised the idea with a smirk. The sunlight coming through the Venetian blinds brought out her freckles and the crinkles under her eyes. "Why not? They'll put anything on these days."

Qualls came back on with the address. It was in Flatbush, not too far from Brooklyn College. As soon as I hung up, Dana snatched it from me, glanced at it, and matched it to the other pieces of information she had gathered on Owen Bronsard since charging into the office an hour before. "The same," she confirmed.

What it was the same as was the address on a two-year-old speeding violation and on the registration for a three-year-old green Jetta that threw in for free the details that Bronsard had been born in Brooklyn 43 years ago, had brown hair, brown eyes, was six feet tall, and wore glasses. The registration picture reminded me of the Wolfman in the middle of being transformed, but most registration pictures did. The only other item in front of her was a credit for some student film that had been shown at an NYU festival. What the address wasn't the same as was an address on a gun license, which apparently didn't exist. All in all, her collection didn't look much better than what I had put together for my Gary Stein hope chest.

"Want to see this tape now, Lieutenant?"

"Put it on, Herman. Put it on."

"I thought you sent that to the Feds."

"Qualls gave you a copy, I gave them a copy of the copy," she said, loving herself as Loschen fed the cassette into the VCR. "Or maybe it's your copy of the copy. Unless you made another copy for yourself before giving us that copy of the copy Bronsard made for Qualls."

"Never."

"No, I didn't think so."

Loschen pressed the Play button and stood back next to her desk to watch what he had wrought. Whatever copy it was, it was the same fan parade outside Citi Field answering Bronsard's same two dull questions. I didn't know what Dana and Loschen were looking for, but I knew what I was. The guy's steady hand was evident not just with the tote bag of my priest friend, but in every second of tape. If there was a centimeter of camera movement up, down, or sideways, I missed it.

"Why's that so odd?" Loschen said, scratching his sunken chest. "He's a pro or wants to be. And you have these shoulder rests and things."

"The hand on a bronze statue is shakier."

I caught Dana's half-nod out of the corner of my eye, but she stopped it before Loschen looked back at her for a reaction. "I don't see any," he said to her, disappointed.

"No," she agreed.

"What're you looking for?"

"A clock, a watch," she shrugged. "Something to give us a tighter timeline between the shooting and the interviews. We can pretty much cut down to a range of three or four minutes when Carey was sitting alone in that press box. What would really be nice is to have one of these people wearing a Swatch on his forehead saying Bronsard got downstairs too fast for his own good."

"While you're ordering that, get some military record that says he was the Army's all-time sharpshooter."

"Yeah, well . . ."

"What?"

"The Lieutenant thinks that can wait a couple of hours," Loschen said, looking at me with a new air of concern.

Give me enough time and I would have beaten a snail across the finish line. "Let sleeping eagles lie?"

"For a few hours anyway," she nodded. "Let's get a grip on Mr. Bronsard before we start having to share it because red flags have gone up in cyberland. And Herman has heard none of this, by the way."

"I've heard it, Lieutenant."

"You'll hear what I tell you to hear. Go get the Leong tape. Let's make doubly sure there's nobody on that subway station who looks like this guy on Bronsard's license. And try Citi Field again. See if there's anybody there yet who can confirm credentials for Bronsard that night."

"Still kind of early for that."

"Then just get the Leong tape."

Loschen went out, but reluctantly. "I think he's afraid of leaving you alone with me."

"I don't need him jammed up on this."

"I think he's the perfect one to have on your side. His juice downtown against Federal juice. We can sell tickets and watch from ringside."

She didn't think I was funny. "He's trying to stand on his own feet."

"Welcome to the club, Herman!"

She didn't think I was all that *unfunny*, either. "One of these days I'm going to ask him who it was," she said, sipping her coffee.

"Who who was?"

"The female, male, or species of another kind who's made him timid about even looking at me sometimes."

"You're being nasty."

"Yes, I am. And I'm going to exploit him totally because he's putting all that testosterone into priorities around here."

"He ever tell you about his father?"

She was astonished. "He told *you*? My god, that's a compliment to you, Finley. I had to have him near passing out at a retirement party before he started whispering it to me."

"He thinks we have emptied places in common."

"Told you he was smart."

"They've saddled you with every misfit in the Department."

"And that's without counting you! Now shouldn't you be going back to Brooklyn and doing what your kind of people do to make money?"

"How you going to handle Bronsard?"

She got up to eject the Bronsard tape from the VCR. "I think you're right, I think he's a candidate. But one step at a time. No more Arthur Thalers. We'll drop around and talk to him about the people on the tape, like Stein and your priest friend. Get him to be helpful. That kind of thing."

"There might be a better way."

"No, there isn't. Go home."

"Qualls told him somebody might call. I'm scouting talent. At least I could get inside his apartment, take a look around."

"Yeah, right."

"I'm serious, Dana. Qualls gave me the address. I just happen to be in the neighborhood. 'Hi, Owen. I thought I'd ring your bell.'"

"But you're not ringing mine. I need this to be quiet, quiet, quiet. At least until I'm sure we're not barking up the wrong tree. You're not quiet, Finley. Even without your Saab."

"I shouldn't have told you that."

"No, you shouldn't have. It reminds me of the thousand and one ways you can be a liability. Go home. I'll call you later . . . And thank you."

I walked out of her office with her grateful eyes and the noblest of intentions. I got all the way through the bullpen separating me from the floor door committing nothing worse than a cheery hello to a blonde detective with bluish lipstick. She looked up at me from the bran muffin on her desk, decided I hadn't fled from a holding cell, and returned the hello. I was already working myself up to ticking off my depressing tasks for the rest of the day when I reached for the door, only to have Loschen pull it open from outside first. With another cassette in his hand, he was beginning to make me think of an old Blockbuster clerk running between the counter and the back room.

"Keep her out of trouble, Herman."

"I still like the emptied places."

It was another of his boy-that-valium's-something-isn't-it looks. He was definitely staring in my direction and trying to be pleasant, but who knew if I was the one he saw? "Great. If it's useful, see where it leads."

He didn't move; I was beginning to wonder whether he ever had a thought that wasn't realizing his shoes were glued to the floor. "I know you think they've put the lieutenant in a bad place with the squad she has," he said. "But we're not going to let her down."

So, I felt like a *schmuk* again. I was back on the West Side Highway at the Karen Rosen crime scene and playing the cop who knew what cops were supposed to be. "Too many nostalgia pills lately. I'll get over it."

He nodded more generously than I would have in his place and continued on inside. I went downstairs and out into a sweet mist of violets from the house garden next to the precinct. I thought of the difference between me and Loschen: I was being protective, he was being protective *and* helpful. Instead of nursing my wounds over that competition, I should have at least been earning a few pennies of the money the Professor and his friends had put to-gether. Right?

Right?

CHAPTER 30

Owen Bronsard lived in a weathered, peeling graystone a couple of blocks behind the bus hub at Flatbush and Nostrand avenues. It was an aloof building on a street that otherwise seemed all black, all Caribbean, and all Men at Work rehabbing facades, stoops, and pipelines. I hadn't seen so much plywood and so many sanders and other power tools in one place since I'd taken the Professor to an Office Depot back in the days when I'd been living in his basement. Except for a couple of gutted three-family houses that seemed to be awaiting a wrecking ball, in areaway after areaway on both sides of the street, hammers were banging and drills were spitting out chunks of rotted wood or faded brick. Hanging over all the morning clatter was a thick layer of dust, the sort that said EXCUSE US FOR THE MESS, BEAR WITH US A LITTLE LONGER. The show didn't seem to have too many outside contractors, either. Most everyone in sight—men, women, a couple of kids giggling with their chore of filling pails of water in one house—looked to be working on houses they lived in; the only commercial truck jutting out from the curbs belonged to a glazier. In the middle of it all, the graystone stood with the smugness of a haunted house; there might not have been anything spooky Gothic about it, but every curtained window in the place carried a message of KEEP OUT. Norman Bates was dead, but that didn't rule out one of his cousins being inside.

I had no great confidence in any of the next moves that occurred to me. Helping my mood were the two bruisers in the areaway next door to Bronsard's: Shovel the dirt, glance at my car, shovel the dirt, glare at my car. They didn't look any more charmed when I threw them a friendly wave. Driving down Flatbush Avenue 10 minutes before, I'd still been bopping along to an endless horizon of smart tactics in the offing. There was what I had suggested to Dana, for instance: Just going up, ringing the bell, and introducing myself to Bronsard as that big-time producer Bobby Qualls had mentioned. Then there was the safety position of just waiting until Dana and Loschen got there and taking in the action purely as a spectator. Or, who was to say? Maybe Bronsard would leave the house, I'd tag along, he'd set up another target, and I'd save the day for the teeming metropolis. And let's not forget option number four: go home and do the work my landlord and utility companies had come to depend on. The two linebackers digging down to the foundation of their areaway definitely voted for number four.

I should have known by then that when I had four scenarios to choose from, a fifth ended up carrying the day. A green Jetta came down the block cruising for a parking space. That matched the information on Dana's sheet, and the athletically-built guy with the tortoise-shell glasses behind the wheel passed muster as a member of the Bronsard family. He looked even more familiar in person than he had in his picture, but I didn't know from where. He stopped to look over and ask with a shrug if I was moving out. I needed a couple of hours to analyze that question, and without them just did the stupid thing by nodding and hitting the gas so he could have the space. He nodded back in thanks and did a wide U to claim my spot.

I moped down the street, but he was too slow to park for me to get a better look at him out of the car. I told myself I didn't have to. If Owen Bronsard lived in that beat up graystone, it wasn't because he had gone apartment hunting in a neighborhood that had been black for decades, but because he had grown up in the place and had never moved. For all I knew, his parents were still decaying corpses in one of the closets. When they had been alive, they had watched their white neighbors drift away house by house to suburbia and the block fall into disrepair; now that they were stinky skeletons stuffed into a closet, they couldn't see the neighborhood coming back to life, and probably wouldn't have cared anyway. For sure, their son didn't feel part of the renaissance. He was too used to living in the mother of all emptied places.

I couldn't leave it at that. I hadn't come all the way to Flatbush to confirm only that Bronsard's house existed. Been there done that with John Wells, the Wisters of Lakeview Avenue, and too many other people lately. Whatever problems it caused with Dana, whatever it said about the rest of my pressing schedule or about a suspicious need to match the Feds in inventing an "involvement" with the sniper, I wasn't about to go home and stand vigil over the phone for the rest of the day to hear what she had found out. At the end of the day, Scenario One, as inspired by Bobby Qualls, was still pretty viable.

I found a parking spot around the corner, in front of a clapboard house being torn apart from the roof down, and walked back to the Bates Motel. The linemen digging next door gave each other I-told-you-so looks as I passed, not caring if I saw them. I took Bronsard's stoop in a bounce, announcing to them I was delivering happy news. I made sure not to turn around when the shovels paused a long moment between scoops.

Bronsard came thumping down from an inside staircase, opened the vestibule door, and took a long look out at me at the street door. Never underestimate the importance of bad timing. I suddenly remembered where I had seen him before: at the Dodger banquet. He had been one of the cameramen shooting the guests as the Professor and I had made our way down to the front table.

"Yes?"

"I'm looking for Owen Bronsard," I shouted through the glass. "I'm a friend of Bobby Qualls at Channel 11."

He needed a second to remember who Bobby Qualls was, the diggers next door needed one to remember that any friend of Bobby Qualls was a friend of theirs, and I needed one to reassure myself there had been nothing especially ominous about Bronsard's presence at the banquet, that it had been perfectly natural for a free-lancer covering the Citi Field shooting to drop by the function that had brought Ralph Carey to the city in the first place. Not counting the likelihood that he had shot Carey, of course.

Then Qualls's name clicked, and Bronsard's eyes bulged behind his glasses. He crossed the vestibule and pulled open the street door so eagerly I immediately pulled back—and almost off the top step and down into a nice rear-ass tumble to the sidewalk. "You're the TV guy!"

"Right . . ."

"Well, what're you . . .? Come in, come in!"

I stepped inside expecting to be hit by the rancid odor of the parents rotting in the closet. Instead, the place smelled of orange blossom aerosol. There was no sign of the Collier brothers beyond the vestibule door, either: a polished wooden floor, a neat coat rack with jackets and woolen caps, even three umbrellas in the umbrella stand. Who had three umbrellas besides the guy peddling them on a street corner?

"You really caught me off balance, Mr. . . .?"

"Finley. Paul Finley. I didn't realize that was you before . . ."

"Either did I! And I bumped you out of your space!"

"No problem. I found another one."

He looked ready to pay me for it. "Sorry for that. But what . . .? Well, what brings you here?"

He had my name; one fact deserved one rush of bullshit. "I was over in Brooklyn College and realized the address Bobby gave me was nearby, so I figured why not give it a try?"

"Fabulous! Come on in here and sit."

Here was what another age called a sitting room: oversized chairs and tables fit for lace doilies. Whatever colors the wall landscapes of beaches and hillsides had were bleached out by the light coming through the two street windows. Looking somewhat out of place was a crucifix on the wall between the windows; it made me think of a Catholic parish house study I'd once sat in while working on Long Island.

I took an easy chair, managing to whack my leg on one of the knee-high tables crowding it. "Careful there," he said unhelpfully. "That thing has a sharp edge. Can I get you something? Coffee, maybe?"

"No, nothing. I'm good."

He gazed at me once again as though he couldn't believe his good fortune, then looped his leg over the footrest of a recliner and plopped down. His polo shirt might have made him look more ripped than he was, but he still worked out regularly—one of those 43-year-olds determined to celebrate his 42nd birthday next year. What his DMV picture hadn't done justice to were his stiletto nose, tiny ears, and chipped front tooth—a cartoon mouse on a boxer's torso. "You weren't out there long, were you? If I'd known you were coming, I would've skipped the gym."

"Like I say, I didn't know I was coming, either."

"Right . . . Bobby didn't really tell me what you were after . . ."

The drilling across the street told me what it was. "We're still laying the foundations for an idea . . ."

"We?"

"Monaghan Productions. You're probably not familiar with . . ." He shook his head, but leaned forward enthusiastically, willing to learn. "Well, we're still putting people together. And one of the first things we need is a cameraman who really knows Brooklyn."

He gave it his imitation of a hayseed with a crick in his neck. "Lived har my whole life, stranger. Not just Brooklyn, but this house. This har's always been the old homestead."

"No kidding!"

"Thanks to my dad," he nodded seriously. "Way back when, he got in on copy machine franchises when other people thought Xerox was good only for offices. One good fortune deserved another, and he started buying the *Wall Street Journal*. Within five years he was able to quit his job at a real estate firm and concentrate on his own real estate."

"Good for him."

"We used to just live on the second floor. Then he bought this floor and decided not to rent it out, have it as kind of a duplex. By the time he died, he didn't really need the tenants on the third floor upstairs, either. I let the people stay until they moved to Florida, then put my own stuff up there. Turned it into a darkroom. Probably the biggest one in the city."

There was nothing tinny about his pride—in his father's smarts or in his own willingness to build from them. I could have used a little more blatant neurosis in front of me. "But it's a huge place. Don't you get lonely rattling around in here all by yourself?"

He smiled his broken-toothed smile; he had heard that before. "As opposed to what? Running upstairs to bang on the door because the tenants are making a racket after midnight? No, thanks."

"And your father never thought of moving? I mean, if he had enough of a bundle, this neighborhood wasn't the greatest for a few years."

He had heard that one before, too, and it still miffed him. "He didn't get along too well with the white neighbors, either," he said, trying to make his defensiveness sound like amusement. "Black, white, whatever was around us, it made no difference. Dad wasn't what you'd call a great mixer. The important thing was the house."

That sounded a little better. Maybe Dana should have run priors on the entire Bronsard family.

"So, tell me about this project. Has something to do with the old Brooklyn Dodgers, right?"

"Why do you say that?"

"I guess I just assumed it. You saw the Carey tape I left with Bobby and then you were at the dinner."

He was red in the face, but at least he had the excuse of a job interviewee who had maybe overstepped his bounds. What was mine? I wasn't looking for even a non-existent job. "You were there, too?"

"You wouldn't have noticed me. I had this idea that maybe . . . well, it doesn't make any difference now. It's not about Carey or the Dodgers anymore, it's about some serial lunatic."

"You were thinking of doing a follow-up."

"I shot everyone in that ballroom," he nodded. "Including you. But then you cut out before I could caption you."

"Caption me?"

"Don't tell me you're the only producer in the city who doesn't care about IDing all the faces."

"No. It's just that in a mob scene like that . . ."

"I got as many names as I could, believe me. Thirty-two times bitten, thirty-third-time shy. I've had stuff turned down for the flimsiest reasons. The wrong kind of flag in the background. Some wise guy peeking out to give me the finger. You producers put outsiders like us through hell, Paul! Have mercy! Please!"

He smiled, so I did, too. I began to sense a melancholy underneath all his sprightliness, and it wasn't going to get any lighter with Monaghan Productions. If my chair suddenly dropped me down into a pit of alligators, I wouldn't have had any complaints coming. "Your work isn't the work of an outsider. You know what you're doing."

"Thanks. I appreciate you saying it. But believe me, if some station offered me a gig tomorrow shooting weather horizons from the roof, I'd grab it in a New York second."

"Money troubles? With your rent already taken care of?"

He heard the snooping but decided not to be bothered by it. "No, it's not the money," he said, sitting back and letting his gaze travel around the room. "Unless they discover oil under the basement and it pays to knock this place down, I can see myself living here for the rest of my life without a problem. But sometimes, yeah, you're right, it can get a little lonely being on your own. You wouldn't mind some of the daily bullshit about what Letterman said last night or how the Mets blew another one."

"Over the water cooler."

"Over the water cooler."

"Got you."

"But, hey, I'm not putting down independent gigs in the meantime. So, what exactly about the old Dodgers you have in mind?"

That seemed like a reasonable enough curiosity. The Ralph Carey Story? I didn't think so. "Well, as you know, so many people have made a dollar off the team . . ."

"Tell me about it! No criticism of the gang you were with the other night, but they're typical. They've turned it into a little industry."

"Exactly why we need a new angle." One that the drillers across the street weren't helping me discover.

"I couldn't agree more. I'm not saying nostalgia doesn't always have a market. But you want more people than that."

"People who can learn."

"*New* things."

"They're old things for some people, but not everybody."

"The younger people."

"What picking up on history's always about, right?"

"Exactly."

At least we had that straight.

"And angels have guided your path today," he grinned, reminding me too much of the Kraken rising from the sea as he rose chest and shoulders first. "Got a second? Let me show you something."

Why *not* get up with him and follow him out of the room over to the staircase? If those guiding angels hadn't wanted me to do it, they wouldn't have left my .38 back home in my bureau.

"Be careful," he said, leading the way upstairs. "These runners aren't what they used to be. All that gentrifying going on outside has almost got me thinking of throwing these away and laying new ones. Mind you, I said *almost*. I'm not there yet."

He was right about the carpeting: a herd of rats seemed to have been working on the stairs. "The neighborhood's really getting a face-lift."

"Isn't tearing down things what made America great?"

"But you, no, huh?"

"For what? I like the house the way it is."

The second floor was a walk-through past four or five closed doors, twice the length of my apartment. The orange blossoms were even stronger in the air, as though Bronsard had been spraying this particular area when I had rung the bell. There was another crucifix on the wall.

His destination was the room at the very back of the landing. "You haven't seen anything like this before, believe me."

I kept my eyes fixed on his hands as I trailed along; if he had some Igor of an accomplice behind the door, that would have just been too bad for Finley Investigations and its official spokesman. But there was no Igor. Instead, there were Peewee and Jackie and

Newk and the Duke. "My dad's obsession. And I've never had the heart to get rid of the stuff."

It was a square, compact room with the window shade pulled down against the sun, and it had been turned into a museum for Brooklyn Dodger artifacts. Team banners and photos hung on the walls, every flat surface was cluttered with picture pins, score-cards, trading cards, autographed baseballs, figurines, and more photographs. There were even a couple of signed bats on the walls. "Whenever I show it to someone, they tell me it's worth a fortune, that one of these memorabilia dealers will give me thousands for it all. I tell them my dad collected these, not dead presidents."

I was a second or two late, but I gave him the laugh he was watching me for. "Got you."

"My mom used to go crazy the way he had this junk all over the house," he said, going over to raise the shade on a still back-yard. "Finally, she put her foot down. Told him he had to put it all in one place or she'd throw it away. He got the message."

I almost jumped when I saw that baseball bats weren't the only things on the walls. Behind me, right next to the door, were four mounted and glass-encased rifles. One of them looked like an old Garand, and that was as close as I came to recognizing any of them.

"Another collection," Bronsard said. "A lot more expensive and he started wondering if he was doing it just because he had money and didn't know what to do with it. The second one from the top, that's what they call a Buckskinner Black Powder Per-cussion Carbine. I dare you to say that ten times fast. He sure as hell used to have me say it!"

"It looks valuable."

"The Buckskinner? Not that much. A few hundred. The real prize is number three." It was a very long shotgun that ran the length of practically the entire wall. "It's what they call a Parker SC. When they hit the stores back in the 1930s, they cost about $150. Keep it in good condition like that one and you can get five K for it today."

"You keep up on the market."

"You see things in magazines."

"Not the ones I read. Hunting magazines?"

"Yeah. I don't know why I read them. I never go hunting myself. I think it's just habit. I used to see them around the house, so I kind of still like seeing them around the house."

"So, your old man was a hunter."

He stifled a smile to himself as he looked at the rifles from some longer distance. "He wanted to be. Took me out after ducks a couple of times, once after deer up in Rockland County. But his heart wasn't in it. I think he had more than enough gunplay in Vietnam. These rifles were like he was trying to convince himself they were something every macho guy with a little money should have."

"But you keep them around."

"I don't know why, to tell you the truth."

"Sure you do. Same reason as the magazines. Your old man got you into the habit and you don't want to break it. And why should you?"

I had intended being clever and he heard tact, and neither interested him. "Maybe it's because, for good or bad, the rifles were also part of who he was," he said with the clarity of having decided the point a long time ago. "Not the manic Fred Bronsard, but the uncertain one, even the slightly phony one. When you remember people, you should remember the whole enchilada or you're just fooling yourself, right?"

Who could argue? I had anticipated abnormal, maybe abnormal playing at normal, but what about normal having made peace with abnormal? He might have been more depressed than the average videocam operator, but I hadn't known enough of them even to swear to that. The bottom line was that the baseball stuff, the rifles, the house, even his peculiar looks, were fast bagging another Finley idea for the trashcan.

He leaned against a bookcase and slapped at his crossed arms. "So, what is it I have to do to persuade you to stop looking, that I'm the guy for this project of yours?"

"Nothing you haven't done. You might even have a leg up."

"*Might* have a leg up? Uh, oh."

"No, no. Everything you've said and showed me . . ."

He wasn't impressed, glancing over at an old wooden desk with a roll-top cover as if to say they had both heard that one before. Above the desk on the wall was a third crucifix. Even in his enclosure, Fred Bronsard had kept his Dodger heroes within his idea of perspective.

"Your father was a religious guy."

"The crucifixes? No, that was my mother. The supermarket didn't have a cross over the door, she didn't shop there. My father let her have her way. The only time I saw him in church was his funeral." He laughed awkwardly. "Mind if I ask something, Paul? What was *your* reaction when you heard about Ralph Carey?"

It was one of the two questions from the tape; instead of a serial killer, I'd found a broken record. "Same as everyone, I guess."

"Shock, you mean?"

"Maybe that's a little strong . . ."

"Right! We hear about shootings in the news every day. 9/11—that was a shock. New Orleans—that was a shock. But an old guy like Carey? Not really shock. Kind of like, 'Oh, gee whiz, that's terrible. Wonder what he was doing in that press box. Wonder if they'll catch the shooter.'"

"What's your point, Owen?"

He gave me the same bulging eyes as he had at the door; it was what he might have been fretting about before I had rung the bell. "Just that it takes so much to get people's attention these days," he said. "It's not even always about quantity. Okay, sometimes. I know news editors, you tell them three average taxpayers were killed in a car crash, they think of it as filler. Tell them it was four taxpayers, and they want to lead the telecast with it! What's so important about that one extra corpse? But other times, just one person gets killed and that's good for station bulletins. Where's the rhyme or reason to any of it? It's like it's all whim . . ."

Maybe it was the close quarters in a room that wasn't exactly in the middle of Times Square or maybe it was the drop in his voice to something chewed to death, but I suddenly didn't mind feeling the keys in my jacket pocket. Okay, I'd decided he was only a sad sack, but it was also reassuring knowing I had as many jabbing instruments at my disposal as he had firearms on the wall.

". . . What the telecast needs that night. Maybe the station's helicopter got a special shot of the red lights on the EMS ambulances. Maybe the victim was about to graduate from the Gibbs secretarial school after overcoming a stuttering problem. You never know. There's no standard for measuring yourself by. You know what I'm saying? It's very important for me, for any freelancer, to try to anticipate these things, but you can't anticipate. There're no rules."

"Except the rule of whim?"

He nodded. "Except the rule of whim."

"So, when you're asking about reaction to Carey . . ."

His smile was almost pleasant. "Sometimes the whim overwhelms me. It's just not worth trying to figure out what number's going to come up on the wheel. So that night out at Citi Field, I didn't go at those interviews like a news reporter. What I was actually trying to do was paint a picture. Why I made sure to ask the exact same questions of everybody. Get a montage, know what I mean? Think of it all as a whole, not for what somebody, in particular, might have said about a shooting, man-in-the-street style. No one gave a damn about Carey. We both know that. He was dead, and only a couple of those people knew he'd ever been alive! You don't count on getting great insights in those conditions. I was after something else. What the old newsreels used to call the passing parade. And the parade was pretty depressing, don't you think? People just reciting what they thought they *should* recite because I had a video cam pointed at them. One after another."

"I see what you mean." I thought.

"Really?"

"Really."

"You caught that?"

With his insistence, less and less. I also moved over to the bookshelf before I began believing he had shifted over to the window deliberately, so I would have to look into the glare from the sun. "Why I'm here."

"Everybody thinks because you're a cameraman quote-un-quote, you're into news. I don't mind somebody like Bobby Qualls thinking that. That's why I went to Citi Field in the first place. Who knows? You might come up with something on the field or in the stands the big outfits miss. Buys a bottle of wine every once in a while. But that's not what I'm really interested in, not at all."

The books on the shelf were an odd mixture of baseball biographies, histories of the sixties and seventies, and westerns. "Art."

"Too hoity-toity?"

"I don't think they've come up with another name for it yet."

"Thanks."

He looked genuinely grateful. And I was glad I'd said what I had.

And then the front doorbell rang, and I didn't know which bum steer I should have apologized for first—the one I had given Bronsard or the one I had given Dana. For either one, the crucifix was saying, I owed penance.

CHAPTER 31

I trooped back down the stairs after Bronsard rehearsing lines that didn't have words. What words would make things right with Dana? None that I could think of.

I could have saved myself the angst. When Bronsard opened the door, it wasn't to Dana and Loschen, but to a pair of friendly FBI agents. I could tell they were friendly because I didn't know them, they were respectful in showing their badges, and they both wore striped dress shirts. Unlike some of their brethren, they seemed to have aced all their exams in Affability 101. "If you have a moment, Mr. Bronsard," the one who introduced himself as Andrew Fox said, "we'd like to talk to you about that footage you shot out at Citi Field the day Mr. Ralph Carey was slain."

Bronsard looked back at me with a dawning crack in mind, and I had to move fast before I heard it. "I'll call you later, Owen, and we'll go over some more of the particulars."

"Are you sure . . .?"

"Go ahead. Talk to the gentlemen. Looks like official business."

Fox and the other one whose name was Lombardo or Lombardi made a nice aisle for me, and we all had smiles for one another until I got past them out onto the stoop. I had the feeling they were reading my license plate on the back of my jacket and would be checking in with me again at some point. Or maybe I was just feeling needy.

The diggers next door were looking up at me as though I had brought rain to the desert: In 30 years they hadn't seen anybody going into Bronsard's house, and suddenly there was a Barnum and Bailey circus marching up the stoop. "How's the work going, guys?"

Maybe it was what they had been waiting for all along. The bigger guy looked even friendlier than the Feds. "Goin' good, man, goin' good," he said, returning his attention to the pit he was making.

The second one wasn't so sure, but he had company. I couldn't see a Saab parked anywhere on the block, but then again, I too had been forced to go around the corner for a space.

CHAPTER 32

When I got home, I found the mailman doing his lobby slotting. He seemed to know he was going to brighten my outlook with the envelopes he handed me. "Have a nice day, Mr. Finley," he said, clapping the boxes closed and chirping like one of those messengers who dropped by every once in a while to hand you a million dollars.

It wasn't a million, but it was a noble start. Mrs. Lefkowitz had decided not to wait for my invoice (prolonging my presence in her life); her check was for $75 more than I would have asked. Jake Early had also thrown in a bonus, though it was the smallest fraction of what I would have collected if I had put aside 20 years to sue Francis Forte all the way up to the Supreme Court. The donation that surprised me most, though, was the $725 from the Professor and his association pals. Despite his grumblings, he had apparently concluded I had done something for the money. Since he hadn't heard about my inspiration about Owen Bronsard, I hadn't a clue about what that might have been.

Dana was waiting for me on my machine when I walked into the apartment. "Credentials confirmed for that evening" was the extent of her message. I didn't know if that was good news or bad news. If Bronsard had been prowling around the stadium's press box tier without credentials, wouldn't that have been much more incriminating? Did she really think I would be satisfied so easily? What kind of a person did she take me for? Put me at a roulette table and I wouldn't have been content unless I shoved every chip

I had on every spin of the wheel. Surely, she should have known by now that I played for the whole shebang every time out.

I grabbed the Tropicana from the refrigerator and sat down at the kitchen table with the treasury the mailman had brought. Aside from the checks, there was a renewal lease from the landlord asking for a rent hike that would have demanded contributions from Mrs. Lefkowitz, Jake Early, and the Professor about twice a month. That restored my sense of equilibrium. When you live a balanced life, you don't want to be caught leaning too drastically in one direction or the other.

Then the phone rang on my desk to make sure I didn't get too heady about having accomplished something at Owen Bronsard's.

"She's back," the voice said, not sounding at all like Dana.

"Who?"

"Christine. Who else?"

"Hello to you, too, Shari."

"Just came back this morning like nothing had happened."

"So maybe nothing did."

"You're not listening. She's got this weird calm about her. Like she's done something and is trying to forget it with her meds."

I had really started getting used to the idea that Shari Glynn and her sister were out of my life. Maybe I wouldn't have felt that way if, say, I still had her check in my hand along with the Professor's and the others, but I had already deposited the last $510, so Beads, Beads, and whatever the hell the place was called was no longer what an investigative conglomerate would have termed an Active File. "Wishing won't make it so, Shari."

"What?"

"You heard me. The more I talk to you, the more I think you could use a session with Dr. Freedman as much as Christine."

"Who the hell are you to talk to me like that?"

"I have no idea, love. Probably just a number in the White Pages you picked at random. Because I sure as hell don't know why you're calling."

I heard the store door close in the background. My watch reminded me it was the hour for Christine to be upstairs making lunch. There was more control in her voice when she came back a register or two lower. "Suppose she did something to this Wells?"

"Then sooner or later you'll find out. If you want sooner, make it a topic of conversation over lunch."

I should have anticipated the answer: She had already given it to me a couple of times before. "Why would I believe anything she says?"

"Because she's not Pinocchio!"

"That's not funny."

"Okay. How about this for a revolutionary idea: You don't like the answer she gives you, you give Marty a call and pass it on. It's supposed to be one of the vows you take at the altar."

"You're not helping, Finley!"

"Like you said last time, it's important to know our limitations."

"You could find out where they went and see if . . ."

"What, Shari? If there's a body somewhere?"

"Well, isn't that the kind of thing . . .?"

I slammed down the receiver. It was one of the advantages of not having a cellphone. When you slammed down my phone, it really sounded slammed down: A nice crack of hard plastic hollowing itself out. Petulance, indignation, rage—they could still all be served on my desk. And there was no way I was going to listen to Shari Glynn tell me I was the guy you hired to look for bodies. Fuck her and all her beads tables. What I really should have done was go over there and kick over all her little compartments. She and Marty and Christine would be on the floor for a year trying to put the beads back in their proper trays. See how they got along without their neat little order of this here and that there. Nothing was supposed to be that pat, anyway. Reagan could shove his jelly beans.

CHAPTER 33

Supper that night was Sal's weekly hamburger. I gave him a big hello walking in, but he had run out of Ralph Carey recollections and answered me by barking over to the counterman to refill the coffee urn and do it fast. I had taken along my book from the Professor on the Greeks and Turks for eating company, mostly so I could tell him something negative about the thing besides how boring it was. Knowledge might be power, but irritability was *real* power. I didn't get any further than opening to my bookmark, though, when a body dropped down in the booth across from me.

"So, what's good?" Andrew Fox asked cheerfully. "The burgers? You should order something better than that, Paul. This one's on the government. A token of gratitude for your heads-up."

I had been expecting him since Bronsard's place, but not quite as soon. "If I'd known, we could've met at Peter Luger."

He liked a good joke when he heard one and waved to the waitress to bring him the same burger and coffee I had ordered. He had an oddly square head; that and his freckles made me think of Alfred E. Neuman.

"Where's your partner—tuning up your Saab?"

"Funny you say that because the efficiency experts who talked us into that model were absolutely right about the Swedes. They really know how to make cars over there."

"Okay, so he's ransacking my apartment."

Fox tried to look offended. "What do you say that for? I'm serious. You gave us a shortcut with Bronsard and we're grateful.

I'm not saying we wouldn't have gotten there on our own a few seconds later, but you got there first and you get the medals. Metaphorically, of course."

"What're you saying—you can nail Bronsard for it?"

"You met him. You saw his place."

"What I saw was a guy . . ."

"Who fit all the parameters you gave Lieutenant McGill. What did you call it—emptied places? Look at that neighborhood. Only Bronsard and an old lady up the block go back to when it was white Irish and Jewish. The priest says he's the only white guy in church Sundays. The population he grew up with abandoned him, *emptied out* like you might say."

"He doesn't seem to have a problem . . ."

"Hey, Paul! I'm not talking race here. Psychology, not sociology! And you get a look at that museum he's built to his old man?"

"He took you up there?"

He smiled. "Well, one question about Carey led to another. You know how it works. And those weren't just baseball bats on the wall."

"No. And they weren't proof he even knows how to load them."

"Granted, granted. Do we know how many rabbits he shot last time out in the woods? No, we don't, not yet. But we will."

"I didn't see any Glocks on that wall."

"Jesus, you're so glum! But you're right. We still have a lot of work to do. And there'll be no rush to judgment like in the old days. It's all going to be airtight before we . . ."

"Give somebody a detention cell for a year or two?"

"Ah, now there's the Joseph Carroll influence! Am I right? But never mind. For the moment we're satisfied with surveillance while we go one teensy-weensy step at a time."

"You're a bouncy guy, Fox."

He spread his arms out across the booth; the glitter off his tiepin in the shape of a scimitar was all part of his glow. He might not have been sitting on a made case, but he seemed to be sitting on something close to it. "Why not? We nail him and I *will* get a medal. A little less metaphorically, if you follow. And we won't have to share the credit with anybody. That's why consulting can be a lot better than these merged task force things."

"I'd love to hear some of this wise advice you've been sharing. I guess the NYPD knows the East Side from the West Side by now, huh?"

"Everybody loses direction once in a while. So, how's the Sam Spade business? I've played with that idea for when I retire, but it seems like a lot of penny-ante grubbing. Doesn't that drive you nuts?"

There were several things driving me nuts, but at that precise moment, Finley Investigations wasn't at the top of the list. For one thing, he had ordered a burger and was counting on eating the whole thing with me. For another, he couldn't have come up with anything more solid at Bronsard's than I had. Call it ego or his Alfred E. Newman resemblance, but I hadn't slowed down with possible suspects *that* much.

Unless, of course, he hadn't been looking for the same thing I had been. "You're going to split off Carey, aren't you?"

At least he had a blush level. "Whatever that means."

"It means, Fox, you've got all these Nebraska congressmen on your back about their local boy and you got Bronsard roaming around the press level of Citi Field, so one and one make two. And who cares about Leong and Rosen? Local citizens equal a local New York problem. No headlines in *USA Today*."

He seemed to want to drop his arms but decided against it. "You've got friction in your soul, Paul. I was told you did."

"Yeah, my regards to them, too."

"But you're not being logical. We make a case against Bronsard for just Carey, and aren't we going to look silly a few months down the road when New York's Finest digs up somebody for *all* the shootings!"

The Turks and Greeks never looked so inviting. "That's tomorrow's apology. Headlines today, worry about tomorrow's bullshit tomorrow."

"Jesus! Talk about short-sighted!"

"Must be in the air you've brought to town with you."

He leaned forward with his hands clenched on the table. I was supposed to see he had turned gravely serious. "You have your row to hoe, Paul, and I have mine. And there's no reason for you to jump over into mine and none for me to jump into yours."

"The new training includes *The Farmer's Almanac*?"

His smile wasn't as goofy. "Oh, right, we're not in Nebraska. But we are in New York. And I do have one serious question for you, my friend. A footnote for the report, you know?"

"This'll be good."

"I was just curious—call it officially curious—how receptive the NYPD was to your Bronsard insight."

There it was again, and I might have been mad except my stomach was too busy curdling. From the beginning, Dana had been acting as though she had been staked out as much as the sniper. Even when I had believed it, I hadn't quite believed it. Until now.

"I understand you have some personal relationships here and I'm not asking you to betray any . . ."

My bile finally got itself together. "We can do this one of two ways. I can stay here in the booth and you can eat up at the counter. Or I'll go up to the counter. You decide."

I couldn't even run that call. After a woeful shrug Job would have admired, Fox got up and went over to the counter to say he wanted his burger to go and skip the coffee. He lingered at the cash register for a good five minutes before his bag finally arrived. In between snatches of Aegean Sea history, I had some satisfaction seeing that his conversational gambits with Sal got him no more than two grunts and a dismissive wave. The trouble was, he didn't look discouraged. He still seemed to be savoring the way he had deliberately provoked me.

CHAPTER 34

Dana opened the door breathing heavily and sweating in her sweats. I had interrupted a session on her stationary bike, and she hadn't planned on being interrupted. Without a word, she immediately padded back inside in her white socks, leaving it up to me to walk through the door or drive back to Brooklyn. I hadn't come that far to do the smart thing, so I went in.

She made it clear how much she was interested in my *mea culpas* by getting back up on the bike behind her couch and fixing her gaze below the window while she resumed pedaling. Her first words after I had finished babbling could have been worse. "For a whole minute after you walked out of my office this morning, I considered having one of our patrols pull you over to check your license, birth certificate, and birthmarks. Because I sure as hell knew where you were going."

"So, I'm predictable."

"No, you're fucking interference!"

"It was a clean shot, Dana! Qualls set it up perfectly."

"Right. And you learned . . .?"

Well, if she wanted to get technical. "The Feds were there, too. Guy named Fox and another one."

"No shit, Sherlock! Herman and I brought up the rear."

"You went, too?"

"Earth to Finley: I told you we were going, didn't I?"

"So, this poor son of a bitch had a parade going through his house?"

She slowed down her pedaling to look over at me; she would have thrown me a quarter if I had a cup. "You're big buddies now?"

"They're going to jam him up just for Carey, forget the others."

"How about if that's a possibility?"

"And how about we skip the wisdom of Washington conferences? You saw the guy. What do you think?"

She went back to pedaling. "You were the one who was so hot for him," she said, pretending interest in something on the street. "You've been hot for a lot of things lately that you cool down about five minutes later. Not an especially endearing trait, Finley."

"Trial and error, and it made sense."

"My trial and your error!"

"Bronsard?"

She hated stopping, but she had to fix the band on her hair. "He was pretty frayed by the time we got there. But thanks to you and Fox, he knew what questions were coming. I'm grateful."

"And?"

"What *and*? Shook his head a lot, said he'd been doing the free-lance life too long, needed a job."

"He show you the sanctuary upstairs?"

"Volunteered it."

"And?"

She gave me a long sniffle as she considered saying what she was thinking. I didn't deserve it, but . . . "There he is being harassed all day by you and the Feds and me, but he . . ."

"Never mentioned calling a lawyer."

"That's right."

"His lawyer's on the wall. In every room."

"The crucifixes? Yes, that's what Herman said. For what it's worth, Loschen doesn't like him for any of this, either."

"Thank you, Herman. What about Lieutenant McGill?"

"Lieutenant McGill thinks Finley's sent me on his last wild goose chase. If we have to start from scratch, that's what we'll do. Maybe they're not going to like that downtown and they'll find someone else. I don't give a damn at this point. I'm tired of chasing my tail. Especially because I've been listening to another free-lancer who needs a job. We're back to square one tomorrow. Starting with that stadium guard who needs an eye test, an ear test, or a brain test."

It happened so quickly she seemed to be remounting the bike twice as the whistle came through the window. She was still standing stupidly in her gray sweats and gym socks when the back of the lounger in front of the couch let out a whoomp. She saw the hole in the chair, I saw the one in the window, and we dove like cartoon creatures for the floor. I counted to three. "Across the street," she said coolly from behind the couch.

"That much I know!"

She didn't bother answering. As she crawled over to her desk where she kept her weapon, I wrote off the lights: She had every one in the room on, and two of them were directly in front of the window. I heard the desk drawer being slid open. Then she was speaking into her cellphone. "This is McGill. 67 Jane Street. Officer in distress. Sniper attack. Opposite rooftop source. Numbers 58, 60, or 64 . . . Hudson Street approach. Right."

She clapped her phone closed and, a second later, was back under the window with her weapon. "Raise your head, Finley. It'll make up for a lot."

"What's with every fucking light on? You got to tell the whole block you're keeping an eye on your thighs?"

"Just a hunk across the street."

By the third minute, I had convinced myself the single shot was it. "58, 60, and 64? Pick one."

"You're not going anywhere."

"I like 64. One of those numbers you can divide everything into."

I had never really pictured myself crawling out of Dana's apartment and I hadn't missed the fantasy. Its only redeeming feature was that I was able to kill two lights with the switch near the door. And the nice thing about going down rather than up when you shouldn't have been going anywhere was you had less time for second-guessing yourself: The stairs were leading outside, so that's where you had to go, too.

Jane Street was a joke. People just moving along with their shopping bags and their ice cream cones, not knowing what the maniac charging out of Number 67 was after. It turned out I had little choice about 58, 60, or 64 anyway: Only 64 had a roof level with Dana's window. The other two were a medium-rise and a one-story laundromat. A woman was fishing for her key on the stoop of the brownstone that was Number 64. Before she could tell me the rules of the vestibule and street doors, I dug out my Nassau County badge. If that meant she was going to show up with Monaghan and some slug of a friend in a day or two, so be it. More to the point was that she let me take the key from her hand, thoughtfully pointed to the right one, and said nothing as I got inside and told her to stay where she was.

The hallway was stuffy, and I decided that meant nobody had gained access to the roof from the front door. There should have been *some* whiff of fresh air if doors had been opened and closed, I cheered myself as I took the first of the three flights. And what else could that mean except that I wasn't in any danger since the shooter had probably crossed over to Number 64 from another roof and had already fled again the same way? It was a heartening thought, almost as good as common sense.

And, strangely, accurate. I needed three tugs to unloop the inside roof door hook. Since it was time for smarts to put in an appearance, it took me almost as much time to nudge the door open and step out onto the roof as it had getting across the street from Dana's and up the stairs. The moon was full—that might or might not have been a clue. The Washington Square Monument was still standing—that definitely wasn't. The east side of Number 64 did indeed lead directly onto another roof at Hudson Street, where a door was swinging off its hinges—and that definitely was a clue.

I reminded myself I wasn't a cop and didn't go any further. I couldn't see any fresh tar on the rooftop over to the Hudson Street door, but I didn't need a crabby Crime Scene guy telling me there was and that I had fouled up clean prints. I looked across the street to Dana's place. She had gotten every light in the living room out, but I could still see the hole the shooter had made. I assumed the mass of an object right behind the window was her bike. I went back and forth a few yards to see if the Magi had left some precious gift—a shell casing, a cigarette butt, a business card. But not even the tarred together pebbles looked disturbed.

I gave her window an exaggerated shrug. She didn't show herself, but I knew she was in the darkness there somewhere.

So many people were.

CHAPTER 35

Everybody was excelling at professional behavior. The Crime Scene technicians were keeping their eyes hooded between the hole in the window and the one in the chair, avoiding all reviews of the furniture tastes of a superior. Dana had put on running shoes, taken off her headband, and tied a black sweater around her waist so nobody dwelled too long on her rump. Loschen stood against a wall being casual about making notes of the questions being asked by the command detectives in charge. The blue on guard at the door wasn't hearing anything anyone was saying. A diplomacy school grad would have been bowled over by all the correctness.

But everything was also so stiff it was brittle. When the woman tech started going at the back of the chair with her tweezers for the bullet, Dana had to catch herself not to recommend a less destructive way of going about things. The lead detective, a beer-bellied blond named Carrington with a tic for greeting every answer with an "oh, yeah," didn't appreciate Loschen's monitoring, and liked it even less when Herman pointedly ignored the three distinct glares thrown in his direction. The near-breaking point came when Dana's pal from the West Side Highway, the captain named Wendell, rammed his way through the front door followed by two older Police Plaza types. She looked like she was going to cry to have so many unwanted bodies squeezed under her low ceiling.

When Wendell nodded for her to follow him and his friends into the kitchen, she flared as though he had asked her to whip up some eggs, but then took a breath and went along. That was the second most interesting thing that happened. The first was how one of the Police Plaza types, a poster executive civil servant with his puffy red cheeks and very barbered gray hair, gave Loschen a slap on the shoulder as he walked past him into the kitchen. Herman gave me a wan smile: He wasn't responsible for his uncles, the smile said.

Since I hadn't been invited into the kitchen and Carrington didn't want to risk confirming he hadn't been, we were left with each other to go through the drill a second time. I might have pointed out he could have spent his time more profitably with the blues on the rooftop across the street, but I also could have yanked at his nose hairs. What really got him cringing, though, was the uncle peeking out from the kitchen after a couple of minutes to summon Loschen into the gabfest.

"Spiral staircases," I couldn't resist saying.

"What?"

"You know. Not a ladder or something that goes straight up. One of those staircases that twists around on itself."

Carrington almost gave me a smile. "Oh, yeah," he said, making me wonder if he was asking, agreeing, or writing me off as a smartass. "That's all I need for now. You can go."

"When I've said goodbye to the lieutenant."

Carrington wasn't having a good day, so just stomped over to the window to see what other poisonous clouds were blowing in. Since the kitchen was taken and the bedroom would have been oafish, I flopped down on the couch for my wait. The glimpse I had caught of the bullet dug out of the chair told me only that it had come from a rifle and that I didn't know what kind of rifle. On the other hand, the woman tech said Good Night to me on the way out as though I belonged where I was. I liked the feeling.

Wendell didn't emulate her. With the same buffalo grace he had shown on the West Side Highway, he charged out of the kitchen to the front door, shoving two sticks of Juicy Fruit into his mouth and looking ready to ping the balled-up wrappers at the first eye he saw. He took it for granted Carrington and his partner saw his beckoning finger. Then the downtown brass came out, doing their best not to see a single object in the living room on their way to the door. Only after the blue on guard realized his duty was over and went out after everybody else, closing the door quietly behind him, did Dana and Loschen emerge from the kitchen. Both looked deflated.

"It didn't *have* to be our sniper," she said, making sure nobody had upset her little secretary of knickknacks and travel souvenirs. "So, we should spend a couple of days in the office concentrating on possibles from old cases. How long's that really going to take, Herman? Ten minutes?"

"Five."

"And while you're doing that, who's going to be handling the sniper? Captain Wendell himself?"

"With those two who were here," she nodded. She brightened with an evil thought. "Hey, but there's a positive side! That means they've knocked *you* to the sidelines, too, Finley!"

"You *were* just shot at, you know."

"Or you were. Maybe you should be the one going through old cases. Who was that dentist who slugged you?"

It would have been funnier if I didn't remember all the neurotic beads associated with the Shari Glynn family. Monaghan, in particular, seemed to know how to pick up the odd fact here and there about what people did for a living and where they lived. "I'm serious," I said anyway. "Keep low for a day or so. At least until they find out it was a kid having target practice."

"We should have somebody keeping an eye on this place," Loschen seconded gravely. "Just in case it wasn't a kid."

"No, thank you."

"But, Lieutenant . . ."

"I told them outside, Herman, and I'm telling you."

He shriveled up so much even I felt relieved when she walked him to the door. When she was sure he was going down the stairs, she looked back at me guiltily. "How many of them you think are going to be watching this place? A dozen? Two dozen?"

"They're sure as hell not going to listen to you."

"I shouldn't have snapped at Loschen."

"No, you shouldn't have. Why'd they want him in the kitchen?"

"I want some water. You want some water?"

"No, I don't want any water. Why Herman in the kitchen?"

"Uncle Edward wanted to ask him if he could think of somebody else we might have annoyed lately."

"There are more tactful ways of doing it."

She went into the kitchen for her water. By the time she came out again with her bottle, she had settled on an answer both for me and herself. "You had to be there. Wendell was licking his chops to get rid of me. Uncle Edward didn't like the reflections being cast on his nephew because of my stupidity in being shot at. So, all in all, he decided, 48 hours at our desks would make a nice compromise. Herman stood there looking embarrassed. I stood there wondering why getting shot at should be a reason for a demotion. And Wendell stood there seething he wasn't going to get his pound of flesh tonight, but okay, he'd settle for a couple of ounces for now. I guess that's why Uncle Edward gets paid the big bucks he does. And you know what, Finley? I don't give a flying fuck!"

"That's good."

"Goddamn right."

She thrust her hips hard past the arm of the couch to go over to the window. I didn't look after her. I thought she was just making sure the police garage of patrol cars in front of her door had finally broken up. But then the wheels of her bike started going. They sounded almost musical.

CHAPTER 36

Magic powders kept the shooting out of the papers. The closest thing
to a leak was a squib in the *Post* about the hunt for a gang of
Village vandals who had taken to throwing rocks through apartment windows. That didn't quite cover it for Fox because the Jane
Street marksman had cut loose while he had been parked outside
the Brooklyn graystone where Owen Bronsard had been very vis-
ibly eating a solitary supper in front of his TV set. I liked thinking
that brought on a case of Homeland Security runs. On the other
hand, it gave Fox all the more reason to endorse Wendell's theory
that the shooting had nothing to do with the sniper. Wendell?
He couldn't have been happier. Since Bronsard had been a Dana
trail, the faster it was shown to be false, the better his dump-
lings tasted. Having the Feds go down with it was just extra duck
sauce.

Not being in the middle of all this official camaraderie, I was
free to sympathize with Dana and to dodge the Professor's calls
about what his retainer was getting him. I didn't want to talk to
him or anyone else who had heard of Ralph Carey. Somewhere
in the middle of all the murk was an itch about how things like a
bullet through a window might not have happened if I had done
or not done something. But I also knew merely mentioning that
would have earned the accusation I was still honing my self-importance, intent on inventing a connection to the sniper I didn't
have. I cursed the day I'd gone to the synagogue to Rennie Miller's
funeral service.

Luckily, I had a rainbow of job delights to keep me distracted. There were so many of them in wildly different hues that I had to stare stupidly for a second to remember what was in a specific file whenever I fished one out of the Finley Library and opened it on my desk. Some might have regarded this as a symptom of yet another existential crisis, at the least of indifference to anything besides the sniper; I thought of it more as a commentary on Office Depot's failure to come up with a greater variety of file colors.

Then the Forces of Moron Evil put in another appearance.

About once a week, I rewarded an especially virtuous day with a couple of shots at the Green Fox. It was usually around ten when I checked out, not up for those increasingly drowsy conversations that kept saloons going until closing time. For once I would have been better off staying to listen to Johnny Yeager and Blanche Walsh debate whether the Portuguese were slaves brought back to Europe from China by Marco Polo. Standing in front of my building was Kitty or his ugly clone. I saw him before he saw me because he kept looking nervously up at the windows, as though afraid a water balloon was about to land on his head. I didn't have time to second that motion because I was suddenly awash in Old Spice. "This time I got one," Monaghan said happily, coming out from between two parked cars and showing me a silver-plated .22 in his hand. "We missed you, Finley."

"There's a way to stay in touch with that feeling."

"Ah, you're a funny lad. Come along now."

I blamed the booze for it all: for my stupidity in not having seen Monaghan between the cars, for my anger the two dimwits were back in my life. Kitty couldn't wait to hustle me into the unlighted archway entrance of my building and show Monaghan how a pat-down was done. "You see now? He's got nothin'. And we know he's got nothin' because I checked him out. That's what you should've done last time."

Monaghan had counted on something like the little scolding because he ignored it. "You have a crystal ball, Finley," he said, his eyes roaming out to the sidewalk every couple of seconds to make sure no other tenant was returning home. "Exactly as you predicted, Johnny's gone off to the Bahamas or some blessed place with all my dreams and money. He's not down in Rockaway with his clan, he's nowhere."

"You've been busy, Dennis."

"Oh, yeah. But guess, would you, who *has* surfaced? That's right. The skinny little blonde in her store."

"And you're going to get us all together," Kitty said with a poke.

For a moment I found the idea appealing. Not so much for reuniting Christine with Johnny Wells's friends as for bringing sister Shari together with the people she had been paying me to keep away from her. But then the moment passed. "You're spending a lot of energy for two grand."

"We can't all be rolling in it like you, lad. Besides, I like to realize my dreams. And that means the beads lady."

"So, go talk to her. I'm not going to stop you."

"Oh, you're going to do more than that," he said, producing a cellphone from his jacket pocket and thrusting it at me. "You're going to have her invite us around to the store so we can discuss the little ins and outs of our situation here."

"She doesn't care about your situation."

"We'll let her tell us that."

"While anybody passing by wonders why the store's open so late?"

"I told you, Dennis . . ."

"Shut up, Kitty. We're doing a special inventory, is all. And in fact, that's exactly what we'll be doing."

So much for Kitty as my ally in reasonable behavior: He whinnied a laugh at a line he had probably already heard a dozen times. "Christine doesn't know me," I tried anyway. "I call her down to the store, she's going to hang up and call the cops."

"No, no, lad. You're going to call the other one. The one that writes the checks. For you, too, I'd wager . . . Oh, yeah. Been conducting my own little reconnaissance to see what's what. What's her name?"

"Shari," Kitty was proud to remember.

"Indeed. Shari. You're going to tell her it's really important you meet to discuss her sister's little escapades with Johnny."

"I don't think so."

"I think so because all I'm asking for is what's legally mine. I don't know if Johnny pulled this off with your connivance, but I'd be willing to say so unless you can prove different."

"And you don't help us," Kitty said with another poke in my chest, "we'll go to the twitchy one and maybe it won't stay so legal."

"Could you close your trap for two seconds in a row, Kitty?"

"I'm just making it clear . . ."

"He understands. Don't you, Finley?"

What I understood was that it was always a bad idea to under-rate the havoc imbeciles were capable of. But even granting that, I still couldn't see either of them holding up Shari for more than money they would be lucky to have an hour to spend before the cops grabbed them. Like someone else I knew, Monaghan and Kitty seemed to spend all their time figuring out the smartest way to get from home plate to first base so they could get picked off a pitch later. "There's nothing in that store, boys. I'm telling you now."

"Wouldn't think of it," Monaghan said, reminding me of the phone. "Just trying to get back what's mine. Sorry that turns out to be this Shari. Next time she'll be more careful about picking a sister. Call her."

"Don't have the number on me."

"989-3415," he said with another happy smile.

"That's good, Dennis. Makes me wonder how you were ever screwed by somebody like Johnny Wells."

"Trust, mate. It's a weakness. I trust people. Go ahead and call."

If I hadn't been so flustered by the corner the cellphone had left me in, I would have sworn my mission bells had just tolled down the street. But then and there I would have preferred think-ing about anything else. "Last chance, Dennis. This is a mistake."

"Like the judge says to the lawyer, noted."

Kitty thought that was funny, too.

CHAPTER 37

Sometimes you need all the planets and their satellites to be aligned just-so around the moon to create a celestial phenomenon. Getting through to Shari Glynn for what Monaghan wanted required the same synchronicity of conditions. One, I was prevented from bluffing with a call to the weather or the time because even Kitty would be able to tell the difference between Shari and a robot operator. Two, Shari had the same command of her telephone at home as she did of the cash register in the store, ensuring that neither Marty nor Christine picked up. Three, she had just the right mix of defensiveness about her private investigator, apprehension about her sister's adventures, and curiosity about the goons threatening her beads to agree to see us. Four, I had the perfect blend of cowardice and relish for gathering all these pains in the ass together not to try to disarm Monaghan and have a go at Kitty. Naturally, it was the spinelessness part that was nagging me the most as Shari opened the door of Beads, Beads, and More Beads to let us in. If I ever redid my resume, I couldn't see including in the testimonial section the part about leading two troublemakers over to a client.

There was a single desk lamp on, next to the register. The bulb must have been five watts since it barely lighted the floor in front of the counter, leaving the beads tables in cave darkness. Aside from the tiny pearls she apparently kept on around her upstairs apartment, Shari didn't look so bright herself when she turned back from relocking the door. "Whatever's so important," she said in a half-whisper, "say it and get out."

Give Monaghan this much: He was delighted by the little rendezvous he had organized. (Kitty, on the other hand, kept glancing around the store with the same anxiety he had shown about the water balloon attack back in front of my building.) "What it comes down to, Missus, is you owe me a couple of thousand dollars and I'm here to collect."

There were several possibilities in the look Shari gave me: had I heard the same lunacy she had, what scheme had I concocted with the Druids in front of her, why had she ever hired me. I suppose all three reactions were reasonable from her point of view. "I have no idea who you are," she said. "And I certainly don't owe you two thousand dollars."

"No doubt there're ins and outs you're not familiar with," Monaghan said, making an effort at drawing room suavity. "And for that, I can only pass along apologies for individuals you wouldn't want any truck with. But since they're off the scene now, it's left to you and me to total up the accounts. And, as I say, that comes to two thousand."

"With interest," Kitty put in.

Monaghan gritted his teeth instead of leveling Kitty with the .22 he was keeping palmed out of Shari's sight; his smile instantly gained more of a hyena's look. "Not a situation I wanted any more than you, Missus, but it is what it is."

She almost made the mistake of responding to a squeaked floorboard in the apartment above. "What it is, Mister Whoever You Are," she said coolly, "is some cheap attempt at extortion and it's not going to work."

"Hey, lady, we're here, aren't we? You didn't say no, don't come over when we called. You know you owe us as much as we do."

I understood Monaghan's grin: Kitty had finally hit one. Celestial phenomena and cowardice aside, there really *had been* much less resistance than there should have been.

"You're here because I want you and your friend Wells to know once and for all that, if any of you come anywhere near this store again, I'll bring charges. No matter who gets hurt."

For some reason, she directed the last bit as much at me as at Monaghan and Kitty. WARNING, FINLEY: I'M A SERIOUS PERSON AND I WON'T STOP AT BRINGING DOWN CHRISTINE IF THAT'S WHAT IT TAKES TO GET SOME PEACE? But why should I have cared if she brought down Christine? I wasn't the one sending so many mixed signals while making a show of shielding baby sis. In fact, why *didn't* she bring her down? She had already told me what a burden her sister had become, had hardly put on sackcloth when Christine seemed to have gone off with Wells to points unknown. She had been truly distraught only when telling me Christine had come back . . .

"No need to go all dramatic, Missus. We've just had a little bit of a misunderstanding thanks to a rogue neither of us wants to see again . . ."

I sagged against the counter. The more Shari and Monaghan went back and forth with each other, the clearer I pictured the check for $510 she had given me and the other one I had taken off Monaghan. I felt like vomiting a rock. Even when the last jeering imp had snapped off a salute to me and gone jauntily down the street, I told myself to keep quiet, that Monaghan and Kitty had four ears between them, and would try to use whatever I said for some new brainstorm. It took me a long second to remember I didn't give a good goddamn if they did or didn't. "Still afraid Christine might have left Wells bleeding in a motel room?"

Shari looked as if I had violated a sacred pact between us. "What are you talking about? Why would you say such a thing?"

Monaghan and Kitty were waiting for one another to sputter first. "My imagination, then. But do me a favor, will you?" Monaghan came alive when I reached into my jacket for my notebook, but relaxed again when he saw I wasn't after my .38. "Write your name here."

"What for?"

"What're you up to, Finley?"

I knew from her face I was right: The signature on the check she had given me and the one Christine had given Monaghan were the same. There had never been a forgery. All the little pearls around her throat were drops from the same glass. She hadn't been merely glad when Christine had taken off; that had been the completion of what she had set out to do before even hiring me. I was just supposed to have checked out Wells for her so she could have a more precise idea of how much of a bitch she could be and maybe regret it every fourth or fifth Sunday morning.

All of which added up to? "I screwed up everything for you, didn't I, Shari?" I said, feeling sand falling out of my knees. "I wasn't supposed to bring that check back. You gave that money to Christine to run off."

As Jenny had warned me, the largest pearl of all was her thin lips. She gave it another of those what-is-this-absurd-man-talking-about looks, but she had already used that on Monaghan, and he wasn't impressed.

"When Christine took off, you weren't worried about what she might do to Wells or what he might do to her. You were worried about our two friends here catching up to them for that money. Money you'd written off until I brought you back the check."

"Ridiculous."

"You owe them that two thousand. They might not have cashed that check with uplifting intentions, might've had some dimwit con in mind. And Wells, he might not have leveled with them the way honest citizens are supposed to. But you still owe it to them."

There were hands on me and a .22 suddenly lighted by passing headlights gleaming in my direction, but I kept my eyes on Shari—in the darkness, where she belonged even more than Christine. "I don't know how far you expected her to get with two thousand bucks, but I suppose love is blind, right? That what you were counting on?"

There was another heavy shoe on the ceiling, and it saved her from answering something dumb. It was never going to be hubby Marty's business, the new insolence in her stare said, so go figure how it was ever going to be mine. "I have no idea what you're talking about, Mr. Finley."

Kitty grabbed more of my jacket with more of his water balloon look. "What're you saying? What's all this shit about Wells bleeding in a motel? What's he mean, Dennis?"

Monaghan knew he had to improvise. "It's bullshit. He's just playing with your head, lad. That's what Finley does for a living— plays with people. Tell him, Finley."

There comes a time in the fortunes of men, and all that kind of rhetoric. I thought of it as the Disgust Bomb. There was just so much ticking it could produce before its mere threat became tiring. At that point, it either exploded or it didn't. Mine did. It was what I should have done back in front of my building when Kitty had been patting me down. Or maybe back when Shari had been telling me I was good only for finding corpses. Or maybe the last time in the store when I had cut my finger in the interests of listening to her indignation at how much Christine had been ruining her life. Whenever I should have done it, I finally did do it, slicing my left hand across Kitty's jaw so hard my forearm felt like it was trying to leap up from my arm and off my shoulder.

Kitty went tumbling back against the nearest table like one of those movie drunks trying to catapult himself through the swinging doors of a saloon. At first, it was just fun seeing his wildly swinging arm clip the edge of a single tray and push it to the rim of the table. But even as I was thinking I wanted more for my money than that, Kitty was losing a second round to his balance and trying to fend off the inevitable by dropping both hands fully into another couple of bins. I loved it, even with Monaghan getting over his distraction and remembering what he was carrying. I'd once had a cat who was so sloppy he had put his paws in his food and water bowls as though they had been extensions of the ground. But not even Bandito could have created Kitty's mess. One tray after another hit the floor, bouncing little shells and cones and pebble-like things all the way to the door and the street window. Shari was yelling and Monaghan was backing up with his useless .22 against the hordes of red ants advancing on him, but for a few seconds in the middle of all the hard hail hitting the floor, they were only sideshows. Far funnier—ironically funny, as the Professor might have said—was that the cause of all the destruction was a guy named Kitty. Kitty had wanted to be a bandito, but at bottom was just a Bandito without paws and whiskers. How many times can a circle close so neatly in your life?

The thumping upstairs sounded more resolute and Monaghan was getting over his retreat from the beads. I had no reason to stick around to meet Marty and the rest of the family. I had done just fine without them. "If she doesn't give you the money, Dennis, get it from the husband. His name's Marty and he lives in a bubble."

The faces Monaghan and Shari gave me made me think of one of the Professor's Wednesday night pontifications about French courtesans from some century. They had entered a room, he had said, confident of drawing spite and hatred from every woman present. As I opened the door, smashing a bead that had rolled after me, wondering when Kitty was going to stop thrashing around behind me, I wondered how hard it would be to change my name officially to Fifi.

CHAPTER 38

When the local precinct hadn't rung my bell by noon the next day, I figured Shari, Monaghan, and their respective armies of dupes and liars had worked out something. This made me optimistic enough to think I would never pick up a paper to read about Johnny Wells's body being discovered and Christine Sewell being arrested for leaving it in its decomposing state. The same positive frame of mind told me that wherever Wells had absconded with his few bucks, he joined me in an exclusive club—the only ones to have made money from Beads, Beads, and More Beads.

The Professor thought I was hilarious. He wanted to hear every detail of the Monaghan Strategy twice over, so what if that meant containing himself about the real purpose of our latest Brooklyn walking tour—the update on Ralph Carey I'd avoided giving him on the phone. Even when he was laughed out about Shari Glynn and sister Christine, he had enough good cheer left over to dwell on the historical significance of one of those gray slate high school buildings with drab fluorescent lighting he had stopped us before. "A hundred years ago this was an athletic club. A hub for the hoity-toity in Bay Ridge. You belonged to the club, you belonged to society."

"Did you belong?"

"Yeah. Then they found out I knew you and kicked me out. There should be a plaque around here somewhere . . ."

He went waddling up to the entrance where a security guard had been watching us since we had stopped. On another day I might have been irked by the guy's beady-eyed stare. But what the hell? Why couldn't I be a bored security guard's entertainment as much as Shari Glynn's? What was the guy supposed to do all day—look up at the classroom lights that threatened homework and final exams and other teenage delights?

"He says he thinks it's inside next to one of the offices," the Professor reported back. "Like it's some goddamn poster for the Friday night hop!"

"They don't do hops anymore, Joe."

"And are we better for it?"

"Yes, we are."

"Right. You're a rapper now. Coolio Finley, Private Dick."

We ended up in a Fourth Avenue pub neither one of us wanted to be in so early in the day. It was the Green Fox without Cynthia and with stools sturdy enough to fit sumo wrestlers but bad for any knees you might have wanted to stick under the bar. We asked for two beers from the pockmarked Seamus anyway because the smells of the place demanded it. I felt like asking Seamus for his green card just to spice up his day.

"So, you think the certifiably loony one . . ."

"We're going to end this soon, right?"

"I'm just trying to dot the I's here. She likes to be 'interesting,' as her sister says, so she probably even told this Wells she'd forged the check. Keep him more interested in her."

"Possible."

"That's great."

"It is, huh?"

"Okay, your big symbol for order—these beads—turns out to be a pack of lies . . ."

"Were they my symbol for order? I don't remember that."

"All those neat little bins. Each kind assigned to its own tray. Maybe subdivided by color or alphabetical order . . ."

"You're having a really good time, aren't you?"

"Goddamn right! Here's to the Monaghan Strategy!"

Leaving aside little things like humiliation and not wanting beer, how could I *not* drink to it?

"Not for me to point it out," he said with an exaggerated smack of the lips, "but if you really wanted your sense of order *and* wanted to earn that check I sent you, you could've been concentrating on the sniper."

"Tell Dana. She doesn't want to hear any more about emptied places."

"She's right. Get to my age, most of this city is an emptied place. That's why your shooter has to be a younger guy who thinks his melancholy is so special. Kind of like you."

"Thanks."

"I'm talking about something else. Something less Finley."

There were many irritating Joe Carrolls (I'd stopped counting after the low hundreds), but one of the worst was the teacher inviting the goofball student to see what everybody else in the classroom had already seen. "You going to help Dana out now, too?"

"If she hasn't figured it out by now herself, she sounds like she's as good at her job as you are at yours. Escalation."

"Escalation."

He twisted uncomfortably on his stool. "Don't they lay out pretzels or something in this place?"

"It's noon, and they're bad for you anyway."

"The only thing that'll kill you, son-in-law, is not seeing the obvious. Carey was one-on-one on foot. This Chinese cook gets shot from a moving train. The one on the highway—moving vehicle against moving vehicle. This guy's escalating the challenge each time. Whatever else he's doing, he's competing with his own marksmanship ability."

He was right, of course: It *was* obvious. But so obvious the pattern was also meaningless? And then and there that hadn't struck me as the most important thing he had said. It had been years since he had called me son-in-law, even dismissively. I still seemed to be back at Beads, Beads, and More Beads trying to gather up my brains.

"Well? Hasn't that occurred to anybody?"

I needed an objection, any objection. "Nice. But what's so escalating about shooting through Dana's window?"

"Assuming it's the same guy."

"I'm assuming."

"Really don't see it, huh?"

Some people liked imagining themselves living in the Wild West, others back in the Age of Chivalry. I suddenly had no doubt before his pop eyes that I was back in the Age of Density where I had been much too preoccupied minueting in great ballrooms and tossing coins to beggars. "No, Joe, I guess I can't."

Instead of coming at me more gleefully, he relented to take another sip of beer. I wasn't expecting the new sympathy in his voice: "Totally understandable. You like the lady and you want to protect her. You don't want to face some dark possibilities. You'll even reach for the bullshit this Wendell and the FBI want you to buy."

"Joe . . .!"

His face reddened in impatience. "For Christ sake, Finley, you can find that escalation in the paper once a month! It's called suicide by cop!"

Seamus didn't like the raised voices echoing off his bottles and walls. I didn't like Seamus. "That's . . ."

"Too logical? Yeah, probably. And I have no explanation for this rifle instead of the same handgun. His latest escalation is going up against people who can shoot back. To me, that fits the pattern."

"If you squeeze it in hard enough. She was across the street and could never get to him in time. Big bravado!" He was down to shrugging over his glass. "But let's even say you're right. What does he do next? Rent a plane and attack some jets at Andrews Air Force Base so he can start a dogfight?"

"Maybe. Something like that. One way or the other, you're dealing with somebody who won't be satisfied until he's raised the stakes so high he has to wind up in the morgue."

"Sure of that, are you?"

He found something funny. "And I don't even sew my patterns on skirts and dresses! They just come to me. Gifts from on high. Carroll, Carroll, and More Carroll."

Drinking my beer seemed better than pouring it over his head. But not by all that much.

CHAPTER 39

I could have gotten any number of things out of my outing. I could have learned more about the athletic club for the rich that had become a high school. I could have advised Cynthia on the kinds of bar stools fit for saloons. I could have meditated on how many realities I wanted to ignore in the interests of continuing to skim along with Dana. But why dote on the minor questions when, as the old man had reminded me, nobody had been saying much at all about the sniper rifle used on Jane Street?

I called Dana to get together for dinner, but a voice I took to belong to the blonde last seen eating a bran muffin said she was out on a job and probably wouldn't be back for the day. When I asked for Loschen, she acted surprised I knew the whole duty roster but passed me on. "There was a robbery on Union Turnpike she's taking a look at," Herman said with his usual vivacity. "Then I think she's going to her brother and sister-in-law's for dinner. I can call her if you want."

I didn't want. I could have called her on her cellphone myself, but the best that would have gotten me was an invitation to go with her to brother Gregory's, and that wasn't much of a best. Gregory lived in Westchester and, based on the one time we'd met, had a warehouse of stories about the idiots who walked around in shoes they hadn't bought in his Yonkers store. What I wasn't sure I wanted was to ask Loschen what I had planned to ask Dana *tête-à-tête*. I decided I did. "So, how's the investigation going?"

"The robbery on Union Turnpike?"

It was the second funny thing Herman had said, though I couldn't immediately remember the first one. "I was just curious about the rifle because nobody's mentioned it in the press."

"Yeah," he said, sounding like he was turning away from the blonde. "That's because they don't want to. Talk to you soon."

For about 15 minutes after Loschen hung up, I debated if his signoff had been a brusque goodbye or code for saying he was going to drop around and tell me all the latest developments. Then I spent almost as much time going back and forth between cursing myself for having compromised him with my stupid questions and reassuring myself he could never be fatally compromised as long as Uncle Edward was sitting down in Police Plaza. In other words, it was a prime example of why Verizon should have tapped a new market with a special plan for halfwit phone calls.

I tried, really tried, to forget the sniper. I stayed tied to my desk for hours looking up the medical records of two Jake Early clients, talking to school and hospital people, and then creating new computer files for shoveling in what I had gleaned. I didn't take a break until I went into the kitchen around seven to broil a piece of salmon. By then it had become clear Loschen had not been sending me any coded messages and would not be dropping by to unburden himself. I faced an entire evening without having to think about anyone connected to the sniper.

Until Bobby Qualls called about Owen Bronsard.

"Guy sounded really anxious," Qualls said, not sounding so calm himself. "Like whatever you told him really got his hopes up."

"I didn't promise him anything!"

"Yeah, but I told you about free-lancers, Paul. You live on the hope. The possibility becomes the probability."

Where did I start? I would have never gone near Owen Bronsard if Qualls hadn't fed him the line about the producer. Even then, I still wouldn't have gone near him if it hadn't seemed like a shortcut to helping Dana. And how could anything related to Dennis Monaghan (*Monaghan Productions!*) not bring a thousand painful cuts? I couldn't believe how many people were to blame for forcing me to make others miserable. "So, what're you saying, Bobby? I should start a TV station to make this guy feel better?"

"I don't know, man. Just that he sounded so down. Wanted to know how to get in contact with you."

I knew it was useless to even cringe. "And you told him . . .?"

Qualls was perky again; this time he hadn't baked the pie, merely supplied the ingredients. "I said I thought you were in the Brooklyn book. I didn't want him showing up on your doorstep. I mean, in a way this all started because I made up that . . ."

How many eons ago had it been that I had been closing the file on Shari Glynn and her original notions of being *sort of* responsible for her sister? On what heavenly throne had I been sitting when I had been snickering down at all the liars in the Glynn and Monaghan clans? If dissembling had been one of those labyrinths on an English estate, I would have been in the middle of it nibbling at the hedges for survival.

I sat mumbling to myself through the first scenes of another showing of *Once Upon a Time in the West*; with Morricone's music as background, it felt suspenseful. It was nice to remember that Fox had been watching Bronsard eat his supper when the bullet had gone into Dana's chair, so at least I didn't have to crawl under my window when I had to go to the john. And being the professional he wanted to be, Bronsard would hardly show up at my door without calling first, right? But the more I sat on all these reassurances, the more Charles Bronson and Henry Fonda seemed to be shouting at me they were slowing down on the fiftieth viewing, that the action that night was in the vicinity of Brooklyn College, around a spooky graystone house. That was not only where Owen Bronsard and his gullibility were, but where my good friend Andy Fox undoubtedly had all the information I needed about the make of the rifle used on Jane Street. Why should he have shared that with me? Why not? He was personable, I was personable. We both believed in the Constitution and all the penal codes based on it. We were both outraged that the rifle might not have only killed Dana but could have killed me just as easily. How could he *not* have helped somebody with such a personal interest in everything?

I got over my hallucination, but not over being antsy, so took a drive over to Coney Island for a frozen custard. Since the weather hadn't warmed up enough to wear a suit jacket without a sweater, there were as many rides and booths closed as open on Surf Avenue, the Boardwalk, and in between, and most of those open were wasting their electricity. As I waited for my cone from the old Arab woman who had been running her stand for as long as I could remember, I thought about the only time I had brought Susan to Coney Island. She had pointed to the chocolate custard spout, called it vanilla, and insisted it was the only vanilla she wanted. The then-younger Arab woman had given her the chocolate cone calling it "Susan's vanilla." The only other memory I had of that day was going on the Ferris wheel—not the Wonder Wheel or any other thing that would have passed muster for a movie called *State Fair*, but a rinky-dink toy model that belonged to some sideshow park for the smallest kids and their terrified fathers. The damn wheel hadn't risen higher than a couple of apartment house floors, but when it had stopped at the top, I had been ready to jump without a parachute. Only Susan's giggling had kept me from screaming at the guy to let us down.

I took my cone for a walk down chilly Surf Avenue. I knew the Professor had been right about overlooking the obvious in the suicide-by-cop thing, but I still balked at accepting it was because of my defensiveness about Dana. I just wasn't used to being accused of clinging to people to such a point; just the opposite, even with something as stupid as "Susan's vanilla." Whatever charm the Arab woman might have lost in Susan's eyes, I'd made sure going home that day she had understood the difference between vanilla and chocolate if she expected people to give her what she asked for. How was she to have become independent otherwise? And now I was supposedly neglecting far more lethal facts because I hadn't wanted to admit the extent of my own dependency? That just wasn't me. And what would it have accomplished? In the end, whatever I was ready to admit, Dana would have ended up with the wrong cone anyway.

There was one guy—lanky, barely out of his teens, wearing a hooded Jets windbreaker —at the target range booth. The concessionaire was doing his best to sound enthusiastic every time a duck went down but then spoiled the effect by rattling the change in his apron and following whatever car crept down the street. The kid doing the shooting had more than a couple of beers in his eyes as he aimed his pistol—something that looked inspired by a German Luger out of a track and field starter's gun. The ducks couldn't have cared less: They streamed by, knowing that even if they got knocked over, they would be back up as soon as they dipped down at the end of the booth. There seemed to be a behavioral model in that, but I wasn't sure whose.

I watched the kid spend five dollars' worth of shots, ending up with a piece of plastic in the shape of a keychain bear for his trouble. He tossed it in his palm for a second, thought about flinging it away, then put it in the pocket of his windbreaker and loped down the street. The concessionaire shrugged to me as though we had both just seen another illustration of life's mysteries. By then, I'd had one of my own. Granted I had been working on my cone for some of the time, but I had stood watching the kid for a good five minutes without a single attempt by the concessionaire to get me to splurge for my own three shots. He thought I was being funny when I asked him about it. "You're on the job, right? I got a season comin' up, pal, and I need every stuffed piece I got here. But if you want one for your kid or somethin', I could . . ."

"No, no. Just curious. I like people thinking I'm a librarian."

He gave me another crooked smile. "And I like women thinkin' I'm a movie star. But it never works out. They see right through me."

He wanted me to laugh, so I did. And thought more about why the sniper had broken his pattern to use a rifle against Dana. The Professor was uneasy with it because, whatever he said, it didn't fit his scheme of things. But the only thing really odd about it, I thought, was that resorting to it in place of the Glock felt hurried, even a little desperate. I wished I knew why, and why I thought I should have known.

CHAPTER 40

I was no expert on foreign trade, but I was pretty sure more than one black Saab had found its way into New York either from Sweden or from one of those multinational plants in the Ozarks. That was why, coming back from Coney Island, I didn't make much of the car parked in front of my building and why I stepped off the elevator into a trio no horror movie had prepared me for—Mrs. Chalian in her bathrobe and curlers, Jeffrey Chalian in the pajama bottoms and T-shirt he seemed to wear all day, and Andrew Fox in his sharpest charcoal gray. Standing in the hallway in front of the Chalians' door, the three of them looked at me like I had taken too long to bring the wine for our party. "This gentleman is from the Federal Bureau of Investigation, Mr. Finley," Mrs. Chalian informed me in the patient tone of a kindergarten teacher, "and we've been explaining to him that you don't tell us where you go when you go out."

Fox didn't object to spending a few seconds of government time watching me squirm. Jeffrey looked relieved his mother wasn't going to have to invite a Fed inside closer to his bedroom. "Thanks, Mrs. Chalian. I'll take it from here."

Her bulldog face dropped with the end of her evening adventure. "Well, it was a pleasure meeting you, Mr. Fox," she said in the same ring of delivering some basic moral lesson. "And we look forward to that literature in the mail. Jeffrey will be very interested to read it. Won't you, Jeffrey?"

I had my door open by the time Jeffrey had finished saying he would be interested in reading it. Fox was practically walking up my legs. I didn't even attempt to guess why he was there. And he didn't keep me in suspense. As soon as he had used his back to close my door against the lingering Mrs. Chalian, he said: "Owen Bronsard's dead."

I clicked on my standing lamp, playing the announcement back a half-dozen times before the light seemed to come on. One of us—the lamp or me—needed to be rewired.

"Suicide. Single shot in the mouth. We heard it, but he was gone before we got in the house."

"And you're here because . . .?"

"He had your phone number on his desk. Looked like one of the last things he did. Phonebook right next to it, open to your page. What'd he want to talk to you about?"

I suppose I should have appreciated the plain-as-can-be information, but I didn't. I was more interested in how many lights to turn on in the room since I planned to catch the late news and then go straight to bed. Plus, Alfred E. Neuman sounded too much like Bobby Qualls saying I was responsible for something I wasn't responsible for. "A job he thought I had for him. A bullshit story I used to get into his place. Wasn't that lousy of me? Yeah, it was, but who among us dares cast the first stone? And no, he never got around to calling me. Thanks for dropping by."

I hadn't really expected him to move, and he didn't. Instead, he gazed around my living room and workspace as if the official part of his business was over and now he wanted to get down to the prospects for subletting. "You don't give yourself much elbow room."

"They haven't finished air-conditioning my new high-rise office."

"There's some thought he couldn't live with the guilt, decided to end it before he shot somebody else."

I heard the mockery; it was a lot like the conversation trying to get started in my head. "And now some bolt of lightning's told you that's not true? Sorry. I know how much you put into believing it."

"You're sure he didn't call you?"

"Check his phone records."

"I'm asking you."

"I told you he didn't. Or maybe I forget how he confessed to shooting Carey and the others before he left us."

Silence. Then: "They might still run with it. For a while."

I hadn't misheard the *They*, either. Suddenly, I wanted a drink and I didn't mind having company for it. "I'm having a J&B. You can go, watch me drink it, or have one."

I didn't wait for an answer, but when I came back from the kitchen with the bottle and two glasses, he was on the couch; he even had his jacket unbuttoned and his legs crossed. Because he had taken the end cushion, he also looked like he was being swallowed up by the upholstery. "You really hit the bullseye with all that emptied places stuff . . ."

"Good for me."

He tried again. "Wherever he went, it was yesterday. He liked this old camera store on Nostrand Avenue. I bet the place still has Kodak Brownies in the cellar. Who the hell goes to a butcher shop when it's all there in the supermarket freezer for you? Owen Bronsard did. We almost blew everything in church. Just him and old ladies. I thought the priest was going to wave us up to one of the front pews to make it more intimate."

"And this told you . . .?"

He took his glass and didn't wait for a toast. "It told me you didn't deserve your medal anyway. The reading on Bronsard was right, but it had nothing to do with taking out your neighbors."

"I see. My fault."

"I think the shrinks call it projection."

"Then you better take a closer look at me."

He thawed out a half-smile and took another glance around. "I don't know New York well, Finley," he said, as though surveying all five boroughs on my walls. "My idea of a manageable place is Pittsburgh. You see somebody brooding, you know it has to be because he's still not over the steel industry tanking or the Steelers losing. Clear cause and effect. But this is a goddamn snake pit. Everybody's nursing some private grievance and a lot of them don't mind splashing the whole city with it."

"What can I tell you?"

Down to it, he wasn't too sure. The lamplight in his eyes made him look sensitive—a searcher with a scimitar tiepin. "He knew we were there the whole time. We set up in one of those deserted houses across the street up a few doors. We might as well have hung a flag over the front door. Couple of kids kept jumping up at the window to see what we were doing. Not what you'd call your classic covert surveillance. But what were we supposed to do? Sit in a parked car? How would that have been any better?"

"What do you want—a critique of your techniques? Get more black Feds. Then only their clothes and jolly eyes will give them away."

He made a loud show of tasting his second swallow. "Couple of times I swear he was peeking at us over his shoulder and looking happy."

"Like anybody being harassed is."

"I'm not kidding. Like he'd finally gotten somebody's attention."

I remembered the conversation in the upstairs Dodger museum. What I didn't remember was understanding how truly starved Owen Bronsard had been. "Yeah, he didn't seem to have too much of that."

"Not that he needed it financially with that house."

"Not that he needed it. Financially."

A door slammed across the courtyard. It sounded like Fagan tramping in for the night. I wouldn't have minded Fox hearing one of his scenes. It would have made me a credible witness when the wife finally dragged the bastard into a courtroom. I might not have been all that believable by myself, but with Agent Andrew Fox backing me up? I could have sent Fagan to Attica for life!

He was still looking at me with the candor face. "What I can't figure is whether you're feeling left out or not quite left out enough."

"An official question?"

"Until tomorrow I don't have official questions."

"It started off as a favor for my father-in-law."

"Yeah, I know about that. And then there's the lieutenant. But neither one of them completely does it for me."

"Sorry."

"C'mon. I told you I was wrong about Bronsard."

"Worse. You always knew you were."

"I didn't say that."

"We'll pretend you did. As for the rest of it, stick with what you said the other day—I needed a break from all the 'penny-ante grubbing.'"

"Why? Because that hit home?"

"If I say yes, can we talk about the Pirates and the Penguins?"

He didn't waste time polishing off his drink—or reaching over to the bottle for another one. "Tonight's answers won't become official tomorrow, either. Just curiosity. I'd like to know."

I got the bottle out of his hand before he blew my liquor budget for the month. Suddenly I felt a little too close to Owen Bronsard. I didn't owe confidences to the first stranger through the door. But I told him anyway about my rush on the West Side Highway the night Karen Rosen had been killed. For once, he listened as though he hadn't anticipated what I was going to say. "You didn't have that feeling before? I mean, you're off the job a pretty long time now."

Of all people, Ralph Carey popped into my head. "Think of Carey the first time he went to the ballpark as an announcer instead of a player. Before the game, he's clowning around on the field with the players like he always did. Then somebody says it's time for the game to start, Ralph, you got to go up to the broadcasting booth now, you can't go back in the locker room with the players. All his instincts and habits said he belonged in the locker room, but time said that's not where he belonged anymore. Instincts and habits can get ornery when time comes down on them."

He nodded, but not as much as I thought he should have. "Yeah, okay. But why the Rosen crime scene in particular?"

"I don't know. One of those emptied places. Who cares?"

"Right. *One* of them. But why that one?"

"You must get straight A's for the sweatbox."

He loosened his tie so perfectly on cue I wondered whether I had taken his after-hours pose too much for granted; even loosened, the tie still had its gleaming sword. "I do all right."

"Somebody close dies, Fox, it doesn't mean you're going to turn into a wailing Greek in the funeral home. Maybe it doesn't hit you for years. You hear a certain word, walk into a certain street. There's an old movie on the tube you saw with the dead person. Whatever. It happened to me on the West Side Highway the night Karen Rosen was killed. End of story."

He didn't believe it, but the glass in his hand reminded him he was a guest. "McGill says Carey's the key."

"The lieutenant isn't here right now."

He nodded with something like grace. "I think he is, too."

"She'll be happy to hear it. Give her back her job."

"That's local business."

"Yeah, right. A blowhard like Wendell, he's going to defend the Alamo against the Feds telling him what to do."

He didn't have an Alfred E. Neuman gap in his teeth; he just gave the impression of having one. "Anyway, we ran the patterns. Came up with a few after Carey that might have been misses, but nothing before the ballpark. Carey gave this guy balls. He pulled that one off, so he got more daring. Ever notice, by the way . . .?"

I refilled my glass so I didn't have to look at him as he was explaining the Professor's escalation theory. I wasn't feeling particularly humble; I just wasn't going to advertise more of the egg Loschen had left on my face when we had been talking about the shooting ranges.

". . . Anyway, that's part of what went into Bronsard. He was in the press box and we don't have anyone else at the other scenes."

"*Nothing* went into Bronsard."

"Except you, you mean?"

"Except me. And so what? Let's just drink off our guilt here for hounding the son of a bitch to death."

"It may be a little more complicated than that."

"It can't be."

"I hope not."

He said it so confidently I knew right away he hadn't just dropped by to talk about my telephone number on Bronsard's desk or the ghosts to be visited on West Side Highway crime scenes.

"I don't even know what's the good news and what's the bad news," he said, shifting up to the couch's higher cushion. "Okay, it's good news for the Bronsard family, I suppose, that we can eliminate him from the shooting at Lieutenant McGill's. I saw him eating and watching the TV myself. But the bad news, Finley, is that the gun used against McGill was a Buckskinner Black Powder Percussion Carbine—the same curio Bronsard has on his wall. What does that say to you?"

"Nothing sensible."

"Right," he said behind another sip. "It's almost like there's someone else living in that house we've missed. Someone who's not at all against the idea of implicating Bronsard."

"You must've . . ."

"The damn thing hasn't been fired since Eisenhower was President. There was a goddamn dead fly in the barrel!"

"Same model, different gun."

"I've never been big on coincidence."

"You're going to have to be. What's the other side? Someone who knew you liked Bronsard for Carey but couldn't blame for Dana? How many millions fit that description?"

"Not too many."

"So, you start counting all the Buckskin rifles in the city . . ."

"Already started."

"And?"

"Started, I said. And there're already too many."

Fagan seemed not to have found any beer in his refrigerator; the slam of the door rattled my teeth. "What are you saying, Fox?"

"Nothing," he shrugged. "Maybe we should just search that house for hidden panels, find some hunchback hiding there."

"Dorsally challenged."

"Dorsally challenged."

I knew where he was going, but I was in no hurry to get there with him. The trouble was, old man Fagan wasn't helping me out.

The loudest thing in the courtyard was hip-hop music somewhere upstairs. "Somebody's playing with you," I said finally.

"Beginning to look that way."

"And?"

If nothing else, my couch was good for getting people to struggle before they could sit with enough leverage to look earnest. "Last time I asked you something that pissed you off."

"Then don't ask it again."

"When you first mentioned your emptied places idea to Lieutenant McGill, was she receptive to it?"

For once I'd hit one: He *was* going after cops. "And for a minute I thought we were having a friendly drink."

"Was she?"

"As a matter of fact, yes." He nodded; he didn't look at all surprised. "Do you guys ever do anything but justify yourselves? I mean, you know what that insinuates, right? You *have* no justification."

"Lots of people circulate in that press box area with credentials of all kinds. It just wouldn't be smart to overlook all the possibilities."

"No, it wouldn't. But sometimes we can get so obsessed with scoring, we miss all the bases going around to home plate."

"We're still not clear on how the investigation ended up in her lap. There were a dozen other candidates. Major Crime, for starters."

"There was a lush problem or something."

"Yeah, that's what we've been told."

"But you don't believe it."

"I believe one of your friend's people is very connected and he may have made a call to Police Plaza."

I didn't like thinking of Herman Loschen in that connection in front of Fox; it seemed to make the cricket a little more aggressive than I was used to thinking of him as being around Dana. "So, what're you asking—how McGill got the case or why hasn't she checked out the guy who claimed he was an FBI agent and then stuck around to shoot Carey?"

"Maybe he was a real FBI agent. We don't rule that out, either."

He was smiling and I was supposed to smile back. I didn't.

"Okay," he said. "We're swinging in the dark."

"No, you're not. You're mainly being superior. We know you have all the money and the technology and the paranoia to use them, Fox. You don't have to keep telling us."

"You could've fooled me tonight when I saw Bronsard on the floor of his living room."

I should have laughed or told him to go fuck himself; my father would have called him a millionaire whining because the bank gave him used bills. But one of the troubles with my drinking was that it usually made me mellow. "For what it's worth, Bronsard had run out of people to care about. There probably hadn't been anybody since his parents died. The stuff he shot at Citi Field was an abstraction. He told me himself. It could've been Carey or a pigeon on the roof. Since he didn't care, he had others tell him how much they cared. Most of them weren't much better than he was, but they let him fake it a little longer, gave him ideas about making all of them together a great statement about the human condition or something. You got to the body too late tonight. Last month one of his neighbors would've gotten to it too late."

He stopped looking sensitive; even his sigh sounded genuinely off-duty. It took him a long moment to nod to himself and put his glass down on the table without finishing it off. "We're going back to Citi Field," he said, standing. "If that's where it started, that's where we'll find him."

"That was McGill's intention before she was benched."

"I told you . . ."

"Yeah, I know. You told me."

He didn't expect me to walk him to the door and I didn't. "And suppose Wendell's hero *is* Davy Crockett?" he asked without turning.

"You can remind him how that turned out," I said.

CHAPTER 41

Ernie DeWitt was said to have preferred pounding the pavement to car patrol in Weeksville because he was from that section of Brooklyn and liked schmoozing with the locals. That was fine during the day when he had shopkeepers, housewives, and school kids to talk to, but he had switched tours for a week because of a rotation jam-up and at night the only people to talk to in the patchwork black neighborhood were saloonkeepers and a couple of gas station workers in the 24-hour places on Atlantic Avenue. This made for longer gabfests with those he came across so that everybody was able to recall some of his last words to them. It was a regular from a bar down the street from the Bethel Tabernacle African Methodist Baptist Church who shortly after midnight found DeWitt bleeding from the neck on the sidewalk, his unfired weapon a couple of feet away. There had been nobody else on the street and it had been too late for a call to 911 to mean anything. According to the Crime Scene people, the cop appeared to have simply been too slow about pulling his weapon against his assailant.

It took several days for the papers to connect Ernie DeWitt to Carey, Leong, and Rosen. The ones that didn't jabber about an aborted mugging or an interrupted drug deal speculated that DeWitt had recognized someone with an outstanding warrant and had made a fool's play in trying to nab him single-handed or had been the target of an anti-cop gang. There were so many theories being attributed to those "reliable sources" that just about everyone with a desk at Police Plaza was covered—another way of saying that panic had set in. If anybody had really been in charge of the rumors, he would have been much thriftier, figuring out pretty fast that the more of them there were, the more likely some enterprising soul—maybe a reporter stationed in Singapore—was going to detect a lot of official confusion.

I stopped counting the people who had seen it coming or should have seen it coming. Even the Professor seemed to number them in the multitudes because he skipped the I-told-you-sos until I was the one to call him. As I had been reminded by my shooting range insights with Loschen, when thousands of geniuses around the world are struck by the same vision at the same time, applying for an originality patent gets tricky. In fact, as much as the latest escalation in a psychopath's version of bravado, what hit me most about the killing was its *obviousness*. I realize that sounds pretty bloodless, especially since the idea came to me while I was watching coverage of DeWitt's sobbing children and widow at the inspector's funeral a few yards away from where his body had been found, but I couldn't shake it. Having played with the city for a while, as Fox had said, the sniper had moved on to having it play with itself, getting it to guess about the *next* step up. Wasn't that supposed to be a game only when it came to guessing the next foreign country to be invaded?

"You're talking about a big hater," Dana said.

"You said it that first night at Da Francesco—North Pole blood."

She glanced down the stadium escalator to where two clowns were getting revved up for the game with a chorus about Houston cowboys and the mares they screwed in the stable. It was the first time we had seen each other since she had been put back on the case and she wore a listlessness from having tried to make up for the lost days; she didn't so much eye the clowns as look mystified as to why they should even be in her sightlines. "The North Pole is cold," she said. "You're talking about vindictive heat."

"Best when served cold, etcetera."

"Or something."

We had been fluttering here and there since I had met her in the Citi Field parking lot. I didn't like paying the lot's pirate rates.

She was sure one of the attendants had a jacket but couldn't remember his name or for what. I could see rain coming to interrupt
the game. Was she wrong or were the Astros the ones with the
orange pajamas? No, they had gotten rid of those ages ago. Oh,
too bad, she had liked them. She hadn't been to a game since her
father had taken her to Yankee Stadium to see that steroids guy
back in the early 1990s. And so on. Neither of us touched on what
had happened to get her back on the sniper investigation and I
was holding off mentioning Fox's latest theory about the shooter.
At the right moment, I thought, I would just casually toss in the
idea the sniper could have been a plumber, a candlestick maker,
or, hey, maybe even a cop!

The escalator left us off at the loge level and she added another
inch of stride to her boots as she followed the sign to the press
box; just because she was bone tired was no reason to show it to
others. There were two guards waiting to intercept intruders at
the ramp—an old black troll who had probably lived in the Flush-
ing Meadows swamps before there had been a stadium and a
potbellied white guy with two chins who reminded me of the silly
son-in-law W.C. Fields always got to invest in beefsteak mines.
When Dana showed them her badge, the old guy wasn't the least
impressed but the goofy one stepped forward immediately. "Lieutenant McGill, right? I'm Larry Grabowski. You questioned me
about that shooting."

"Right. How are you, Larry?"

"This is the woman I was telling you about, Johnny."

Johnny still wasn't awed enough to call for the smelling salts,
not even when Grabowski reminded him the second box to the
left of the out-of-town broadcast booth had been reserved for us;
he was barely up to raising his gnarled hand to move us on. "You
need anything, Lieutenant," Grabowski called after us, "just hol-
ler. I'll be here the whole game."

"Thanks, Larry."

"He's . . .?"

"The one who heard nothing and saw nothing," she nodded.
"He still hadn't when we came back the other day and asked
again."

I'm not the ideal target of sports club owners obsessed with having luxury boxes because if I want to have all the comforts of home for a ballgame, I'll stay at home on my lumpy couch in front of the tube; going to the ballpark is supposed to be going to the ballpark. But for one night I could live with the freebie box with the padded seats and the comfort tables as a change from my usual taste for pigeon roost seats behind home plate. If forced to, I could also deal with a waitress being on call for the beers and hot dogs. But the novelty would have been a lot more satisfying if Dana hadn't made it clear right away she had more on her mind than the Mets' pennant chances by testing the doorstop to make sure of an unimpeded view of the parade going past Larry and Johnny outside. When she dropped her shoulder bag on the chair closest to the door and furthest from the field, I knew I was going to have to handle most of the rooting for the home team.

"Something, in particular, you're looking for?"

"What I've missed so far."

She had given me that identical clipped answer to the identical question on the phone when she had called with her invitation. I didn't know if that made me a nag or made her self-absorption scary, but I couldn't have argued against either possibility. And didn't like it too much. How else to say it but that she was further away than my notions of independence were ready for? It wasn't just the job in general or the pressures she was under to tie up this specific case, but the dumpy image I had of myself first detouring her with leads that seemed to have led only to themselves and now saying fussy things to her from the sidelines. Whether she got anywhere or not, some slimy trickle in my gut said, she had to ignore me just to know one way or the other. When had I ever promised to be *that* charitable when granting independence?

By the fourth inning both of us had learned what we had already known: me that the Mets needed another starting pitcher, Dana that the press box level hosted not only reporters and broadcasters, but season ticket-holders, the friends and acquaintances they had given their tickets to for an evening, celebrities and semi-celebrities, retired ballplayers and other guests of the club, and anyone else in the universe who could flash Larry and

Johnny with the equivalent of a ticket or Dana's badge. She might as well have been standing in the middle of Times Square trying to narrow down the passing tourists by the states they had come from.

Since the advertised waitress service had failed to materialize, I gave both of us a break by going out to the john and then hitting the concession stand for a couple of franks. With the game midway along, Larry had vanished from his post and Johnny was reduced to snarling at the stool that kept rocking under him on the inclined ground. On the other hand, I couldn't see anybody the slightest bit questionable getting past the old guy. He probably had the photograph of every would-be gate-crasher in 40 years pasted to his bedroom wall. Which pretty much left only two possibilities: that Ralph Carey's shooter had already passed inspection as a legitimate press box level guest and had been in the vicinity before the killing or he had had to deal only with hapless Larry Grabowski. I preferred the second choice even before making the mistake of going over to ask Johnny if he had been working the night of the shooting.

"What's it to you? I didn't see *your* badge. Hers I saw, not yours."

My guardian angel told me Johnny wasn't the person to try with my Nassau County shield. "There's a friend of mine you should meet."

"Yeah? Who's that?"

"Name of Vince Galassi."

"I don't know no Vince . . ."

"I know you don't. That's why I should introduce you."

"Don't do me no favors."

"No, no, I think the two of you would really hit it off."

"I got enough friends. Don't need no more."

"No sweat."

"And I'll tell you 'nother thing. If I was here that night, you wouldn't be gettin' complaints about people bein' shot and killed in this place. Don't quote me, but that's a fact."

"Between you and me."

When I got back to the box, I found Grabowski looking very fidgety with Dana. He was all but hopping up and down behind jittery smiles while she was measuring him from her chair as if there were a microscope between them. She didn't look tired anymore. "I would've remembered by now, Lieutenant," he was saying in his golly-gee-whiz tone. "You guys certainly got me thinking about it."

"What about official people, Larry?"

She showed nothing—to him *or* me—and I wondered if I was the only one who had been avoiding talking about Andy Fox.

"Official people?"

"You know. Like a fireman. An inspector coming around to check on the wiring. Something like that."

"No, they do that long before the game starts."

"Okay, no fireman. How about . . .?"

She deserved the Oscar. She drew it out so long that Grabowski was up on the tip of his toes to help her get it out—then caught himself and dropped back down into his shoes. When she finally said "cop," his eyes were out on the field, darting wildly around in search of anybody at all to knock him out with a fastball.

"Something that slipped your mind, Larry?" she pressed quietly.

"No, not really."

"Unreally, then."

The hot dogs were getting cold in my hand and I was still hungry enough to devour both, but nothing in them could have been more delicious and chopped up miserable than Larry Grabowski. "There might have been one guy I forgot," he let out.

"Forgot? How could you forget, Larry? We've been through this so many times since Carey was shot . . ."

He started shaking his arms at his sides like someone who had to get to the john and fast. "But it wasn't anybody you'd think mattered."

"Let's work it this way: You do your job and I'll do mine. So why wouldn't I have thought this person mattered?"

"Because he was a cop! One of you!"

She didn't want to hear another word, and my first thought was that Fox had been by to coach the clown. When the stands suddenly sent up a mass groan at another Houston bat cracking another Mets pitch, she looked out at them for a moment of relief. But then, as little pockets of sarcastic braying went up around the park and somebody in the adjoining box angrily banged a table, she came back to refocus on Grabowski. "Go ahead."

Larry looked at me in appeal but didn't see what he needed. I didn't see Fox trusting him to lie about anything, either. "I'd already given the guy a hard time once," he said to her. "He didn't look like a cop to me. You don't know, Lieutenant. Every game you get wise guys coming around with something they bought in a dime store. Or the newest one—these phony IDs they make on their computers . . ."

"Larry?"

"Yeah, right. Well, I just started feeling like an asshole. Know what I'm saying? First, I'm practically biting his badge to be sure it's real, really insulting him, then, later on, he's asking me official questions about the shooting. I thought he was really nice about it all and I wanted to forget the whole thing. I didn't think you meant somebody like him."

She went straight for the answer she didn't want whatever it was. "And why didn't this cop look like a cop to you?"

"He was so scrawny! I mean I'm not saying everybody has to look one way. But if I see this gentleman here, for instance, and he tells me he's a cop, I'll believe it. But this Detective Loschen, he didn't look like it at all."

Dana was looking in my direction, but she wasn't seeing me. She was so pale I wasn't sure she knew where she was sitting. What wiseass thing had I told the guy at the target range in Coney Island—I liked to think I struck people as a librarian? I wondered what he would have said if I brought Herman down to shoot some of his metal ducks.

CHAPTER 42

The worst part of getting out of the ballpark was the wide, empty ramps. Even the most skeptical Mets fans were still hanging on in the stands with their hopes for the second half of the game and there were no single-file staircases or escalators to negotiate, so Dana and I had to tramp down side by side in unnerving silence. All the way down I could hear the same calculator working in her head as was tallying up the numbers in mine. Herman had been the one to suggest (brag about?) the peek-a-boo angle in the shooting of Carey. Herman belonged to the 107 and could have made a persuasive case with Uncle Edward that his command, his department, and his superior should handle the shooting, keeping everything in his lap. Herman had been up in the Bronsard museum and seen the Buckskinner Carbine on the wall.

"But he can't hit the side of a barn!"

She stood swaying on her heels at the bottom of the ramp defying me to contradict her. I gave it a try. "He's been cramming in private."

"Bullshit! And his Acura's as gray as he is, not red!"

"Then you'll have a little talk with him and he'll clear up everything for you and we'll forget about Larry Grabowski."

Her anger couldn't have been more torrid, so why did it also sound soft in the center? "You really expect me to go tearing up my command because of what that idiot up there said??!! Give him a day or two and he'll be telling people it was you!"

I didn't like the way she was booming or the way a scorecard vendor and a couple of ticket takers were looking over at us from their jaw session at the gate turnstiles. I have nothing against public scenes, but I've also noticed I prefer them when I'm the one causing them. I told her she had a point and kept walking. Accomplishment: I made it to the brilliantly lighted sidewalk outside the gate without her ordering me to stop or be shot. Surprise: When I turned back, she was coming out under the eyes of the vendor and the other leerers lighting a Parliament.

"When did you start that?"

"When I realized other things were going to kill me first. You want to go on the list or you want to say something useful?"

A monkey couldn't have done more chattering. I knew so much about what she was feeling I couldn't wait to share it with her as we stopped and started through the reflected stadium light of the parking lot in the general direction of her car. If Larry Grabowski was right, *of course* she wanted to shiver at the thought that Herman Loschen—the same Herman Loschen who had been working with her every minute of every day—had been the one who had shot at her. If there was anything at all to what Larry Grabowski had said, *of course* Herman Loschen had been mocking her through all the Arthur Thalers, Gary Steins, and Owen Bronsards. *Of course,* it was beyond accepting. She had relied on the guy so much she had asked him to take notes of Carrington's interrogations in her apartment, had made common cause with him against the Feds and the Wendells, had gone out of her way to protect him against any bureaucratic retaliations against her. *Of course,* she wasn't just going to take what Larry Grabowski had said at face value. Nobody in her position would have. And yet she could hardly dismiss it out of hand, either. Who better had summed up her situation than one of the great philosophers? No, not Plato or one of those Germans, but the inimitable Dennis Monaghan. Why had Dennis Monaghan ended up out of pocket two thousand dollars to Johnny Wells? Monaghan couldn't have said it more clearly: Because he had *trusted* the bastard!

Okay, I left out the part about Monaghan. I thought it, but I didn't say it. I'd had more than one vision of my end over the years, but none of them had been about being run over in the Citi Field parking lot. When I finally shut up, she had her car keys in her hand but no lock for fitting them. "I know he wasn't in the office when any of the shootings happened," she said, trying to sound decisive, "but that's the first place to look. Just one overlap and Larry Grabowski can go fuck himself."

I nodded—with another bad thought. And unlike the Monaghan one, she sensed this one across her car roof. "What?"

Also unlike the Monaghan one, this one seemed worth saying. "If there's anything to it, you have to be the one to nail him."

"Meaning what?"

"Meaning you don't want Fox or his friends getting there first."

"What the hell do I care about that? If that son of a bitch is . . ."

"You care, Dana. It's shitty politics and isn't worth a damn in the big world picture, but you care. You don't need them coming in and saying you don't know who's working next to you."

She laughed; incredulously. "Bulletin, Finley: I don't!" She got her door open on the third try, then stalled with a thought. "How did Fox miss this, by the way? He's been back here, too."

That answer I could imagine. "He was too busy looking for something else. How the chain of command shook out."

"You don't say. And how would you know that?"

"That's what those guys do," I said, dusting off another little seat for myself in Purgatory. "The credits, not the movie."

She didn't believe me for a second, but she had already opened up too many fronts to add another. "I'm going to drop by the office."

"Then what?"

"How the hell should I know?"

It was another one of those moments like the day in Beads, Beads, and More Beads when I should have stayed mum about how to extricate Christine Sewell from Johnny Wells; obviously, not even Shari Glynn had taught me anything. "Whatever he handled by himself, that you weren't there for, you're going to have to go back over that ground, too."

"There's nothing like that."

"You sure?"

She leaned in to throw her bag on the seat and came back out with a candidate. "The witness on the West Side Highway who made the red car," she said irritably. "I was still pissed Wendell had let him go home. I knew nothing was going to come out of it, so Herman did that interview himself the next day."

"How far did this guy cut it down? Make? Year?"

"Four-door, that's all I remember. No plate, of course."

"The plate, okay. But if Herman or somebody else rented the car, what about a company tag? Most companies have tags front and back."

She seemed on the verge of saying something exasperated, but then checked herself as an Alitalia from LaGuardia practically used the roof of her car to get going to Europe. "I get your point, okay?"

"Hey, you wanted to start from scratch, didn't you? So here you go."

"Not funny, Finley."

"Let me take that red car."

"No, sir."

"Dana . . ."

"I said no."

"If there's anything at all to this, you can't shake the hive too soon. You'll have plenty on your hands working up an approach to Uncle Edward and keeping Fox away."

She knew it; she had never wanted to be on an Alitalia flight so much in her life. "Tell me it's bullshit, Finley. Tell me Herman had a good reason for not mentioning being up there."

I remembered something idiotic. "The day I brought him the Bronsard interviews, we were sitting in the roll call room and this cop twice his size couldn't get his apple juice out of the machine. Loschen went over and got it out with one smart bang."

"And this Zen moment is brought to us by . . .?"

"Herman doesn't flaunt all his Hermans."

"If you believe Grabowski, that's *all* he's been doing!"

"You know what I mean."

"Yeah, you're as squirrely as the idiot up there. Call you later."

"I'll be outside the station house when you're finished."

"Look, I don't need . . ."

"Yes, you do, Lieutenant. If you find some overlap, we'll go out and have a few drinks on it. If you don't find anything and have to move on to the next square, you'll want to remember it was probably Herman who fired a shot through your window, who might really have a taste not just for killing the Careys and Leongs for fun, but for shaking you up."

After such a big speech, I still stood watching her Chevy wind toward the exit gate too long, not moving toward my car until her tail lights dipped down into Roosevelt Avenue under the El. An American Airlines plane went overhead. The stadium stanchions seemed unmoved by the roar that suddenly went up from the crowd. I couldn't remember the last time I had walked out on a game before it was over, let alone only halfway through. The only excuse for it, I thought, would be nailing Herman Loschen.

CHAPTER 43

I spotted her car across the street from the station house and for some reason found my own space a few doors down. It wasn't late enough for the street to be asleep, but most of the houses I could see had only one room light going. Every front yard on either side of the block seemed to belong to the Violets of the Month Club, and the sweet aroma was even stronger at night than during the day.

I spent the next hour having one bad thought after another. One was that Loschen had practically confessed to me with his story about his old man and his constant endorsement of my emptied places. Another was that we were jumping the gun on Loschen just as we had on Bronsard and that everything that seemed reasonable at the moment was going to look like a lot of destructive posturing in the morning. The worst of them was that Herman hadn't just gotten Dana into a bind incidentally, but had worked up his whole terror campaign around her from the start. When she walked out of the precinct, I told my Bad Angel, I wanted her to have paper not only exonerating him from the killings for time reasons but documents proving that he wasn't the creep of creeps, that he had seven Mormon wives and 20 children all of whom he loved deeply. I was definitely not in the mood for the little puppy scampering around the Lieutenant at work and turning into a rabid mastiff in her name after hours. Among other things, that would have made me a more likely candidate for the shot fired across Jane Street and that possibility was supposed to have been only a wisecrack.

When Dana finally did come out, she had folders sticking up from her shoulder bag. For a second she stood uncertainly on the top step of the entrance looking up and down the street. I blinked my lights. She started, but then nodded, and crossed over to her car. I had a sinking feeling the folders she was carrying had made her hesitate at the door not just because she hadn't seen me right away, that she had graduated from the dismay and anger back at the ballpark to simply being spooked. For what it was worth, I didn't see any gray *or* red Acuras parked nearby.

I followed her west down Union Turnpike without the slightest idea where she was going. The bars around St. John's University didn't appeal to her, neither did a couple of fast food outlets further along. Just as I was beginning to resign myself to tailing her all the way into her apartment in the Village, she found what she had been looking for on Queens Boulevard, in the dimmest of neighborhood saloons. I had griped about the gin mill where I had gone with the Professor? This one didn't have to worry about the right kind of stools; it was barely lighted enough to make out the bar. The skels spread around the freezing hole might have been miners waiting to be rescued from a cave-in.

Dana had taken a table for her beer under the only wall light in the back. The bartender thought he was being cute when he tilted his head back to her to ask if I should be allowed to take my club soda over to her. She gave him a bug-off smile, but he got something like a growling laugh from one of the skels.

She had washed her face; I wanted to think dirt, not tears. "There were perfectly nice litter baskets you passed to come here."

"It suits my mood."

"So?"

"So, there was no overlap."

"You didn't need an hour to find that out."

She eyed her beer as if it had sneaked onto the table in front of her. "My Inbox was bulging. Ballistics confirms that cop in Brooklyn, DeWitt, was killed with the same bullet as the others. Everybody's escalation theory is in full working order."

"I'm sorry."

"Don't be. At least we know why DeWitt was killed. Which is, of course, knowing we don't know why."

"Calm down."

"I'm perfectly calm. No PMS or anything."

"Good. You're calm, I'm calm, the skels at the bar are calm."

"Captain Wendell would like to see me tomorrow, please call in the morning for an appointment."

"Oh. Pomp and ceremony."

"Exactly. I'm sure he'll have three people standing around him, each one of them with a recorder to swear I was told I'm not doing my job so it isn't Wendell's fault the whole goddamn New York City Police Department is being shot out from under him."

"Now you're being uncalm again." My eye caught the word CORSO on one of the folder tabs in her bag. "And what else?"

"Isn't that enough?"

"Not for all the time you were up there."

Instead of going for her beer, she reached over to my club soda and drank half the glass in a swallow. "The range scores," she said. "I'd forgotten they really weren't as bad as some of the snide cracks said until the beginning of last year. He was never Olympic team material, but he fell off so much he was sent for an eye test. When the doctor said there was no deterioration, I suppose I racked it up to just a bad day at the range he'd correct next time around. For some reason, that day never came."

"You're not that sloppy an administrator."

"What do you want me to say? I have my insecurities."

"And Herman's never been one."

"Just the opposite," she said evenly. "Okay?"

"Then the question becomes what happened 15 months ago to make his hand so unsteady. He go on a toot?"

"I guess I'm going to have to find out. Meanwhile, Anthony Corso."

"Who's Anthony Corso?"

"A landscaper in Bronxville who worries about putting his kids to bed without seeing police stations and finds it odd cops should be calling him after nine o'clock. Don't we have office hours, or what?"

"And Anthony Corso told Loschen . . .?"

She found a ringlet of hair above her left ear and began working it. "He was definite was Mr. Corso that he'd seen a rental agency sign on the back of the red car. He remembered because it was some agency in Jamaica and he's from Jamaica and never heard of it. Even though he hasn't been there in years, he likes to keep up on the old neighborhood. He figured it had to be one of those gypsy kinds of outfits. You know the kind. They're usually run by what they call mi-nahr-ities."

"And none of this was in Herman's report." The faster twirling of her curl seemed like answer enough. "So not Hertz or any of the biggies."

"He would've remembered that, Corso said. Some plain name but one that didn't mean anything to him."

"Plain."

"Plain. Acme Cars, like that."

"Meaning you've already looked it up?" She nodded. "So? Is that what it's called—Acme Cars?"

"There are two candidates. One is Acme and the other one is Daily Rentals. I ignored the illegal telephone hours in the Corso household and called him back. He couldn't say for sure. Could've been either one. I had to remember he had a restless kid in the car, then there was the shot and Rosen's sudden veering not to crash. So much to do and so little time for doing it. Fuck him, too."

She stared down at the flat beer she hadn't really wanted. She might have been drawing pictures with it: images of the Lieutenant who hadn't looked too closely at a serial killer because she had had his devotion.

"How about a friend instead of a worshipper?"

"I thought you were already both."

"Corso's one folder. What else you got in there I'll find helpful?"

Down to it, she hated giving in. "Look."

The first folder was a stack of transcripts. "My bedtime reading. The interviews at Citi Field after Carey. The other one."

It was a copy of Loschen's personnel file. The photo looked about ten years old, but the eyes had the familiar wool-gathering gaze. Aside from the periodic fitness reports, there was only the most uninformative boilerplate under it. Herman had a living mother, two living sisters, and a dead father. He had gone to school, had gone to another school, and had been recommended for the Academy by Uncle Edward, an Uncle Martin with the Transit Police, and an Uncle George with the Corrections Department. He had graduated from the Academy, had done six months with NSU 8 in the Bronx, had moved on to the 105 in Queens South, then over to the 107. He had a couple of commendations that might have been for supplying the strudel for a precinct Christmas party, never been involved in any heavier arrest than a grand larceny, had never been forced to fire his weapon. His psych profile ("no apparent tendencies detrimental to the performance of his duties") could have described a fire hydrant. Friends, hobbies, and organization memberships didn't exist. "This thing looks scrubbed."

"Doesn't it, though!" she said, finally letting go of her hair.

"So, what's Uncle Edward expunged?"

"Obviously, everything personal, including the father's suicide. He's a cipher, Finley, and Uncle Edward seems to like it that way."

"Nobody's this much of a cipher."

"Know something? At this point, I don't give a damn if he's been shooting these people for psychological or astrological reasons. I'm judging his candidacy on its own merits. Is or isn't the sniper the nephew of Uncle Edward, Uncle Martin, and Uncle George? The rest can wait."

"Okay, okay. I can hit the car agencies in the morning. You should put off Wendell for the late afternoon."

"I'm not going to schedule him at all until I hear from you," she said tartly. "And then depending on the answer you give me, I might need you downtown to help me with a wire job."

"That's not going to help, Dana. You think Wendell's . . .?"

She could have lifted the table with the metal in her eyes. "I'm not talking about Wendell. You place Herman at one of those car rental places, I'm going to be talking to Uncle Edward while he's still digesting his lunch. *That's* what I want on tape. I don't know what I'm walking into here, Finley. For all I know, the whole goddamn family gets its kicks shooting the electorate. Even if they don't, Uncle Edward is not going to like his nephew spitting on the family crest and isn't going to buy it just because I have suspicions. And even if he has to buy it, that doesn't have to be great for the good guys, either. Bundle Herman quietly off to the country and tell the *Post* McGill's been taken off the case because the job proved too much for her. Ain't gonna happen. Follow?"

I followed. And wondered why I had been worried about her.

CHAPTER 44

The easiest part was the rental agencies. I never got to Acme because I went first to a hole-in-the-wall storefront on Hillside Avenue, only a couple of blocks away from where Arthur Thaler had exploded. A silver sign announcing DAILY RENTALS on a blackened-out window made it anybody's guess if they were renting cars, movies, or hookers, but inside was another story. Six or seven desks had been crammed behind a reception counter, with telephones buzzing and computers clattering all over the place. Every inch of wall space was covered by rate estimates or blown up photos of some African prince on one of those wicker throne chairs. The prince must have known something about his employees because his gaze over them wasn't all that benevolent. In Ghana, Nigeria, or wherever, he looked as warm and cuddly as Donald Trump.

The young woman working the counter wore a rose dashiki and had spilled a bottle of silver glitter over her eyes. She also had that happy-to-be-of-service smile city agency employees have been trying for years to get down right. "And who would this gentleman be?" she asked brightly when I showed her Loschen's photo.

"One of your customers a couple of weeks back. On the 12th, to be exact. We just have to confirm he was in the car he said he was."

More happiness. "*We?*"

"Oh, sorry." I showed her the Nassau County shield; for once, it dazzled. She looked at me with a respect somebody had once told her to save for special occasions and went over to a file box at the end of the counter. "A red Acura."

"I remember that one." A bald, paunchy guy with a spotted scalp stood up from the desk closest to the counter and, as though eavesdropping on the woman was standard practice, all but pushed her away from the file box to do the digging himself. She smiled at me not to worry about his manners—as good a reason as any to worry about them.

"The 12th, right," he said, finding the slip he was looking for. "Took it for only three hours."

"That's why you remember it?"

"No," he said, taking a stiffer look at me. "What's this gentleman in the middle of?"

"Let's be sure we're talking about the same gentleman. Loschen? First name Herman?"

"Could be. But you haven't told me the problem here."

"Nothing that'll get you in trouble."

Some of the desk people were deciding I was more interesting than whoever they had in their ears. The paunchy guy thought I was funny. "The thought never occurred to me, sir," he said, now booming like a politician at an election rally. "We rent vehicles to legally licensed drivers in need of them, we don't cater to trouble."

"Then tell me why you remembered this rental and I'll be gone."

It was like the U.S. Open: The woman in the dashiki and the two others behind her at desks swiveled their heads over to their boss's side of the net. He needed to think about it but finally relented. "Because I left for the night right after he brought the car back," he said. "Had to be just after ten o'clock. He was about a half-block ahead of me going up to 144th Place. That's where he'd parked a gray Acura. Whatever he needed our car for between seven and ten I don't want to know."

"But you keep track of the mileage."

He thought about some legal advice he had once gotten, but then just glanced at the slip. "Not very far. Brooklyn and back. Manhattan and back. Something like that."

I thanked him and asked to use the office telephone to tell Dana. His idea of a yes was to return to his desk and leave it up to the counterwoman to decide one way or the other. She handed me a cellphone that might have belonged to the office or just been hers; she was happy to do that, too.

Dana was at home, hadn't gone to work yet. She didn't sound knocked out by what I reported. When I told her I was thinking of going over to the second place, Acme, to see if Loschen had rented from them on the 11th, the night of the near-miss on the QBE Herman had mentioned, she said it wasn't necessary. In fact, she had been so sure of what I was going to turn up she had already made an appointment with Uncle Edward.

That was my first surprise and had me second-guessing her all the way into Manhattan to her apartment. The second surprise was when she let me into the apartment in jeans and a sports bra where the blonde with blue lipstick, introduced as Detective Alice Kaufman, was amid helping her wire up. Both had Parliaments going.

"Kaufman will be with you," Dana said. "This isn't the moment to economize on credible witnesses."

Whatever Kaufman had been told didn't make her greet me as a fellow conspirator. In boots, a leather jacket, and a scarf tied around her throat, she looked like one of those barnstorming pilots who communed only with the clouds and God. The one time her eyes drifted in my direction as she checked the wire around Dana told me that in her opinion three was definitely a crowd. "Suppose I got another answer at the car rental place?"

"You weren't going to." She nodded over to one of the Citi Field interview transcripts on the coffee table. "My bedtime reading."

It was the interrogation of a reporter who had apparently been the last one to speak with Carey. The guy had been shuffling out after the game and had seen Carey waiting alone in his box. The passage underlined by a green Magic Marker said:

A: We'd talked a little during the game and I asked him if he was going out for a drink. He said yeah and laughed. He said he and [Mets announcer] were going out for a couple of malted milks. That's what he called it—going out for malted milks.

She was waiting for my reaction. "It's an expression," I said to her. "Carey's generation, when they were being coy about drinking."

"But the wrong expression in the wrong place at the wrong time if you're Herman Loschen."

"So, after all these years he just snapped at being reminded . . .?"

"That's the way it is with ciphers, I guess."

"You're looking for things, Dana."

"Yes, I am. And guess what? It's not the worst way to proceed."

I wasn't going to have an argument with her in front of Kaufman. In fact, she wasn't going to argue with me alone or in front of anyone on the planet Earth. "Herman in the office?"

"I told him to go through all of DeWitt's arrests. You didn't know that was the knee-jerk solution of the brass to keep people on the sidelines?"

Kaufman laughed dutifully, but I heard the tremor in Dana's voice as she took another unconvincing puff before stubbing out the cigarette. She was so far out in the middle of the river she didn't dare think about anything except swimming. I told myself to shut up.

When Dana went into the bedroom to test her mike, it came through in stereo in the earpieces Kaufman and I were wearing. We spent another few minutes talking about distances and dead areas around City Hall Park, where Uncle Edward had agreed to meet. "One last thing," Dana said, sticking her shirttail under her jeans and buckling her belt. "He saw you up here that night. So, if we end up walking somewhere, you stay out of his field of vision. Alice will handle it."

For that, Kaufman indulged a blue-lipped smile at me.

CHAPTER 45

We went ahead in Kaufman's car and found a parking space near the Woolworth Building in view of most of the park benches. The only thing I learned on the drive was that Kaufman had been assigned to the 107 to replace the Indy 500 ace Ronnie Hersh. Other than that, she said nothing and seemed to expect the same from me. But once we were parked, the silence became a bit much. "You think the Lieutenant's wrong?" I asked.

Alice Kaufman unzipped her black leather jacket and slumped back against her door with a more distant measure of the lunchtime workers hustling along Broadway. She had spoon-shaped cheekbones, a lot of curls in her hair, and probably hadn't missed a gym session in years. The clothes and the lipstick said she wouldn't have minded being noticed more than she thought she was. "We'll see where it goes."

"But you're not shocked by the idea."

"No?"

"No."

"You say so."

"Okay, I'll say so."

"Look, Finley, I don't know Loschen. I'm there less than two weeks as a sub for Hersh. Probably why the looey tapped me for this. All I know about Herman is he hasn't left me in a bad place the things we've worked on together. A nerd? Some people call that just being shy. For sure he's got brains. In some companies, he'd probably be raking in millions. But Herman, he likes being a cop and has the relatives to say great, Herman, go to it. More than that I don't know."

"But you're still not shocked by the idea."

"Put enough effort into it and you can believe anything. In McGill's place, I would've turned the whole thing over to IA. But it's her call."

She saw Uncle Edward first, coming down the far Park Row side of the park. He wore Police Plaza mufti: a sharp blue suit that minimized the bulges, a blue shirt, and gray-red silk tie. He also walked like someone who did it regularly for exercise. "He's early," she said.

"One of those walkers who doesn't know his own speed."

She did an odd thing—she giggled. "They sound dangerous."

I relaxed, only then realizing I had to. Kaufman's blasé cynicism had been an extra knot on the rope around me. "They're all over," I said, watching the well-groomed little man try to be subtle about searching the benches for Dana. "People who run so fast they take it for granted everybody's keeping pace with them. They get where they're going and then wonder why it took you so long."

She turned her dry smile to an old-timer cadging coins from a passing tourist couple. "I'm what you'd call a little slow in rat games."

"Everybody's good at them when they have to be."

"That a test question?"

Dana crackled in our ears with a One-Two-Three test before I went further down my stupid road. A second later I saw her scooting across Broadway to where it converged with Park Row at the tip of the park. She zeroed in on Uncle Edward before he spotted her. Her final mike test sounded like a prayer to Jesus, Mary, and Joseph. Edward tried not looking surprised at having her come up behind him, but plainly didn't like it.

"Thank you for coming, sir."

"This better be important, Lieutenant."

"Yes, sir, it is. Would you like to sit?"

"Just get to it. I'm assuming this has to do with concrete leads in the investigation, not some internal matter."

"I wouldn't bother you about that, sir."

"Good to hear. Well?"

Hands flattened in his jacket pockets, he began moving leisurely away from the tip of the convergence and back in the direction of City Hall. She stepped ahead of him just enough to steer him within the benches path, and he was old school enough not to contradict the woman, even the inferior employee kind. I had never seen her clasp her hands behind her back before, like some old man strolling on a boardwalk, and hoped it wasn't her idea of avoiding accidents with the mike. If Edward had any sensors at all, he would have picked it up.

"I've got to ask you one very sensitive question, sir."

"Only one?"

"I've been assuming all along this investigation was thrown my way in part because of your nephew . . . No, no, this has nothing to do with Captain Wendell or anybody else. I'd just like to know off the record whether Detective Loschen spoke to you about it after the Carey shooting."

"Herman? He might have. He was at the ballpark that night. He had a sense of the crime scene. He spoke highly of you. I wouldn't be candid, Lieutenant, if I didn't say he may have been a little *too* flattering. There are many people, not all of them named Wendell, who believe our investigation began going wrong right there."

"I agree with them, sir."

"You do?"

Kaufman looked at me with a sickly expression. I told myself I would have said the same thing. And didn't believe it.

"I think it was meant to go wrong right there."

"What the hell are you talking about, McGill?"

"I believe the shooter may be one of us. A cop."

A cement truck grinding every gear it had rumbled past us, and I had the urge to cover my ears so Edward wouldn't hear it coming from Dana's chest. Kaufman just looked annoyed at the interference.

"You wouldn't be talking about my nephew, would you?"

"There are questions we have, sir."

"Let's stick to English. It'll save time."

"Detective Loschen rented a red Acura from a fly-by-night outfit in Jamaica. Their records indicate he used it for only three hours the night of the Rosen shooting."

"So?"

"The rental hours cover the time Rosen was shot . . ."

The more she explained, the more inept it sounded and the less I liked her leading with my morning visit to Queens. There had been more than that, hadn't there? But for the moment I couldn't remember what it was.

". . . The rifle used at the shooting at my house . . ."

I didn't get the order at all. I would have led up to the car rental, not started with it. She shouldn't have tossed in the rifle as an item in the middle of the list: It had almost killed *her*, hadn't it? And besides, I still hadn't heard a good explanation for using it in the first place.

"You're really serious!"

"I'm trying to do this right, sir. And I'm not the only one who's gotten to this point in the investigation."

Kaufman looked as flabbergasted as Edward sounded. I hadn't expected the Fox card; she hadn't even hinted at it.

"Since when are you privy to what the FBI is doing?"

"We're supposed to be cooperating, aren't we? Besides, there are also private investigations under way headed in the same direction."

I showed Kaufman my best Mount Rushmore. Here I was accusing her of being capable of selling out people and Dana was the one shooting me down the river into the rapids.

"What I'm suggesting is that Detective Loschen answer a couple of questions, ideally this afternoon. I think you should be there for it."

"What's she doing, Finley?"

Only one thing occurred to me. "Don't you watch those poker games on TV? This is the part where one of the players stands up, shoves all his chips into the middle of the table, and says 'All in.'"

Except that the two of them had gone behind a tree and I couldn't see which one of them was standing more cockily.

"Loyalty doesn't seem to mean very much to you, Lieutenant."

"I don't think it's more important than the job at hand, no."

"How laudable! Boy, did my nephew misread you! I could've had him transferred to something more visible a dozen times. But he liked you and the Garden of Eden, wanted to stay right where he was. I guess he didn't know the snake was a woman, too."

I wanted to slide under the dashboard, but I thought Kaufman would have beaten me to it. She settled for rubbing her palm across her knee.

"How about the beginning of last year—was that one of the times you suggested Detective Loschen might need a transfer?"

"What's that got to do with anything?"

"Trying to establish a timeline, sir."

"For what?"

"He's not answering," Kaufman muttered. "What's so important about the beginning of last year?"

I didn't dare say. I didn't want to hex what Dana knew Edward was sitting on—her last frail doubt about Herman Loschen.

"What I'm asking, sir, is whether you proposed a transfer to Detective Loschen around the time his range scores went south."

Kaufman got it, but Edward didn't want to. "Your tone is becoming offensive, Lieutenant. If you can't find this maniac, it's really not an option to start chewing your own ass and blaming fellow investigators."

"Then I'll just say it, sir. If you proposed something concrete to your nephew about a year-and-a-half ago, his response was to sabotage his own standing by making a mess out at the range. There may have been other things he did, too. I haven't had time to check them yet. But one way or another, he was determined not to leave the 107."

They reappeared from behind the trees at the end of the lane at the back of City Hall. Dana still had her hands cupped behind her back. Edward had a misty look in his eyes as he scratched his temple and looked past her. He had begun to hear what she was saying.

"Manhattan South."

"Sir?"

"We were down to the paperwork. Then the scores came up. I don't know how, but they suddenly became a big issue. Was I sure I wanted to expose my nephew to all the whisperings, especially with two other candidates ahead of him on the merits? I considered it even he wasn't restricted to desk duty until they straightened him out at the range."

"Sir, it wouldn't surprise me if Detective Loschen himself blew up the range story so it would have the effect it did."

"You have no proof of that!"

"Not right now, no."

"And even if you did, what? He didn't want to be transferred because he's lazy, has no ambition, has gotten used to the easy duty out there?"

"No, sir."

"Oh, right. Because now he's a serial killer suspect."

"At the moment, a person of interest."

"You're out of your mind, McGill."

"I realize what it means talking to you like this."

"You damn well better!"

"Yes, sir."

He turned away from her as though she might disappear if he gave her enough time with his back to her. But she was still there when he turned back, and his voice was quieter. "Why he didn't accept the transfer—is that what all this lurid conjecture is based on? Just that?"

"It's one question of several we've developed."

"Ah! You haven't just been sitting out there polishing your toenails and banging that ex-cop, you've been *developing* things! And I suppose this Paul Finley is one of these *investigators* who's decided a member of the Department has been behind these shootings?"

It was her chance to push me right through the rapids and over the waterfall, but she didn't take it. "I don't think that's helpful, sir."

"Then I'll ask you, Lieutenant: Why didn't he want a transfer?"

That answer I knew: Because Herman Loschen wasn't in love with his seven Mormon wives and 20 children.

CHAPTER 46

My cat Bandito had had more tricks than planting his paws in his food and water dishes. Another favorite was grabbing a careless sparrow in the backyard and, after breaking its neck, proudly trotting over to show my parents how neatly he had clamped it between his teeth. Ralph Carey, Michael Leong, Karen Rosen, and Ernie DeWitt had been Herman Loschen's trophies for Dana. They were tribute, vanity, and obsession rolled into one. She had been right that first night at Da Francesco about having been set up for a fall. But it hadn't been by Uncle Edward, Wendell, or anyone else above her, it had been by twisted Herman, and probably not even he would have copped to it as his intention.

Dana had laid out enough that Uncle Edward couldn't dismiss her. But he hadn't risen as high as he had by accepting a back seat to his juniors, either. Instead of agreeing to go back to her office to confront Herman then and there, he whipped out his cellphone and tried to look like he was back in charge as he stabbed out a number. The brief static in my ear might have been Dana gurgling in protest.

"Herman? It's me. Free for lunch? . . . Those files will still be there when you get back. Your lieutenant won't miss you for a couple of hours. Meet me at Gianni's on Gold Street. Say an hour . . . Then use a siren and get through the traffic! I'll be waiting. The usual table."

"You got to give the old fart credit," Kaufman said as Edward clapped his phone back into his pocket.

"Yeah? Why?"

"At the very least he knows he's got an administrative problem on his hands with the looey. That's not going to do much for him with the boys at the Big Brass Club. And if it's worse than that, if his nephew's what McGill says? But there he is, still standing out there on the burning deck issuing orders to everybody."

"I've been on that ship. Everybody ends up in the drink."

Kaufman looked at me in disapproval as Edward and Dana started over to the curb, to cross Park Row. He took it for granted Dana would follow without objection. Dana took it for granted she had shot her bolt for the time being. Kaufman took it for granted there would always be a chasm between a working cop and an ex-cop.

"You realize, Lieutenant, there's an explanation for all this. Not one I'm particularly proud of, I'm sorry to say because my sister's children have always been a little low in the energy department. But you're going to owe me an apology for your little fantasy."

"I hope so, sir."

"And right now, I'm not ready to accept it."

We waited until they crossed Park Row and slipped down Beekman before we moved after them. For the next hour and a half, we sat in the car on Beekman, around the corner from the Italian restaurant Uncle Edward and his nephew seemed to know intimately. We didn't fall in love exactly, especially when she started streaming Parliament smoke around the car and nervously clicking her Bic, but compared to what was going on inside at the back table in Gianni's, Kaufman and I became soulmates. At first, there were only long silences, background laughter from other tables, and small talk with the restaurant manager. Then there was Uncle Edward's officious cross-examination of Dana's work on the case. Somehow she managed it without mentioning Loschen except as somebody who had done this and that with the rest of her team. Then, as the 90-minute mark passed, he began dropping in more allusions to Herman as one of the nephews and nieces he had tried his best to "straighten out." Dana's only reply seemed to be pouring more mineral water into her glass. At least until she said: "Maybe you can phone him and find out how close he is."

"There's traffic at this hour." Even with the restaurant wall between us, his voice sounded shaky. "All right, let's get this nonsense over with. I can't sit around here all afternoon."

Kaufman flexed her knee, wincing as the blood returned to her leg. I would have traded her that for the briefs pinching the hell out of my crotch.

"Answer the phone, goddamn it!"

"He may be in a dead zone, sir."

"Right. Order a glass of wine if you want."

"No, thank you."

"We're taking up one of their best tables. Should get something. A cheese platter, maybe? They have good cheese."

"He's losing it, Finley."

"Close."

"How long they going to give it?"

I would have bet not another minute, but Uncle Edward was made of sterner stuff, giving it 20. Then even he had enough motivation to call the 107 squad room and hear that Loschen had hurried off as soon as he had been summoned almost two hours ago. His next call was to his own office, to make sure he hadn't been playing telephone tag. He had been—sort of.

"What're you talking about? *Who* asked you that? . . . And you told him yes? . . ."

The phone cover was closed impatiently again. "Somebody called my office to ask whether I had gone to lunch with you. My secretary says it sounded like Herman."

There was a long moment, then: "He's running, sir. He has to be. Where would he go?"

"You're taking a lot on yourself, McGill."

"I didn't want it this way any more than you. But we need answers."

"Yes."

"I suggest we drop around to his apartment."

"Yes."

"Stay off the radio as long as we can."

"We're hardly to that point."

But they were. And once they had taken Dana's car over to Loschen's apartment on East 11th Street and got no answer from the downstairs bell, they were past it. Edward's last gasp was a call on the sidewalk to his sister. Whatever he heard on the phone didn't calm him.

"All right, Lieutenant," he said, barking to the end. "I'm sure you've gone through his personnel file. If you can't find him through anything there, we'll go to an APB. But I will give that order personally."

"Yes, sir."

"Call me by five at this number."

He showed her his phone screen, leaving it to her to grab for a notepad and write it down. She swung her body around so hard to get at the pad in her pocket I had a vision of the mike falling out of her bra. But it stayed there until she finished writing and he started up the street toward Second Avenue. Either she had let him go deliberately or had to win a debate with herself; one way or the other, it came out as a rabbit punch.

"I really won't find anything through his personnel file, sir."

"Excuse me?"

She waited until a woman pushing a baby carriage went by. Even in those three seconds, he seemed to wilt a little, knowing what was coming. "There's nothing to find there. We both know that."

He came all the way back to her, hating every step. "You really have no sense of your boundaries, do you, McGill?"

"A lot of people are going to be thumbing through that file in the days ahead. Shouldn't it be a little more complete?"

"That's not my jurisdiction."

"Computers are computers, sir. And then you have printers that don't always kick out the copies they should. Those kinds of accidents happen. But there are going to be a lot of questions about the blank that's Herman's personnel file right now."

He looked up and down the street as if searching for a heavy truck. But he didn't know who he wanted to throw under it: Dana, nephew Herman, or himself. "Sometimes being a blank is more useful than being who you are," he finally spat.

Kaufman reached for another cigarette, but I got one out of the box before she did. My hand was shaking, and I knew it wasn't only because of the toasty relations within the Loschen family. Uncle Edward was a master of understatement: From some pit in my mind, a fiend yelled out that being a blank could *always* seem more useful than being who you were.

Kaufman looked at me oddly as she flicked her lighter at my cigarette. "You all right?"

"Never better."

"Useful, sir?"

"You heard me. If we were forced just to work with Herman's facts, he'd be a night watchman on a landfill."

Even a quarter of the way down the block, I could feel her dismay. I wouldn't have known what to say to her if she had been sitting alongside me instead of Kaufman. "He's had involvements, experiences. Good ones, bad ones. Something that might have . . ."

"And you want to have them all down on one piece of paper. You want your little clues to what could have turned him into what you're accusing him of being. I don't blame you for that, Lieutenant. Everybody likes neatness. I myself am tempted to think it started with that spineless brother-in-law of mine who made the kid responsible for his suicide. But that's neither here nor there now. That kind of thing has nothing to do with the job. A cop proves himself out on the firing line, not in his causes and effects, not in whatever special bug he's got swimming around in his mind. Why be limited by that garbage? Is it going to help him when he finds himself in an alley some night with two thugs?"

"I don't think that's even in question, sir."

"Oh, you don't!"

"No, sir."

"So, you're looking at the head of the caveman clan right now."

"I don't think you should have touched those records."

"Did I say I did?"

"For starters, your shame may not be somebody else's."

"And there's the rub, isn't it, McGill? Maybe it should have been. Then I wouldn't have to be standing here with you right now hearing you feel more superior to me every time you open your mouth."

He went back up toward Second Avenue. Dana watched him a moment, then looked down in our direction and shook her head. She might have seen us, she might not have. She would have shaken her head at some god in the sky, anyway. I was sure I'd introduced her to a lot of them.

A few minutes later I returned to civilian life. Dana took off directly for her office, Kaufman dropped me off at my car and then also headed back to Queens. They couldn't have accomplished very much for the rest of the afternoon because a bulletin about the search for Queens Detective Herman Loschen broke into the evening news. Then there was the commissioner "regretfully confirming" that Loschen was being sought as what Dana had said—"a person of interest." Nobody said a word about Uncle Edward, who stood with Wendell, Fox, and assorted waxworks from the Police Museum in the rear while the commissioner dodged follow-up questions. Dana was nowhere to be seen, but her name was mentioned twice as the "lead investigator." Uncle Edward had the look of someone wondering how the second sledgehammer blow would feel.

I suppose I shouldn't have felt good about anything. There were still the four victims, along with whatever fuses Loschen had helped light in Arthur Thaler and Owen Bronsard. And that was without including the hole through Dana's window and my there-but-for-the-grace-of-God moment on 11th Street. But I did feel good for her. She had negotiated an obstacle course that absolutely everybody, including me, had set down in her path and come out the other end bruised and battered but standing tall. I thought of her sitting on the edge of my bed after we had made love after the shootout with Thaler: She had been shaking up and down with every reason to be crying, but in fact, she had been laughing. And apologies to the Carey, Leong, Rosen, and DeWitt families, but I liked it that she was.

It's always a hex to laugh too soon.

CHAPTER 47

Caller ID was supposed to insulate you against the worst. Even if you had to answer the phone, you had seconds of cushioning for dealing with people who wanted a piece of your soul or all your money. When Dana's cellphone number flashed just as I was going to bed, I jumped to the thought that the hunt for Loschen had brought her to Bay Ridge and that she wanted to crash for the night. A second later, I was the one doing the crashing.

"I would like to see you."

I wasn't without experience talking to lunatics. Winston Lewis, for one, had been enough experience for a lifetime. But the Winston Lewis who had held a gun to the head of a nine-year-old girl in a Valley Stream school cafeteria had been a shrill screamer who wanted to be sure I knew he was serious. And the louder he had gotten and the more he had heard the panic breaks in his own voice, the more doubts had crept into his head about how he wanted things to end. Herman Loschen had nothing like that in his voice. He might have been calling to ask me out for a beer.

"People are looking for you, Herman."

"That's not the first thing you thought of."

"So, you stole McGill's phone before you took off."

"Really?"

I stopped the sudden lava flow from going into my chest. It swamped the hairs of my arms and my legs, but I refused to let it go further. You gave up the dispensable, not the vital, so it was an absolutely dispensable fact that I had called Dana on her cellphone from the Jamaica car rental agency, long before Loschen had vanished and before she had returned to her office. To have her phone he had to have her.

"You understand the situation now?"

Old Academy lessons kicked in. He was textbook: He wasn't going to use my name because that would have given me an existence he didn't want me to have. I wasn't supposed to give him anything but replies to what he said, keep him on whatever still passed for his even keel. But the trouble was, I didn't give a shit about textbooks. *I* was Winston Lewis. I wanted to rage at everybody, even nine-year-old school children. Knowing how the lunatic had been obsessed with Dana, how could they have let her walk around so vulnerable? And she was no better. How did an armed police officer let him get so near and—apparently— overpower her?

"What do you want, Herman?"

"I want you to come to Rodman's Neck. They've got the place pretty locked down by now. But they'll let you through. I've warned them what'll happen if they don't."

"Proving what?"

There was a long moment, then: "Is it important to know that?" he asked, sounding genuinely stumped.

"I want to speak to Dana."

"Don't take more than an hour."

"I said I want to speak to . . ."

It wasn't my moment for insisting. I was dressed and out of the house three minutes after he had disconnected us. In the elevator, Rodman's Neck felt like Los Angeles. It didn't get any closer in my car. Up in Pelham Bay Park near City Island, the place had been the NYPD range for decades. Anyone authorized to carry a firearm and wear a uniform on the East Coast had been there at one time or another. I could have done without it as the scene for Loschen's last stand. Worse than the setting for his personal embarrassments, it had been the setting for his *deliberate* personal embarrassments. Slyness was now demanding recognition, and that didn't promise anything good for anybody.

It was better to think of Anybody than of Dana.

I had another Monaghan Choice at the Belt. I could have gone toward Manhattan, across the Kosciusko Bridge, and through Queens up to the Bronx, or I could have gone away from the city, from the Belt to the Van Wyck to the Whitestone. Why change the distancing tactics that had been working so spectacularly the last couple of weeks? I headed east away from Manhattan toward the Van Wyck.

For once I hadn't forgotten my gun, which clinched how useless it would be. All the way up to the Bronx I tried to picture the wooden range barracks Loschen had probably boarded himself up in. From what I remembered, there were any number of them without windows or with an easily watched single window, leaving only a narrow entrance door. The nimblest SWAT team in the world couldn't have rushed in without leaving time for Dana to be hurt. How long had Herman been figuring in that little detail? Retreating to the range might have been a lot of things, but improvisation didn't seem to be one of them.

It was a good thing he had Anybody cooped up with him, not Dana.

Thanks to the thin traffic so late on the damp weeknight, I was still well within an hour when I hit 95 North for the short cutoff to Rodman's Neck. Of course, my euphoria was based on Loschen's deadline and my trust that Wendell or whoever was in charge would honor it. How could he not honor it with Uncle Edward undoubtedly on the scene? I blanked out thoughts about how easily he could have.

As soon as I reached the cutoff, I found myself in the middle of a motorcade. Squad cars were ahead and behind me. Every patrol in the city seemed to be converging on the park's forest road to go to the range. Why one of them didn't stop me I had no idea; maybe they were as spooked by the thick fog hanging over Long Island Sound as I was. I finally ran out of luck when a car from the 40 precinct came alongside and ordered me to pull over. But it was too late by then: The chain-link fence to the range was only a hundred yards ahead. I kept going, the cop in the suicide bucket kept screaming, I kept going. By the time he thought of his roof honker, I was sliding between two TV trucks and getting strange looks from everybody in and out of uniform. I was about to get out to explain my hurry to the two blues manning the sentry post when somebody pushed my door back into me so hard I took a nice jab in the side from my steering wheel. I couldn't make out the pusher until Carrington, the beer-bellied bozo from Dana's apartment, had crossed completely behind and around my car and jumped in beside me. He pounded impatiently on my roof for the sentries to move faster about dropping the chain fence. "Go!"

I went, escaping a charging posse of microphones and video-cams and following his stubby finger toward the wide parking lot. "No one's going to be happy to see you except Loschen," he said.

"What the hell happened?"

"She took an ice cream break around eight. Loschen was waiting."

"In front of the station house??!!"

"Oh, yeah. Guy's got stalactites for balls. They're the ones that hang down, right? I always mixed them up with . . ."

"Carrington?"

"Yeah?"

"Fuck yourself."

The perimeter was on the far side of the lot—a raggedy line of squad cars, Emergency Services trucks, uniforms, and brass. It ran from an elevated set of bungalows that looked like portable toilets past a half-dozen administrative clapboard shacks over to a rifle range in the weeds. The center of attraction was a square white building four waterlogged staircase steps off the ground; five heavily harnessed SWATs were crouched down on either side of its door waiting for a green light. A sign outside said TOOLS. "At least he didn't go for the gunroom," I said, killing the engine.

Carrington was still back at my indifference to his studies of cave icicles. "Oh, yeah," he said, offended.

They were all there—Wendell, Uncle Edward, Kaufman, some other faces I'd seen around the 107, and of course Fox and his partner Lombardo from Bronsard's house. That was without counting a lot of other braid and flak jacket outfits. Whether or not he was calling the shots, Wendell wasted no time telling me what he thought of my presence. "You want to keep practicing in this city, Finley, you don't fuck this up," he said, chewing gum more rapidly than a teenage girl behind a checkout counter.

"You the one I'm supposed to be talking to?"

"Me," Edward finally asserted himself. "You don't want to do this, you don't have to. Nobody's forcing you."

"What is *this* exactly?"

"Go in there and watch him blow himself away or try to blow you and the lieutenant away." Fox didn't mind the glares at him; he already had his ticket for the show and couldn't be thrown out. "You're not going to talk him into surrendering, Finley. I'm telling you right now."

"I'm still waiting to hear what he wants."

"He says he wants to talk to you," Wendell allowed. "He won't harm you or McGill if you agree."

"Which leaves him with what leverage?" Fox wanted to know. "If he won't hurt McGill, go get him now."

"That what you would do, Foxie?"

"Not our operation. We're here to advise."

"If there's a chance . . ." Uncle Edward broke off in a coughing fit. Wendell didn't need a formal invitation to fill in the space. "My concern is Lieutenant McGill," he said, sounding very much for the record. "I don't care what else happens. Sorry, Eddie, but that's what he's left us with."

"Do what you have to do," the other croaked.

"What about his mother? His sisters?"

Nobody seemed to appreciate my thought, Uncle Edward least of all. Who could forget he was basically just dealing with a cipher? "We're down to you, Finley, because we've run out of other options," he said, his voice back. "Now if you're willing to help, here's the drill."

The "drill" hadn't changed in 50 years, and Uncle Edward, Wendell, and a captain in a vest too small for him seemed ready to take that long to explain it. Fox thought I was funny. I thought he was enjoying himself too much. "Okay, okay," I said, another Winston Lewis spasm coming on. "He can shoot me, but he can't shoot McGill and I'll say the rain in Spain or something as I'm dying so you can charge in. Give me a phone."

Kaufman had hers ready. I was disappointed she had wiped off her blue lipstick. Had she already found somebody among the brass she didn't want to rub the wrong way?

"Who is this?" The voice was no tenser in the Bronx than it had been in Brooklyn; it just sounded closer.

"Finley. I'm here."

"So, come in."

"Any reason I should, Herman?"

"The same one that brought you this far—you care about her."

I could have stood there all night listening for spite, meanness, or simple anger, and I still wouldn't have heard it. Even his jealousy seemed to have been narcotized. "The last few yards are the hardest, Herman, and I've got to know they're worth it. Put on Lieutenant McGill."

"That really isn't . . ."

"No, that really *is*, Herman. Put her on."

Wendell was running out of patience with both of us; we were holding up another charge of the Light Brigade. And no matter what the ads said, the damn trouble with cellphones was that you were never sure if the background noise was the other party moving around furniture or some intercept of whales mating in the North Atlantic.

But it wasn't whales. "Get out of here, Finley," she said.

She was calm, and I didn't care how much my exhale entertained Fox. "Why? You people have fucked this up so bad, how could I do worse?"

"You can't, so let's leave it at that."

"Can't talk now. I'm running up Kaufman's minutes. See you soon."

I didn't know what I'd accomplished hanging up before Loschen came back on, but it felt right, and not only because it evened us for the way he had cut me off at home. I needed him guessing as much as he was having his version of fun by keeping me in that state.

"You're still not getting a medal," Fox said. "Cool it."

If I had been more sentimental, I might have thought Fox was using indirection to get me across the square of gravel and dead grass into Loschen's sights. I had no time to tell him how too late he was, and that was lucky because then I might have had to think about what I was doing. "I'm not going to get to this anyway," I said, handing Kaufman my .38. "Give me your cigarettes and lighter."

"Herman doesn't smoke," Uncle Edward growled.

"McGill does lately. Stress-related."

"Give him the cigarettes, Detective," Wendell said. "Keep in mind, Finley, we've got sensors on those weapons. Get her to light a cigarette and you move as close to her as you can."

"No, thanks. I'm bringing her a cigarette because she may want a smoke. No other reason. Tell your laser beam sharpshooters that."

Whatever seconds of thought he had given to raising his estimation of me fell off his clock with a thud. "You want a vest?" he asked crankily.

"I'm not going swimming."

"You know what you're doing, Finley?"

"No. Do you?"

Granted it wouldn't have resolved much, but I would have felt a little better if he had given me more than a blank stare while he chewed more flavor out of his gum.

CHAPTER 48

I always hated those scenes in war movies where the platoon had to cross a minefield. You knew at least one soldier was going to trip a wire; otherwise, why have the scene? The inevitability of somebody's balls and legs being splattered all over had never struck me as riotous entertainment, and it didn't charm me much more walking toward the range tool shed with my arms raised. The SWATs huddled against the wall were no help. If they saw me as anything except a human battering ram to get them inside, I missed it. The worst hypocrite was the second one to the left of the door, who gave me a big thumbs up. At least I was able to kill a second thinking about where he could shove his thumb more usefully.

Venetian blinds covered the square glass panels on the top half of the door. I couldn't see Loschen watching me through the slats, but I presumed he was. Either way, I didn't know how he was going to be able to open the door without making himself a target behind it or through the cheap wood of the jamb on the other side, and a click under the steps as I climbed them told me the shock boys were looking forward to that fraction of a second, too. I couldn't believe it was going to be that easy.

And it wasn't. When the door opened, it was Dana. Or half of her, anyway. Her right arm was extended so rigidly away from the door and into the darkness behind her, she had to have been cuffed to Loschen. "No wild moves, boys. It's McGill."

There was nothing from anybody underneath or on either side of me, and the crystallizing fear in Dana's eyes might have been mine. "I need an okay from somebody. Right now!"

It took another few passes by the moon, but someone finally gave me back a dispirited "okay."

"Thanks, guys. Going in now."

So much for my sanity as I had no more excuses for not putting my right foot ahead of my left and entering the shed. Dana was yanked away like a puppet on the end of a chain. "Close it and lock it," Loschen said from the left of the door.

I groped an ordinary half-pretzel brass lock until it caught, reassuring myself that Loschen had more flair, even of his demented kind, than to shoot me in the back. It was a perfect illustration of thinking highly of people to encourage them to do high-minded things.

"Put your jacket on the floor, please."

The place smelled of rotted wood and kerosene. The only light came from a desk lamp that had been set on the floor in front of some shelving in a corner. It lighted the concrete floor around it brilliantly, kind of the way Shari Glynn had illuminated Beads, Beads, and More Beads for my visit with Monaghan and Kitty—a *déjà vu* I could have skipped without feeling its loss. The desk itself looked as much like an extra shelf as a place for writing snappy memos; it was sagging under small cartons and old file cabinet drawers. And why not? Like everything else in the place, object and human alike, it too was just waiting to be discarded.

I had to squint into the darkness to make out the Glock Loschen was holding under Dana's chin against the wall near the door. I could barely see more of him than the thin hairy hand holding the gun, but he didn't look particularly jumpy. She showed more skin under her jaw than normally. Her stare also seemed to be waiting for a soft shoe. "I'm not armed."

"Of course not. But throw your jacket on the floor anyway. And then pull up both your pants legs."

Whether it was Dana's expectant gaze or my grammar school nuns coming back for a morality check, I felt absolutely lewd as

I pulled up my pants to prove I hadn't stashed a piece. My calves belonged to a john in a bordello being raided. "Okay?"

"Turn around, please. Keep your arms up."

I gave him what he wanted so he could see I didn't have anything tucked into the back of my belt. I had once heard a war story about a bald East Hampton cop named Alvarez who in a similar situation had hidden a .22 under his hairpiece. Even though he was said to have brought in a couple of junkie kidnappers with the trick, I'd never wanted to meet Alvarez. Something about crudely exploiting his physical handicaps.

I turned back around fighting an instinct to flinch from whatever Loschen was about to do. Instead, there was a moment of metal clicking against metal, then his free hand slid a handcuff off a long iron bar. He hadn't been cuffed to Dana directly but had been using the bar like a grocery store clerk reaching out with a gripper pole for the economy-sized cans on the highest shelf. "Please go back over there and sit down," he said to her, pointing to the floor in front of the desk.

I wanted to crane my neck back off my shoulders as she stepped over to the space near the lamp. If there was any moment when some Darth Vader beam would take him down from outside, it was as he stood watching her camp down, his gun in one hand and the iron bar dangling the cuffs in the other. "Don't worry," he said casually. "I put some insulation on the walls. Their probes can't be all that accurate."

Which seemed to explain not only the slate gray sheeting on the wall behind him but the Tool Room and the thousand and one odds and ends to be found in any one of them worth the name. "Good thinking, Herman."

"Yes."

He wasn't boasting, just acknowledging a fact; we might as well have been back in our little classroom desks in the 107 muster room talking about target practice. Since the question was suffocating the air anyway, there was no reason not to return the favor. "Now you kill us for your grand finale?"

"That's not what Herman wants," she said. "Is it, Herman?"

"Not if I can help it."

"Herman wants witnesses. He wants us to know what a great brain was lost when he faded from the scene."

"You shouldn't taunt me, Lieutenant. I've been holding it together pretty well here and I'd like to go on doing that."

I couldn't have agreed more, especially since it was an opening for me to gain some purchase. "The lieutenant sounds a little tense. I brought her a cigarette. In my jacket pocket, left side."

That seemed like enough notice to hook the jacket with my shoe and soccer-kick it softly in his direction. "Look yourself."

"It's already hot in here. We don't need smoking."

"We don't need short fuses, either."

"You wouldn't be trying to gas us or something, would you?"

"It's a thought."

I must have given off the same pure innocence of a kindergarten child in semi-darkness as I did in daylight because he thought it over a moment, then asked: "Do you need one that badly, Lieutenant?"

She hesitated, as though I really *was* counting on more than tar and nicotine filling the room. "I think so, yes," she said finally.

"I never noticed you smoking until the other day. If you don't start, you won't have to go through quitting."

"You're not in the best place for lecturing me, Herman."

He was still her puppy; he could raze the city with his Glock, but he hated displeasing the lady. Without dropping his eyes from us, he managed to fish the cigarettes out of my pocket and then a single cigarette from the box. He underhanded the cigarette and the Bic lighter to her with fluid perfection. So much for the theory that he had turned into a serial killer because he had been too uncoordinated in the schoolyard to make the boxball or punchball team. "Tell Finley why we're here," she said.

"He knows why."

"You want witnesses. To what?"

"Guess."

"What's the mystery? You're either going to kill us or kill yourself."

"I'm not talking about that."

"Well, excuse me for having that in the front of my skull."

"You're not thinking."

Out of the corner of my eye, I saw her meditating on the possibilities for the lighter; nothing seemed to occur to her. "I hate to disillusion you, Herman, but . . ."

"We're here, aren't we?"

"Can't deny it. And?"

"Absolutely everything under their nose," he said, sounding a little too much like Winston Lewis for my nerves. "Back to the starting line."

"And what would that be?"

"Here! The numbers! What else? They use their range scores to judge you, but they don't have a clue what went into them."

"So, this has all been what—Herman Loschen leading the struggle against supermarket barcodes and credit card numbers?"

"Don't be glib. You know damn well what I'm talking about. When there's a problem, nobody wants to see what's right in front of them. That might be embarrassing. All these people being killed, but nobody ever wanted to look inside. They might find *policey* things. It's more exciting to look outside. Bronsard. Thaler. Terrorists. If I hadn't called an end to it, they'd be looking for Martians."

"*You* called an end to it?"

Even his delirium didn't give him permission for a full smirk; a little one, but then he pulled that in, too. "It took you long enough to go back to the obvious. And you two were the fastest."

Sometimes even the dullest textbooks had their uses, and Dana's crack about Herman's "great brain" reminded me of one at the Academy, in particular of a chapter on vanity as the average psychopath's most common capital sin. For the first time in years, I even pictured the illustration in the Nassau County handbook—a head swollen like a watermelon and all the seeds inside captioned with words like ARROGANCE and POMPOSITY. "You kept us busy sorting out your mistakes."

"I don't think so."

"I know so."

"Everything's clear in retrospect."

"That's where *you* don't see what's under your nose. The lieutenant could've bagged you days ago, but your uncle didn't want to hear about it."

"That's a lie!"

I didn't dare look at her. I didn't need my last image of her to be a doubt about how many heads I had. "Actually, Herman," she came through as she lighted her Parliament, "we were pretty sure last week . . ."

"That's a lie, too. What mistakes? Tell me just one, Finley."

That was good, the textbook would have congratulated me: He had admitted me into his universe. Now there was a straight path from that to him blasting me to kingdom come. "The rifle."

"I wasn't trying to hurt anybody."

"No, you were having fun. You missed because you wanted to."

"That's right," he said placidly.

"Like those other misses? Wall Street? The QBE?"

"I didn't know those people. And they weren't with a rifle. They were two entirely different things. I just wanted you to think Bronsard."

"Because it was more fun."

"I said so."

"Except you didn't get the platinum tour of the Bronsard Museum."

"Meaning what?"

"Meaning if Bronsard had explained to you what those weapons were, he would've told you the Buckskinner wasn't all that rare. If you'd really wanted to have your fun, tie everybody up in knots, you would've used the Parker under it on the wall. That's the really rare one and would have confused everybody. But you only got the silver tour."

"That's . . ."

"What, Herman—a mistake?"

"It has nothing to do with anything. Fox was watching Bronsard. He knew it couldn't have been him."

"And you should have remembered that. Mistake number two."

"So what? None of that mattered."

"Of course it mattered, Herman," she said. "You know how the little things always add up."

He sensed a joke, then wanted to believe it was a joke, then admitted it might not have been a joke. "Add up to what? You're talking about petty things, neither here nor there. Bronsard was a diversion. It had nothing to do with anything. You're smarter than that."

For a tool room, the place seemed oddly short on hammers, crowbars, and other handy weapons; the only one I could see was the bar he had used to handcuff Dana and that he had rested against the wall behind him. What wasn't at all in short supply, on the other hand, were bullet-ripped range targets waiting for a garbage truck; they were stacked five and six deep all over the place and so eerily they looked like the walking dead waiting for their signal to get after some living flesh. "We have to measure up to you or you'll be disappointed? That what you're saying?"

He turned to her with one last hope: She was supposed to reassure him we were just kidding. Instead, though, she just blinked and blew smoke at him. "What is it? We missed some great plan or pattern you had?"

"The emptied places. Like Finley said."

"Yeah, well," she shrugged. "Who doesn't have a bedroom in the house where some loved one used to sleep? Takes forever to get the stink of medicines and death out of the air."

It might have been the first time he had ever thought seriously of hurting her, and she doubled the idea by looking up at the cartons on the desk as though they were the only intriguing thing in the shed. "What do you think is inside those things?"

I got over the Vanity tactic. She was buying into it too well, and he was about to join her. And he still had the gun. "You're playing into their hands, Herman," I said quickly.

It took him forever to relax his glare against her. "So, they can kill me and avoid a trial?" he asked, calm again. "Yeah, I know. Even my uncles will be relieved. They won't admit it, but they'll be relieved."

"Oh, they don't have any problems admitting it. In fact, Edward's already on tape saying he's had it with his cipher of a nephew."

"I'm sure."

"What, you thought it was a family secret or something? 'We might not like each other around the Christmas tree, but that's our business, not for outsiders?' Something like that?"

"If you want."

"If he told anyone in the Department what he really thought of you, there goes your career and his part in it?"

"My uncles are very big on career."

"You mean they *were*. But you they've written off. Uncle Edward's said as much into a tape recorder. Right, Lieutenant?"

"I have it in my office, Herman. We can send for it."

"Sure. Right away."

"Seriously. Kaufman can get it and put it in front of the door."

"I know what they think of me."

"You're not listening, Herman," I said, sure I heard a creak outside the door. "You've lived all your life with what they think of you. They've been holding their noses, you've seen them holding them, and all of you pretend everything's great because Herman has his shield. Nothing new there. But now they've okayed everybody in the Department thinking that way about you. It's Uncle Eddie's last hurrah before they retire him."

He laughed. "He's already figured a way out of that, believe me."

"He'll appreciate your loyalty, but he's not getting out of this one. You've fixed it for him."

"Okay," he shrugged. "All the better."

I didn't know what was more wearying—trying to get to him or not showing I wasn't doing a very good job of it. "But there'll be no credit to you. We won't be hearing about any Herman Loschen Syndrome. We'll just have a cipher who started shooting people because he snapped one night out at the game. That makes him special? I don't think so. Who the hell wants to waste a trial on that? Better just end it here today. Don't you see how much of a loser that makes you?"

"No."

"Not even the fact that it's all come down to you and Uncle Eddie wanting the same thing? Doesn't that bug you, just a little?"

"It would bug me," she said. "It would say to me maybe I really am this nonentity Uncle Edward thinks."

He gave it some of his deepest cricket thought, then smiled— smiled as radiantly as anyone who had never used those muscles could. "Yeah, it probably does say that."

"And that's fine with you?" she asked. "You're just going to take it? Go poof in the night?"

I had heard something and I knew she had seen something. She had made up her mind to keep Loschen distracted, and I should have, too. But knowing what he was up to, what the Professor had predicted would be his ultimate objective and what Owen Bronsard had already done in his quieter way, I suddenly felt that I had been witnessing suicides my whole life and didn't want to see another one. "I think whim deserves more than that," I heard myself say. "Anybody can start off with a whim. 'Oh, there's this guy in the booth next to me making a joke out of malted milks. Why not take him out and see how long it takes people to figure out who did it?' That's the easy part, Herman. It's carrying through on your whim."

"You don't think . . .?"

"Leong and the others? No, that was just as easy."

"Bullshit!"

"That's not what whim is about, Herman. You should've talked to Bronsard about it. He thought he was an expert. Whim is about making other people suffer. Your targets didn't have enough time to suffer. Probably not even DeWitt and he was the only one who had a shot at you."

"I even gave him a two-count."

"Fabulous. But he still didn't suffer. But what about them outside? A big trial and you get to say to everybody what you're saying to us. It won't stay in the family anymore. Won't be our little secret. And Uncle Eddie and all the rest of them will dread every second leading up to it."

"You kill yourself or let them kill you here," she picked up, "what happens? A couple of weeks of conjecture, nothing else. Nobody's going to listen to me and Finley. They'll confiscate that tape first thing."

There was another creak at the door, and this time I saw some kind of body mass outside, too. There was no way they could have burst in without hitting me or Dana, and I wondered who had given that order. "Think it out, Herman," I said, wishing I knew if I should have been inching left or right. "If the lieutenant wants to keep her job, she'll have to give up that tape and keep quiet. The only people who'd take me seriously are those egomaniacs with their Internet blogs."

"You're not talking me out of this."

She must have heard a breaking point more clearly than I did because she squashed her cigarette on the floor and held up her hand with majestic poise. "We already have, Herman. Give me my phone."

"For what?"

"We're telling them you've told us everything you wanted to tell us and we're coming out."

"You, maybe. Not me."

"Give me the phone."

I played the next minute over for weeks. Sometimes I remembered everyone as having been calculating something, but when I was being more honest I knew only Loschen really was. He took her phone out of his pocket and underhanded it as smoothly to her as he had tossed her the cigarette and lighter. She was still catching it as he turned the barrel of the Glock toward his mouth and I was getting over my freeze. I reached him too late for the discharge, but in time to push it off the centimeters from his mouth to his ear. I didn't wait for the shot to rebound around the room. I was already clawing at his tie knot, shirt, and throat, wrenching the gun from his suddenly limp hand and shoving him to the ground as the front door came down with a crash. He smelled like a sanitized toilet, his ear was spouting blood all over my shirt cuffs, and I was going to need a new pelvis, but he was easy to keep pinned.

"Back off, back off!" Dana was shouting to the first two aliens through the door. But they were playing deaf. There was enough of Loschen's head peeking through my pinning to make for a target and they had their orders. In that half-second of choice, I failed Loschen because I had no intention of sticking my hand over the back of his skull to protect him. I would have regretted it, but I would have gotten over it. A whole hand was a whole hand. But then there was a crash as loud as the SWATs coming through the door. Dana had tipped over one of the cartons from the desk and the first two shooters had jumped back, suddenly trying to keep their balance against the hundreds and thousands of spent shells from the target range rolling toward them.

"I said back off!"

And then she was on her feet between the SWATs and me and Loschen. I didn't get it further than my mind that one of the aliens might have been robotic enough to shoot right through her to carry out the orders on Loschen. I didn't have to because they lowered their weapons. For the longest time, there was nothing but the sound of more heavily booted feet running through the door and Loschen panting under my hold.

"Finley?" she asked, without turning back to me.

"Okay, okay."

Some of the shells glistened in the flashlights thrown on them. I wondered how sharp I would look if I sewed some of them on my black turtleneck. They were certainly cheaper than Shari Glynn's beads.

CHAPTER 49

The next week or so went by on Novocain. Everyone did and said the expected things, but as if from memory, from some unsteady, gawky distance. Loschen's lawyers talked about saving their best shots for a trial. There were hints of this, threats of that, and denials of whatever anyone had gotten it into their heads to imagine what the hints and threats had been about. The closest Loschen himself came to speaking in public was in his choice of attorneys—not those who could have been supplied by his benevolent association, but a husband-wife team with a lot of medals from taking on the city bureaucracy. Photos of him at his arrest and arraignment showed the cricket who could as easily have been the suspect's police escort as the suspect himself. He might have still been Uncle Edward's protege and Dana's right hand. Some pictures weren't worth two cents.

The sponging up came from the very top, with Uncle Edward and Wendell referring all questions to the commissioner's office. After a few wormy words about the benefits of cooperation among law enforcement agencies, Fox dropped from sight altogether. The one thing nobody stinted on was Dana's role in the investigation and the arrest—not only because it was true, but because it was always good to emphasize good cops when bad ones were admitted to be on the loose. Police Plaza also did Finley Investigations a huge favor by explaining my presence in the tool shed as being the result of my investigation into the killing of Ralph Carey on behalf of the Professor and his Brooklyn Dodger friends. A half-hour after a spokesman for the commissioner's office let drop that half-fact for the first time, the old man was on the phone to me using up years of suppressed admiration. I really knew I was in trouble when he passed along compliments from Vince Galassi. Being the negative creature I am, I listened to his praise wondering how long it was going to take him to realize I had forced him to squander all his reserves and that he was going to have to start replenishing his hidden stores behind his usual crotchetiness as soon as he got off the phone.

For my part, I wasn't even sure what I was being so numb about. Every time I'd tell myself we hadn't resolved much of anything in that tool shed except getting Loschen and ourselves out of it alive, my Good Angel reminded me we had taken a psycho off the streets. Everything else should have been secondary, right? So why the filmy screen I found myself looking at whenever I thought about what had happened since that night at Citi Field? With all his complexes about malted milk, rabbi uncles, and manipulated target scores, Herman Loschen was still a poster child only for Herman Loschen, and that didn't feel like nearly enough for what I (not to mention the Carey, Leong, Rosen, and DeWitt families) had invested in the case. The problem with that feeling, though, was that I couldn't pin down exactly what I *had* invested in it.

I could have saved myself a few nights of torment, anguish, and other slick moods if I hadn't waited a week to mention it to Dana. We had both been summoned to the courthouse in Kew Gardens where Loschen's lawyers had filed some kind of procedural brief and been told to sit in the hallway in case we were needed. The next time you tell somebody to go sit in an empty hallway of the Queens Borough Hall courthouse in case they are needed, tell them to take along a Groucho Marx mask to give the place some character. There were three public benches about 50 feet apart that looked like sewer gratings and brass handles to the courtroom doors—so much for the interior decorating. The wax on the waxed floors seemed to have been waxed, and certainly smelled like it. I might have used my time waiting to qualify for the Olympic skate team except for the fact that Dana was there and looked more rested than I had seen her in ages. Whatever daze

Loschen had left her in had begun to recede from her face, and I didn't realize until that morning how *uneager* she had looked for weeks while in the middle of the investigation. Simple curiosity was back in her eyes, and it wasn't the kind that wanted to know who was stabbing her in the back or what lead had she neglected or how many hours did she have left before she was replaced on the case. If I had told her I had run into King Arthur and the Knights of the Round Table on the steps of the courthouse, she couldn't have looked more fascinated as I went into the unsettled feelings I'd been having about what had happened at Citi Field.

"Which night at Citi Field?" she asked. "The one when Ralph Carey was shot or the one when Larry Grabowski gave us Herman?"

And just like that, the mountains parted and lightning split the sky. I had—and hadn't—distinguished the two in all my broodings. One second Ralph Carey was going down and the next Larry Grabowski was telling us who had probably done it. I had conflated the two episodes the way they had never taken place. And in between? In between there had been all the other victims Herman Loschen had first been killing and then investigating with us. "Maybe I wanted it to be Herman even less than Uncle Edward did."

"Why do you think that is?"

That answer also suddenly seemed obvious. "That night when we were walking through the parking lot and I was giving you that big pep talk about how you must've felt betrayed . . ."

For some godforsaken reason, she looked merry. "Yeah?"

"That's funny?"

"Go ahead, go ahead."

"I was talking about me, too, wasn't I?"

She took coy counsel with the traffic rumbling past outside on Queens Boulevard. "It's occurred to me. Not that night, but since. In fact, my misery has secretly counted on your company."

"Let's not push it too far. I wasn't promoting him as my staff genius. How many times did I meet the guy? Three or four before Rodman's Neck?"

"Ah, but how many times in your fantasies, Finley?"

"What fantasies?"

"The ones about me, of course! As long as the only pair of pants around me all day was Herman, you didn't have to get your male ego in a knot. He was a brain in a jar, no other body parts. But once you had to think of him as going around popping people . . . Oooh, now there's a betrayal like no other!"

"You've got a helluva inflated view of yourself, you know that?"

"And every day brings more calls and e-mails telling me why I should! I'm too good for you, Finley. Anybody in the city can tell you that. Read your morning paper."

I didn't know if what she said covered it or not, but in Queens that morning it felt like it did. I was also annoyed that, needed in the courtroom or not, she would have to be going directly back to her office afterward. Why did I have to wait the whole day to see her again? Nothing ever happened out at the Garden of Eden, anyway.

CHAPTER 50

Two days after his trial date was set, Loschen was stabbed to death in what was said to be a high surveillance recreation yard on Rikers Island. A coke dealer named Ilario Velez, waiting to be extradited to Florida, was identified as the only person in the yard with him at the time, but there was also an unlocked and unguarded gate leading from the yard to a boiler room that should have been neither unlocked nor unguarded. Since there were no damning prints on the shiv, no confirming testimony on an attack from three guards, and no ostensible motive, charges against Velez didn't get much further than a few headlines. Insofar as Loschen had never been closer to a drug case than a coke bust in an off-campus St. John's University dorm a couple of years before, there was little energy behind pursuing theories of some cartel vendetta. There was even less for taking up the cause of the husband-wife lawyers that their client had been *assassinated* (their word) to save the NYPD and some of its brass embarrassment during the trial about the conduct of the sniper investigation.

I thought the lawyers were right about the attack, but probably wrong about the reasons for it. Regardless of what I had told him in the shed to get his gun away from him, I couldn't imagine Herman producing great revelations on the witness stand outside those relating to the scrubbing of his personnel file. What I could imagine were a lot of people at Police Plaza being skinned to their nerve endings by the prospect of daily testimony from a psychopath who, leaving aside the odd killing here and there, would have impressed as a meticulous, astute investigator. He just wasn't a Department image you wanted to have to deal with in the morning as regularly as Doonesbury. In any case, Velez was shipped down to Miami only a day or so later than scheduled. He ended up with five years on multiple convictions that usually brought five times that much. Some said it was a reward for having turned informant. That might have even been true.

The world hardly stopped spinning without the cricket. It didn't even slow down Finley Investigations, where the Police Plaza endorsements had crackled like a starter's pistol for every cuckolded husband and wife, scarred medical patient, and suspicious heir in Bay Ridge to come running to me for relief. But I was getting too old to be satisfied with reality. I suppose I knew I was going to do something as soon as I heard the news that, after a long delay, the Medical Examiner had released Loschen's body to his family. Right away I ruled out the Manhattan church where the funeral was going to be held. Just one photograph by the media people sure to be there would have made me too ripe for Dr. Phil, "Access Hollywood," and other seekers of spiritual truths. But that didn't exclude going to the cemetery, especially when I found out it was Green-wood in Brooklyn, less than three miles from my apartment.

My last trip to Green-wood had been about a year before, on one of the Professor's educational tours. Since he had dwelled at length that day on the tomb of Charles Ebbets, an early owner of the Brooklyn Dodgers, I was tempted to invite him along so he too could put some cap on the Ralph Carey shooting. But I didn't really want company, particularly the kind that liked finding irony in a loaf of bread. I was also getting a little ahead of myself. Driving down to 25th Street, I wasn't all that confident of putting a cap on a goddamn thing. It just seemed right that I not let Herman Loschen be slid into the ground without taking notice.

The gateman apparently had his list of favorite and least favorite Green-wood corpses. A serial killer wasn't as romantic to him as mob goons like Joey Gallo and Albert Anastasia. When I said Loschen's name, he went through a medley of grunts and whistlings as he consulted his board and directed me to the right area. I thought about asking him if psycho cops also reflected badly on gatemen, but instead did what I was told.

Did warm spring mornings bring out the best or worst in cemeteries? As a tourist with the Professor, I'd found all the grass, trees, lakes, birds, and squirrels a hypocritical disguise for the purpose of the place. But I hadn't driven down from the apartment to start a crusade against the right to bury people somewhere other than in a garbage dump. All the twittering and chirping coming from the trees might not have meant much for the dead, my more enlightened view said, but there was no point terrorizing the survivors with Grim Reaper images of destiny, either. The fact of the matter was, Joe Carroll's lectures on Charles Ebbets, Leonard Bernstein, and William S. Hart aside, I had loved our tour because of all the birds. I hadn't seen such an aviary—herons, thrushes, hawks, kingfishers, mockingbirds, crows—since I had been working patrol as a rookie on the Eastern Shore. For a couple of years, I'd even been something of a birder, if *something* meant the two Saturdays Jenny and I had gone to Bear Mountain to spend the day a little differently and the Sunday I had taken Susan out to the Hamptons to watch the gulls and egrets. Winding through Green-wood's neat little lanes, I liked the feeling, as I had the day with the Professor, that the birds and I hadn't abandoned one another when I had left Long Island.

The Loschen burial wasn't hard to find once I arrived in the right city. Three patrol cars had been laid on in case of intrusions, and I assumed the unmarked van a couple of hundred yards down the lane was some kind of communications vehicle. I saw only one TV truck, and the dour expressions on the people standing around it said they had been told they were going no further than where they had parked. There were about a dozen private cars and a hearse squeezed between the van and the three blue-and-whites. The burial ceremonies were going on in the middle of a simple row of tombstones. I counted about 20 people, the majority of them women. The only mourners I recognized from photographs and TV film were the mother, the two sisters, and Uncle George; no Uncle Edward or Uncle Martin. Uncle George was clearly a man of conflicted priorities since a nice little breeze flapped his black topcoat enough to show a Corrections Depart-ment uniform underneath. I wondered how that had gone over with the mother and sisters, but saw enough of Uncle George's granite face and steel-shoulder posture to know he wouldn't have cared too much how it had. He was there to represent not only a wing of the Loschen family but the legal institutions Herman had violated and that had violated Herman. Uncle George looked equal to the multitask.

The two cops who had gotten out of their car were too busy glowing in their cigarettes to give me more than a glance as I cruised past. I didn't know what else I had come to see, or what I had accomplished, but I knew I didn't want to just go down to the end of the lane, turn left, and head back to the gate. I had al-ready done that the night out on Lakeview, and once seemed like enough for that routine. So, I parked at the end of the lane, killed the engine, opened my door, dropped my legs on the pavement, and watched what was going on at the gravesite.

People being miserable, basically. One of the sisters, as scraw-ny as Herman and with severely pulled back black hair, looked very much in need of the husband or boyfriend supporting her at her elbow. Had Herman been her hero? The cop she boasted about to the other girls in school? It was a good thing she had graduated. Who were the others? Cousins mainly there for the mother? Prisoners Uncle George had sprung from Rikers for the morning to pad the house? They could have been anybody. And if one of them lifted her eyes from the meditation the priest had apparently called for, she would have seen me and decided I too could have been anybody. Herman Loschen had gotten his bright idea to play Buffalo Bill with the city so he could be mourned by people who had never really known him, didn't know each other, and probably didn't know themselves. Bullseye!

As an attendant handed the mother a rose to toss atop the coffin, I felt suddenly drained. I didn't know who was about to be lowered out of sight forever. It couldn't have been Herman Loschen since he had departed in the Rikers recreation yard and had long since joined a long line of people who had left me dumb and stranded. None of them even had names anymore, so it was useless for me to warn Jenny or Susan or Rennie Miller to stay away from the cricket. They would have to manage that on their own. It was none of my business anymore, and nothing—not guilt, not piety, not love, not wounded vanity—could pretend it was. I really had no right even to have them in my head at the same time. As the more stricken sister stepped forward to deliver her flower, I thought of what a great thinker had once told me on a bathroom floor. Maybe if I had bounced Vince Galassi's skull on the tiles the way I had been tempted, he wouldn't have had the time to tell me that "nothin's ever the same as what really happened."

www.ingramcontent.com/pod-product-compliance
Lightning Source LLC
Chambersburg PA
CBHW030403020726
47493CB00003B/930